Let It Snow, Let It Snow, Let It Snow by Andrea Boeshaar
Shari Flannering is driving to her parents' home for the first time since her husband's death. When a winter storm arrives a day earlier than predicted, Shari's folks encourage her to take refuge at a bed-and-breakfast run by a friend of the family. Assuming Miriam Sheppard is alone this Christmas Eve, Shari agrees. That's not the case at all, though, as Shari soon comes face-to-face with an old flame—a man whose heart she broke twenty-three years earlier.

Orange Blossom Christmas by Kristy Dykes
Who would have predicted that church secretary Lois Delaney might find love at a bed-and-breakfast in a remote Florida orange grove? Though romantic sparks are flying, Lois worries that she and the inn owner, Landon Michael, are too different for romance—she's a penny-pincher, he's a spender, she's an extrovert, he's the quiet type. But when Lois takes the psalmist's advice and "commits her way to the Lord," she finds love a-blooming amidst the orange blossoms.

Mustangs and Mistletoe by Pamela Griffin
City boy Derrick Freeborn, at a Texas bed-and-breakfast ranch for the holidays, meets country girl Taylor Summerall—and life is about to get more interesting for both of them. Taylor wants nothing to do with the friendly accountant, yet she's stuck teaching him horseback riding. Derrick does his best to learn and to fit in—and experiences a Western adventure he'll never forget. Can these two opposites find romance?

Christmas in the City by Debby Mayne
Aunt Celia, in the hospital recovering from a fall, needs someone to run her boardinghouse in Soho. It's not the job Kathryn Anderson, a professional chef, has dreamed about, but she is honor bound to the one family member who has always been there for her. When prison minister Stan Jarrett—a man with a past—finds himself stranded in New York City during a snowstorm, the Lord may unveil a special plan to bring the two together.

Holiday
AT THE INN

© 2004 *Let It Snow!* by Andrea Boeshaar
© 2004 *Orange Blossom Christmas* by Kristy Dykes
© 2004 *Mustangs and Mistletoe* by Pamela Griffin
© 2004 *Christmas in the City* by Debby Mayne

ISBN 1-59310-536-3

Scripture quotations are taken from King James Version of the Bible.

Scripture quotations are also taken from the HOLY BIBLE, NEW INTERNATIONAL VERSION®. NIV®. Copyright © 1973, 1978, 1984 by International Bible Society. Used by permission of Zondervan Publishing House. All rights reserved.

Cover image © Corbis

Illustrations by Mari Goering

Published by Barbour Publishing, Inc., P.O. Box 719, Uhrichsville, Ohio 44683, www.barbourbooks.com

Our mission is to publish and distribute inspirational products offering exceptional value and biblical encouragement to the masses.

Member of the
Evangelical Christian
Publishers Association

Printed in the United States of America.
5 4 3 2 1

Holiday
AT THE INN

*Christmas Love Is Dished Up
at Four Bed & Breakfasts*

ANDREA BOESHAAR
KRISTY DYKES
PAMELA GRIFFIN
DEBBY MAYNE

BARBOUR
PUBLISHING

Let It Snow

by Andrea Boeshaar

Dedication

This story is dedicated to two of my favorite
missionaries who serve the Lord in Cambodia.
They don't run an orphanage
(like the one in this story), but they have
adopted two precious Cambodian children.
The missionaries to whom I refer
have hearts to see souls saved and have
dedicated their lives to The Great Commission.
For this reason, a percentage of royalties earned
from this novella will go to support their ministry.

Chapter 1

Oh, the weather outside is frightful, but the fire is so delightful. . . .

Sharon Rose Flannering leaned forward and turned off her car stereo. She always enjoyed singing along with the classic seasonal song, but the weather outside really was frightful tonight, and she had to concentrate on her driving.

The wipers flapped from right to left in a futile attempt to keep the windshield free of snow. Visibility was next to nil. Shari could see only a blur of white on the road before her.

"Lord, I know I said I missed snow on Christmas, but You didn't have to do exceeding, abundantly, above all I asked in this circumstance."

In spite of the situation, Shari chuckled. *A merry heart does good, like medicine.* With everything she'd been through in the last ten years, she'd needed a heavy dose of merriment—that saving medicine referred to in Proverbs 17:22. God had proven Himself trustworthy throughout her life's many trials. His Word rang true. Besides, God's remedy cost nothing compared to psychotherapy and antidepressants. Most likely, those would have been her options had Shari not learned to chuckle in the face of adversity. Moreover, laughter kept the joy alive in her heart. She felt happy. Life was good. God was in control.

Even in the midst of a Wisconsin blizzard like this one.

Shari's cell phone rang, and she managed to flip it open and answer it with one hand without taking her eyes off the road as her car continued to creep along the interstate. "Hello?"

"Where are you?" Her mother's voice held a note of concern.

"I'm not sure. I can't see anything."

"Oh, no! And I don't even know what to tell you. We weren't supposed to get this storm until tomorrow."

Shari laughed. "I haven't been gone so long that I've forgotten Wisconsin's fickle weather."

"We should have all gone to Florida to see you this Christmas."

"We celebrate that way every year, Mom. And now, with Greg gone. . ."

Shari didn't finish the sentence. No need to. Her husband of twenty-three years had suffered with brain cancer for nearly a decade, and Shari's family had endured the emotional highs and lows of his illness right along with her. Surgeries and radiation treatments had kept Greg's disease in check for a while, but the time came when doctors could do no more. Since Greg knew Jesus Christ in a personal way, Shari couldn't feel sad that God chose to deliver her husband from his terrible pain and perform the ultimate healing—taking Greg to heaven. But she still mourned the loss of her husband, and this was her first Christmas without him. That was one of the reasons she had chosen to come home.

Home. Funny how Wisconsin still seemed like home, even though she'd lived elsewhere for more than half her life.

Suddenly, brake lights shone red through the swirling snow ahead, and Shari snapped back to attention. A moment later, she rejoiced. "Mom, a salt truck is right in front of me. Isn't that awesome? I'll follow this truck until I can figure out where I am, then I'll call you back."

"Please be careful, honey. I'm so worried about you. I just knew you shouldn't have driven all the way from Pensacola."

"I'm fine. Don't fret."

Shari quelled her impatience with her mother. Sylvia Kretlow was a pastor's wife, yet she couldn't come close to scraping up enough faith to equal that of the tiny mustard seed Jesus referred to in the Gospel of Matthew. She assumed the worst in all situations. Shari's dad, the minister, wasn't much better. He had a gloom-and-doom outlook on life, insisting he was "serious-minded." However, his somber attitude had caused him to keep a choke hold on Shari and her siblings during their teenage years, which only fueled their rebelliousness. If Shari hadn't run off with Greg Flannering at the age of twenty, she might never have come to trust Christ as her Savior. As it stood now, her sister and two brothers had yet to arrive at a saving knowledge of Him.

And that was another reason for her visit to Wisconsin. Shari hoped to be used as an instrument of God's love during this holiday season. Since Greg's death, Shari had never felt more determined to reach a lost and dying world with the Christmas story—and that included her siblings. Unfortunately, they'd had the salvation message hammered into their heads since birth. Words wouldn't reach them anymore. God would have to do something miraculous in order to reach Mark, Luke, and Abby.

"It seems like tragedies always happen during Christmastime," her mother lamented. "I don't want our family to suffer another loss this year. Greg's dying was hard enough."

Shari grinned. "Mom, your optimism is *so* encouraging."
Sylvia clucked her tongue at the quip.

"Let me figure out where I am," Shari repeated, "and then I'll call you back."

"All right, but please be careful."

"I will. I promise."

Shari disconnected the call and forced herself to relax. Following the enormous truck made driving a hundred times easier. However, ten miles later, the truck veered onto the exit ramp. Shari followed the truck, realizing too late that she'd left the interstate. Then, just to her right, she saw a well lit green and white sign advertising a Stop 'n' Shop. She pulled into the gas station/convenience store and decided this would be the perfect opportunity to determine her precise location.

Parking alongside a pump, grateful for the overhead protection from the storm, Shari filled her vehicle's gas tank before entering the store. The clerk couldn't have been more than nineteen. He was chatting with three scraggly young men who leaned on the counter, smoking cigarettes. They seemed harmless enough, although Shari wrinkled her nose at the noxious smell. She noticed the blue haze lingering over the counter-enclosed cashier area. To her relief, however, the rest of the store didn't seem smoky.

She visited the ladies' room then returned to the checkout counter just as a country-western rendition of "Silent Night" resounded through the speakers.

"So, I'm just now entering Green Bay?" Shari blinked in surprise at the clerk's response to her question. It seemed like an eternity had passed since she'd driven through Manitowoc. Under normal weather conditions, the drive between the two cities would have taken about thirty minutes.

"Where you headed?" the ruddy-faced young man asked.

"Forest Ridge. It's a little town in Door County just on the other side of the bay."

"I know where it is." He finger-combed his dark brown hair away from his forehead. "Wouldn't try to make it there tonight, though."

Shari frowned. "But it's Christmas Eve."

All four young men gave her sympathetic shrugs.

"There are a few hotels on the other side of I-43," a guy with a pockmarked face suggested before he blew a plume of smoke into the air. "You might want to stay at one of 'em."

"Yeah, snow's not s'posed to let up for a while," the clerk said.

Shari shook her head. "I want to be with my family. I've driven all the way up from Florida to spend the holidays with them."

"Should've arrived yesterday." The clerk grinned. "It was forty degrees outside."

Shari had thought the same thing a bazillion times while journeying through several long, uninteresting states; however, she hadn't been able to get off work any earlier. She'd considered flying, but the heightened terrorism alerts made Shari too nervous to board an aircraft.

Back in her car, she phoned her mother. After a few minutes, Shari's father got on the line.

"You're near Miriam Sheppard's bed-and-breakfast. She calls it a 'highway haven,' and it stays open all year long. Why don't you spend the night there?"

"With the Sheppards?" Shari let go with a peal of laughter. "I don't think so."

"Why not? Miriam asks about you all the time. She's

probably alone tonight. Your mother's nodding her head and. . . What? Oh, Karan's at her in-laws' and Brenan is in Africa. No, make that Brazil."

Shari knew Brenan's whereabouts already. Her church supported his mission team and she read their quarterly newsletter. Dr. Brenan Sheppard had come a long way from the quiet, lanky guy Shari dated in high school and two years into college. Back in those days, Brenan had about as much ambition as demonstrated by those young men inside the gas station. While Shari didn't regret breaking off their engagement, she was sorry for the way in which she did it—an unkind, impersonal letter.

Then, she ran off and eloped with Greg Flannering. At the time, Greg and his family were new to the area. Shari met Greg at an infamous, late-1970s disco. It was love at first sight for both of them, even though Shari was engaged to Brenan.

Years later, after she committed her life to Christ, Shari wrote Brenan a much different letter and apologized. He never replied, and she didn't try to contact him again. But she'd heard he never married, and she always felt responsible—like the woman who irreparably broke the poor man's heart. So, she prayed for him, asking God to bring a wife into Brenan's life. Still, staying at his mother's bed-and-breakfast seemed a little intimidating, even though Shari had always liked Miriam. The older woman was a widow, too. Her husband died years ago, and instead of moving back to Forest Ridge where she'd raised her children, Miriam continued to run the bed-and-breakfast, a small but profitable business that began after the older pair retired.

But it was sad that Miriam wouldn't have family around her tonight.

"She's alone, huh?"

"Shall I have your mother give Miriam a call?"

Gazing through her windshield, Shari felt as though she'd been planted inside a snow globe. At once, she saw the wisdom in not attempting the rest of the drive. "Yeah, go ahead. If worst comes to worst, I'll find a hotel."

"Okay, we'll call you right back."

Stepping out of her car again, Shari traipsed back into the Stop 'n' Shop. She purchased a cup of coffee and sat down at one of the four tables near the restrooms. As she sipped the too-strong brew, Shari felt glad she'd donned her comfy, wrinkle-free black knit dress and button-down red holiday sweater this morning. She had stayed overnight in Cincinnati and had felt determined to drive straight through to Forest Ridge today. She should have made it in ten or eleven hours, including lunch and bathroom stops. She had hoped to arrive in time for church, already dressed for the occasion.

Too bad the weather decided not to cooperate with her plans.

Shari's cell phone rang, and she answered it. "What took so long?"

"Oh, I'm sorry," her mother said. "Miriam and I got to chatting. Anyway, she said it's fine. She'd love to have you. She's got plenty of room in her bed-and-breakfast. It's right near the gas station where you are now."

Shari listened carefully to the directions. The Open Door Inn couldn't be more than a mile away.

"Great. I'm off. I'll call you after I get settled." She tamped down her disappointment over not seeing her family tonight. "Merry Christmas, Mom."

"Merry Christmas, honey. We'll see you tomorrow and celebrate then. At least I'll know you're safe tonight."

"Right. G'night."

Shari ended the call and shrugged back into her black wool coat. After wishing a Merry Christmas to the four young men still congregated around the checkout, she ventured back out into the winter wonderland.

*

"At forty-three years old, you're finally getting married." Karan Strang shook her head, and her honey-blond hair swished across her shoulders. "I can't believe it."

Brenan grinned, enjoying his sister's reaction to his news. "Well, I haven't popped the question yet. Elena could always turn me down."

Karan lowered herself onto the floral-upholstered settee. "Doesn't sound like she will."

Brenan didn't think so either. The dark-haired beauty he'd met in Brazil had gotten under his skin in the most unusual way. *It must be love.* Elena said she loved him. It's just that she was only thirty, and the difference in their ages bothered him a little.

Brenan glanced at the doorway in time to see his brother-in-law, Daniel Strang, enter the living room. Brenan's niece, Laura, and her husband, Ian, followed.

"Mom is stunned." Daniel combed strong fingers through his graying hair. "We pulled off our surprise without a hitch."

Karan grinned and lifted nine-month-old Chrissy onto her lap. Brenan still couldn't believe his sister was a grandmother. Or that he was a great-uncle. But seeing Chrissy, a picture of health, reminded him of the Cambodian orphanage he'd had on his mind for some time now. However, he shook off the burden. There wasn't anything he could do to help the missionaries in that part of the world. He'd been called to serve in Brazil. With Elena.

"And here Mom thought she'd spend Christmas Eve alone," Karan said, bouncing the baby on her knee. "Brenan, it was so cool that your plane got in before the bad weather hit."

"Amen to that!"

At that moment, Miriam Sheppard strode into the room carrying a tray of cookies. She looked happy, two rosy spots brightening her cheeks, and Brenan was glad he had made the effort to come home for the holidays.

"We're going to have another guest." Setting the decorated treats on the table, Miriam straightened. She looked at Brenan. "You'll never guess who's coming."

"Who?"

"Shari Kretlow. Of course, her last name isn't Kretlow anymore. But for the life of me, I can't think of what it is."

"Flannering." Brenan hadn't forgotten it. Where he once had rued the day he ever heard it, he felt nothing now as he spoke the surname, nothing other than curiosity. He frowned. "What's Shari doing in Wisconsin? Last I heard she lived in Tucson."

"Oh, that was years ago, Bren." Karan's voice carried above the baby's squeals. "For the last, oh, I don't know, eight or ten years, Shari's lived in Florida."

"Awful about her husband," Miriam said, shaking her head and walking away. "Oh, and Ian," she said to Laura's husband, "would you mind shoveling the walk for our guest?"

"Sure."

Ian stood, and Brenan watched his mother's retreating back before glancing at Karan. "What about Shari's husband?" It had taken years for Brenan to stop hating the guy. But he could hardly be about the Lord's work with something like hatred in his heart. Long ago, he made the decision to give all those wrongful, painful feelings over to Christ. "What happened?"

"Don't you read any of my e-mails?"

"Well, I. . ." Brenan decided he couldn't lie. "I usually skim them, Karan, because I'm so busy."

His sister rolled her hazel eyes in irritation. "Greg died last March. He'd been sick for a long time. Abby told me he'd been out of his mind for the last couple of years and was confined to a nursing home. He used to swear at the nurses and call Shari all sorts of horrible names. But it wasn't really Greg. It was the brain cancer talking."

At another time, Brenan might have felt like justice had been served, but now, all he felt was sorrow. What's more, being a medical doctor, he could well imagine the particulars. "Must have been tough on Shari and all the Kretlows."

Karan nodded as her husband sat down beside her. "In spite of the big scandal they caused when they ran off together, Greg and Shari turned out to be committed Christians. That part has always made Abby nuts."

"Why?"

Karan handed the baby to her daughter, Laura. "Abby felt like Shari and Greg succumbed to the brainwashing she grew up with. Now, she says she doesn't even believe God exists."

"What a shame." Brenan narrowed his gaze. "So how do you know all this?"

"She does my hair." Karan grinned. "I see Abby about every six weeks, and we catch up on all the news."

"Ah." Brenan chuckled, but on the inside a strange, unsettled feeling filled his gut. Shari Kretlow Flannering, once the love of his life, was on her way over.

And she was a widow.

Chapter 2

Shari found the Open Door Inn easily enough and pulled into the back lot as instructed. She noticed other vehicles parked neatly in a row, although they were covered with white fluffy snow. She wondered if Miriam had guests after all.

Trudging around to the side of the house on a freshly shoveled walk, Shari reached an ornate wooden door. She stomped the snow from her black suede shoes and rang the bell. Miriam answered in a matter of moments.

"Merry Christmas!" The older woman enveloped Shari in a hug. "My, my, how good to see you again!"

"Likewise. Thank you for allowing me to stay here tonight. I hope I'm not intruding."

"You're not at all. Come in."

Stepping into the large foyer, Shari noticed the gold wallpaper and polished, dark-tiled floor. Miriam took her coat, and Shari watched as her hostess hung it in the front closet. Then she turned back to Shari.

"Let me get a good look at you."

Miriam gazed into Shari's face. Their height was evenly matched, and Shari noticed Miriam appeared older but still looked very much the same as she remembered her, with her rust-colored hair, brown eyes, and freckled complexion.

"I'd recognize you anywhere, Mrs. Sheppard."

"Please, call me Miriam." She smiled. "And I was thinking much the same thing. You still have that spark of mischief in your eyes."

Shari laughed, and the two clasped hands.

"Gracious! Your fingers are like ice. Come on into the living room and sit by the fire."

Shari thought she'd like nothing better. But when she turned to follow Miriam into the other room, her gaze found none other than Brenan Sheppard standing in the doorway. Tall, with ebony, short-cropped hair, he now sported a neatly trimmed dark beard. He only vaguely resembled the unmotivated college sophomore she had dumped for smooth-talking, ambitious Greg Flannering. And, judging by the way Bren's beige cable-knit sweater fit snugly across his broad shoulders, it appeared he had filled out his once-lanky frame.

Nevertheless, Shari was unsure of what to make of the situation. Was this a setup? A Christmas prank—courtesy of Mom and Miriam?

She chuckled at her deduction then decided to make the best of it. She stuck out her right hand. "Hi, Bren. Good to see you again."

His brown eyes regarded her outstretched hand before meeting her gaze once more. "After twenty-three years, Shari, I don't want a handshake."

She felt her smile fade. Did he intend to finally tell her off? She deserved it if he did.

Brenan grinned. "I want a hug!"

Within seconds, she was enfolded into a smothering embrace. She laughed, relieved by the outcome. Then, inhaling, she got an intoxicating whiff of Brenan's spicy cologne.

"Merry Christmas!"

Brenan released her, and Shari took a step back. "Same to you," she said. "I didn't know you were back in the States—not that I keep track of your every move or anything." Shari laughed at her sudden nervousness and quickly explained. "My church supports your mission team, and I read your newsletters every so often."

Brenan arched one swarthy brow. "What church is that?"

"Golden Shores Community Church in Pensacola, Florida."

"Sure, I know the one." Brenan's features lit up like holiday lights, and it was obvious he was enthusiastic about his ministry.

Miriam's voice interrupted their conversation. "Shari, come in by the fire. I know you're freezing."

Brenan turned sideways and extended a hand, indicating she should enter the room ahead of him.

Shari complied and walked into the cozy living room. Floral-upholstered furniture was placed in a half-circle in front of a glowing fire that crackled in the fieldstone hearth. One glance told her she had definitely intruded upon a family gathering. However, before she could utter an apology, Brenan's sister Karan jumped up from the settee and strode toward her.

"Shari! Wow, it's great to see you!"

Another hug, and Shari felt the sting of tears gathering at the corners of her eyes. These people should hate her, and perhaps they had at one time. But now, they seemed to have prevailed over any negative emotions, greeting her with such warmth and sincerity, it touched her to the very heart of her being.

Karan released her. "You look terrific."

"Thanks." Shari suddenly wished she'd stayed on her diet

and lost those pesky pounds rounding her hips. "You look great yourself."

She did, too. Karan was just as tall and slim as during their high school days.

Totally not fair.

For the next few minutes, Shari was caught in a flurry of introductions. She met Karan's husband, Dan Strang, their daughter Laura, and Laura's husband, Ian. Then, at last, Shari's gaze fell on a towheaded baby, creeping around the plush carpet.

"That's my first grandchild, Chrissy."

"She's adorable." Shari smiled. Glancing back at Karan, she shook her head. "You're about the best-looking grandma I've ever seen."

Karan beamed.

"Shari, please sit down," Miriam said, indicating an armchair near the fireplace.

She did as the older woman bade her then stretched her arms out closer to the screen, warming her hands. "Maybe it'll stop snowing soon, and I'll be able to drive the rest of the way to Forest Ridge. I'm so sorry to infringe on your Christmas."

"The more the merrier," said Karan, reclaiming her seat beside her husband.

Brenan sat on the sofa to Shari's left and Miriam on the other side of him.

"I heard the snow's going to keep up through tomorrow," added Dan, a nice-looking man in spite of his thick midsection.

His announcement about the weather, however, plucked an anxious chord in Shari's heart. She had no intentions of spending Christmas with the Sheppards, especially since Brenan was in town. It felt too weird.

She stood. "Maybe I'd better try to make Forest Ridge tonight after all."

Brenan pushed to his feet. "That'd be dangerous. You can't drive even that short distance in this weather."

"Bren's right," Karan said. "There's a winter storm warning posted for all of Northern Wisconsin, and the weather lady on the news at five o'clock advised folks to get off the roads and stay home."

"That was over an hour ago," Shari countered. "Maybe the snow has let up some. I did see a salt truck out on the interstate."

"Shari, I know we just met," Dan said with a grin, "but I'm a bossy guy. Sit down and relax. You're not going anywhere tonight."

Her gaze slid to Brenan who shrugged. Shari caught an amused glimmer in his cocoa-brown eyes.

She sat, and the room fell silent except for occasional squawks from Chrissy. "Well, thank you for letting me wait out the storm here." She hoped she hadn't appeared ungrateful for wanting to leave. "I'm just looking forward to seeing my family."

"Understandable," Miriam replied.

"Especially after losing your husband," Karan added, a note of sympathy in her voice. "Abby told me about it after she'd returned from Florida and the funeral. Please accept our condolences."

Shari smiled back. "Thank you. I did get your sympathy card but never got around to responding."

Karan waved her hand in a dismissive gesture.

Brenan sat forward, resting his forearms on his knees. He cleared his throat. "I'm also sorry to hear about your loss. I just found out tonight that Greg passed."

"He would have learned the news sooner, had he taken

time to read my e-mails." Karan sent her younger brother a withering look.

Brenan grinned back at her before returning his gaze to Shari.

"Thanks," she said once more. "But Greg's in a better place now."

Brenan replied with a thoughtful nod. "Are you okay?"

"Oh, yes. I mean. . .it was such a long, drawn-out thing," Shari said, settling back into the armchair. "But let's change the subject, shall we? This is Christmas Eve, and I already feel terrible about spoiling your holiday."

"Shari, you are *not* spoiling our holiday." Brenan's voice carried an authoritative tone. "So get that idea out of your head."

She saluted, and Brenan cast a quick glance at the ceiling.

Everyone chuckled, and Shari was again reminded of how much she preferred laughter to tears.

Karan stood. "Shari, would you like to see pictures of your twenty-fifth high school reunion? I got to go because Carol Baskin didn't have a date, and she didn't want to attend alone."

"Some things never change." Shari laughed.

Karan chuckled, too, but feigned an indignant stance. "Did you hear that, Bren?"

He rubbed his thumb and forefinger up and down his bearded chin. "I hate to admit it, but I thought the same thing."

After another laugh, Shari leaned forward and extended her right hand, her palm toward Brenan. He returned the gesture in a modified "high-five" slap.

"You two are despicable," Karan joked as she sashayed from the room. "I'll get the pictures."

"No, she didn't!"

Brenan chuckled as he watched Shari's incredulous expression.

"Vi Taylor married Lyle Koffey? But he was such a dweeb."

"It's the old ugly duckling story," Karan said. "Only it's the male version."

"Hmm."

Brenan grinned as he watched the two women examine the photos of the past summer's high school reunion. He hadn't been there because of obligations in Brazil, and Shari didn't attend, she said, because she couldn't take the time off from her work as a dental hygienist.

Brenan let the updated information on Shari's life digest as he continued to enjoy her exclamations over every picture. She found something hilarious about each one. Karan was in stitches, and Brenan had to confess to finding Shari quite delightful.

In many ways, she had changed a lot over the years. Gone was that intense, serious, almost angry young lady. Now Shari's disposition seemed more lighthearted. Physically, she'd put on some weight, yet that only seemed to soften her all the more. Her hair was just as golden blond as he remembered; however, instead of long, she now wore it chin length, tucking one side behind her ear. Loopy earrings hung from her lobes, and matching bracelets clinked on her wrists. Shari might turn a guy's head, but not like Elena did. Elena's South American beauty could fill a room and draw gasps of awe from anyone in her vicinity. Part of Brenan reveled in the fact that he'd won the prettier woman's heart. Yet, there was something about Shari he found quite appealing.

He sipped his glass of hot chocolate and wondered what her

life had been like with Flannering. Had she been happy? It appeared so. She'd said she loved him.

"Hey, Shari, did you ever have kids?"

The room grew quiet, and all eyes looked at him.

He glanced around at the stunned faces. "Did I say something wrong?"

"No, it's just. . ." Karan seemed to grope for words. "Where in the world did that question come from? We were talking about Ted Meinhardt's car dealership."

Brenan grinned. "Sorry. I wasn't paying attention."

Karan rolled her eyes. "Typical brother. He skims my e-mails and ignores what I say."

Shari smiled and turned toward him. "In answer your question, Bren, no, I never had kids. Greg and I wanted children, but they never came." Shari shrugged. *"Que sera, sera."*

"What does that mean?" Laura wanted to know as she pried carpet fuzz out of Chrissy's chubby fist.

"What will be, will be," Miriam piped in as she re-entered the room. "Dinner is just about ready." Then she began to sing the old Doris Day tune. *"Que sera, sera.* Whatever will be, will be. . ."

Brenan leaned to the side, reclining on a throw pillow while his mother cantered down her own memory lane. He regarded Shari, and when she looked his way, he caught her gaze. "See what you started?"

She just laughed.

Chapter 3

At his mother's request, Brenan brought the Christmas tree in from outside and set it into its metal stand in a corner of the living room. Karan, sitting on her haunches, arranged the colorful, handmade skirt around it. As tradition dictated in the Sheppard home, the tree was decorated on Christmas Eve, and everyone helped. But first, Mom served a dinner of broiled beef tenderloin, twice-baked potatoes sprinkled with paprika, and French-cut green beans.

"Oh, this is delicious."

At Shari's remark, Brenan glanced up from his meal to look across the dining room table at her.

"You're a marvelous cook. Did I always know that, or have you improved with age?"

Miriam chuckled and winked. "I've always been a marvelous cook."

Shari smiled.

Karan cleared her throat. "Shari, did you hear the big news? Brenan's engaged!"

Her blue eyes widened. "No, I didn't." Her gaze flew to Brenan. "Congratulations!"

"Thanks, but they're a bit premature." He looked from his sister to Shari. "I haven't proposed yet."

"But you will, and Elena will say yes." Confidence shone on his sister's face. "You said so yourself."

"I can't wait to meet her," Miriam said. "This summer. . . right, Bren?"

He nodded.

"See?" Karan waved a hand in the air. "The proposing part is a mere technicality."

Brenan grinned. He supposed that was true. His entire mission team expected him to ask Elena to marry him. They were a perfect match, after all. He was a doctor. She was a nurse. They were both unattached and committed Christians. Besides, Elena was crazy about him. What more could Brenan ask for in a woman?

Still, he was sort of waiting for that love-struck feeling to hit him. However, he wasn't fifteen anymore and head-over-heels in love with Shari Kretlow, the pastor's kid. The more he recollected, the more he realized Shari had been one wild young lady back in those days. But Brenan knew why. Pastor Kretlow ran his home like a detention center. The more curfews and groundings he had imposed, the more Shari and her siblings rebelled. Shari had confided in Brenan about everything.

Hindsight told him that, although he had loved Shari more than his own being, she'd viewed him simply as a good friend. When he asked her to marry him, she accepted solely because she couldn't wait to get out of her parents' home. Brenan realized it now. He knew, too, that Pastor Kretlow had mellowed over the years. The man had always loved his congregation, but back then, he was a tyrant of a father. Even when Shari was in college.

"Brenan, I've got to tell you something."

Her voice drew him from his reverie.

"For years, I've felt burdened for you, and I've been praying that God would bring the perfect woman into your life. You know—it's not good for man to be alone and all that." Shari laughed, and Brenan grinned, catching her paraphrase of Genesis 2:18. Then, she dabbed the corners of her mouth with her white linen napkin. "I'm not making this up either." She shot an earnest look at Karan before glancing back at Brenan. "I'd be happy to show you my prayer journal as proof."

"I believe you, and it seems God answered your prayers." He smiled but felt oddly disconcerted. Wasn't Elena the perfect woman for him? When he left Brazil, he'd thought so. Why did he suddenly feel so skeptical?

"I'll also have you know this blizzard is my fault."

"How's that, Shari?" Miriam asked.

Brenan forked some potato into his mouth as he listened.

"I like Florida, but I miss the seasons, especially snow at Christmastime. So I asked God for a white Christmas." She grinned. "God always answers my prayers, even though His answer is sometimes no. In this case, He said, 'Let it snow!' "

"Hey, that rhymes." Sitting at the end of the table, beside the highchair, Laura stopped spooning baby food into Chrissy's mouth long enough to laugh.

"Stop me if I'm being too personal," Brenan began, "but it appears you're a much stronger Christian now than when I last saw you. How'd it all happen?"

"Oh, that's not personal, at least not to me. As you well know, Dad preached the gospel all the time. It wasn't just reserved for Sunday mornings. I guess I sort of tuned him out. I got sick of hearing the same thing over and over and over.

What's more, my impression of a Holy God was a Wizard-of-Oz-like figure. You know, the guy with the booming voice and big white face?"

Brenan smirked and cut off a piece of his meat.

"One night when Greg was away—" She paused. "He traveled a lot. Anyway, I started watching a Christian broadcast, mostly because I couldn't find another program worth viewing. I began to get curious and wondered what made the evangelist on TV different from my pulpit-thumping father. I watched the entire program and had tears running down my face by the time it ended. I realized the problem wasn't with my dad at all. It was with me."

When she paused, Brenan looked up and met her remorseful stare.

"I wasn't a Christian when you knew me—" Shari glanced around the table. ". . .when you all knew me. Oh, I could talk the talk, but the truth of God's Word never penetrated my heart until that night."

Miriam smiled. "Your mother told me years ago. I understand Greg accepted Christ, too, although it was sometime later."

Shari nodded.

Karan grinned. "Abby told me, although she says there is no God."

"I know." Shari nodded her blond head. "The Christmas story has been lost on her—as well as the reason God came to earth and was born of a virgin. Please keep praying for Abby. For my brothers, too."

"Will do," Karan promised.

"Hey, wait a sec," Brenan interjected. "How come I don't know about all this. . .about Shari and her family?" He glanced first at Karan, then at his mother. "Why didn't anybody tell me?"

"I *did* tell you," Karan said in her own defense. "Tonight. Just before Shari arrived."

"You said she and Greg turned out to be committed Christians." He shrugged. "Guess that wasn't much of a surprise." He looked over at Shari. "I figured the two of you *were* Christians."

"Far from it, I'm afraid. But I wrote you a letter, Bren." Shari sipped her ice water. "Years ago."

"I got it." He stared at his plate and remembered how little comfort it brought him, how hurt he still felt after reading it. Still, he forgave her. Forgave them. "But I don't recall you mentioning a turning point in your life."

"Maybe you skimmed her letter like you do my e-mails," Karan quipped.

A soft chuckle emanated through Shari's pink lips. "I know I told you about it, Bren."

He didn't remember. All that came to mind was her apology for dumping him.

Chagrined, Brenan cleared his throat. "I'm not one hundred percent sure, but I don't think you wrote about your conversion."

"Maybe not. Those blank cards will only hold so much information." She looked over at him, and Brenan felt caught in her penetrating gaze. Remorse pooled in her blue eyes. "Sorry."

"No big deal." He sent her a good-natured wink, but like a hot spot after a raging forest fire, the love he once felt for Shari began smoldering somewhere deep within his heart. It was time to snuff out the last of those feelings for good.

※

After dinner, Brenan sat on the back hall stairs with a string of

Christmas lights in his lap. He thought about phoning Elena in Brazil. Maybe hearing her voice would offset the sound of Shari's laughter. He glanced at his watch. No, it was nearing midnight. Elena sacked out early and rose at the crack of dawn. Brenan didn't want to disturb her just because he was having a case of nerves.

Extinguishing the remnants of his feelings for Shari wasn't going to be easy. Already, Brenan felt he was losing the battle. Sitting across from her at the dinner table fanned some inexplicable eternal flame. After all, Brenan once said he would love her until the end of time. Back then he'd meant every word.

Lord, this can't be happening. . . .

He plugged the lights into a nearby electric outlet. Then, slowly, he began unscrewing each large colored bulb, replacing it with a new one in hopes of finding the culprit responsible for disabling the entire string. For as long as Brenan could remember, fixing Christmas lights had been his job—mostly because he was the only one in the family gifted with enough patience.

From the adjacent kitchen, the sounds of clanging stainless steel cookware, accompanied by the scraping of plates, reached Brenan's ears. He heard his mother's voice, then Karan's, and finally Shari's laugh. Odd, how the latter had somehow infiltrated his being and wound itself around his heart.

Lord, how can I still be in love with Shari after all these years? But, maybe what I'm feeling isn't really love. It's nostalgia. Brenan's resolve gained strength. *Right. That's it. Nostalgia.*

Brenan pondered the question and decided his emotions had run amuck due to the shock of seeing Shari again. And then there was all the reminiscing over those high school reunion snapshots. . . .

Chitchat began, and voices were raised over the din of

rushing water from the faucet in the kitchen sink. More clanging and scraping. Brenan tried to ignore the ruckus and focus on the Christmas lights. Maybe he would make his excuses and retire for the night while everyone else decorated the tree. He'd spent a good part of the past twenty-four hours traveling. Spending the night in an airplane seat had left him exhausted.

And that's probably why I'm out of sorts. I'm overtired and not thinking straight. He grinned, congratulating himself on finally making the appropriate diagnosis.

"Oh, Shari, I never knew that! Honey, I'm so sorry!"

His mother's voice extricated Brenan from his thoughts.

Don't eavesdrop.

"Why did you stay with him?" Karan's louder-than-average voice rang through kitchen and into the back hall where Brenan sat. "I mean, if Dan cheated on me, he'd be dead, and I'd be in jail."

Brenan frowned. *Had Flannering been unfaithful?*

"Oh, honestly, Karan," Miriam said. "You say the most outrageous things."

"I'm serious, Mom."

"Listen, I had my own murderous thoughts. Trust me." Shari's voice wafted to his ears, and Brenan couldn't refrain from listening.

Someone shut off the faucet, and things grew quiet, including Shari's tone. Brenan suddenly had to strain to hear her.

"But I realized that I made a vow before God, for better or for worse, in sickness and in health, till death do we part, and I had to live up to that promise. Because I did, Greg became a Christian."

"Abby never said a word."

Brenan rolled his eyes at Karan's remark and unscrewed another bulb. He replaced it. Nothing. He moved on to the next light.

"I kept Greg's infidelity from my family, although they know about it now. But back then, I was afraid they wouldn't support me in my decision to stay with Greg. And I didn't want to stay with him, but when he returned home after his fling and said he'd been diagnosed with a brain tumor, it seemed almost inhumane to turn him away—especially since I carried the health insurance."

"Oh, mercy!" Mom exclaimed. "You've really been through the wringer, haven't you?"

"I refer to it as tried by fire." Shari laughed. "I like to think of myself as pure gold now."

Brenan caught her reference to Job's trials and tribulations in the Old Testament, and he couldn't help but smirk.

"Do you think you'll ever remarry?" Karan asked.

Brenan hated the way his ears perked up at that question.

"I don't know. It takes a long time to train a husband."

All three ladies chuckled.

Brenan rolled his eyes.

"Besides," Shari added, "the world is full of such weirdoes, even within the Christian community. That may sound harsh, but God warned his children about wolves in sheep's clothing. I'm here to tell you they really exist. Take the last date I had. Now, mind you I haven't dated in more than two decades, but. . ."

Shari's voice became nothing more than a whisper. Seconds later, shrieks of disbelief, followed by raucous laughter, bounced off the plaster walls and ping-ponged into the back hall. Brenan didn't think he could stand hearing much more. His emotions were in a jumble. His heart went out to Shari for enduring her husband's unfaithfulness without the support of her family. At the same time, he admired her strength of character. He suddenly wanted to know more about her. In a word, he was. . .interested.

All at once, Brenan felt like a guy who'd stepped into quicksand, and he was sinking fast. Up to his knees. To his chest. Soon, he'd be a goner.

Oh, Lord, help!

The string of lights in his lap suddenly went on. *Thank You, Jesus!* Yanking the cord out of the socket, he stood and traipsed through the breakfast nook. He paused when he reached the main part of the kitchen.

The women sobered when they saw him. Surprised expressions lit their faces.

"I think it's sin to have so much fun doing the dishes," he teased, careful not to meet Shari's gaze. He held the lights up to his mother. "All fixed."

"Wonderful. Thank you, Bren."

After a nod, he proceeded into the living room, hoping to busy himself. No doubt, Dan and Ian would help rid his mind of those unexpected, unwelcome thoughts about Shari.

Chapter 4

Shari wanted to disappear. "Do you think he heard us?"

"Naw." Karan sent her a dismissive wave. "Bren doesn't listen to small talk. I mean, think of how he tuned us out when we were looking at those pictures. We were all in the same room, and he couldn't even keep up with the conversation."

Shari hoped Karan was right, although she'd glimpsed an odd expression on Bren's face before he strode out of the kitchen. Had it been pity? Or was it satisfaction? Did Bren think it had all turned out for the best? He would have never gone to medical school if he married her.

"Elena, being a nurse, must talk his language, because. . ." Karan shook her head. "If women are from Venus and men are from Mars, then Bren's got his very own planet."

"Oh, nonsense," Miriam said while loading the dishwasher. "Bren just has an incredible mind. Smart as a whip. That's why he's such a marvelous doctor."

Shari smiled, recalling he'd always been a good student. She probably wouldn't have graduated from high school if Brenan hadn't helped her.

Pushing up her sleeves, she rinsed plates and salad bowls while Miriam loaded the dishwasher. Then Shari washed the remaining pots and pans, and Karan dried them and put them away.

At long last, the ladies ambled into the living room. The first thing Shari noticed was Chrissy fussing in Laura's arms. Exasperation pinched the younger woman's features, and Shari's heart went out to her.

"Can I hold the baby?"

"If you want." Laura glanced at her daughter, then back at Shari. "She's awfully crabby. Happens every night before bedtime."

Shari gathered Chrissy in her arms, and Laura handed her a crocheted, pink baby blanket and a pacifier. The child squawked, but Shari rocked her side-to-side and began singing soft strains of "Away in a Manager." Chrissy quieted and stared into Shari's face. Seating herself on the couch near the fire, Shari wrapped the blanket snugly around the little one. She rocked and sang to the baby while watching Miriam, Karan, and Laura unpack boxes of decorations. Since she'd barged in on their Christmas Eve, tending to the baby was the least Shari felt she should do. Besides, she never passed up an opportunity to hold an infant.

Shari went through her repertoire of lulling Christmas songs. "Silent Night," "It Came Upon a Midnight Clear," "O Come, O Come Emmanuel," and her favorite, "O Holy Night."

"I don't believe it," Laura said much later. She crossed the room and peered down into her now sleeping child's face. "She looks so sweet and innocent. Who'd believe she's such a terror by day?"

Grinning, Shari thought Laura favored her mother in appearance, right down to her trim figure and hazel eyes.

"You got her to sleep." She stared at Shari. "How'd you do that?"

Feeling pleased, Shari shrugged. "I do have a way with kids. The nursery workers at church adore me."

"I can see why. Will you come and live with me and do this every night?"

She laughed, hearing the teasing note in Laura's voice.

Then, Laura moved to take Chrissy, but Shari touched her forearm. "Can I hold her a while longer?"

"Sure. Just holler when your arms feel like they're about to give way. Chrissy's a pretty solid kid."

"I'll holler, but not too loudly."

Laura's eyes widened and peered at Chrissy. "Right."

She returned to assist her mother and grandmother in trimming the tree. It already looked lovely.

Shari sighed. A glowing fireplace, a sleeping baby in her arms—life didn't get much better than this.

❧

Brenan leaned on the heavy oak doorframe, his arms folded across his chest, and watched Shari rock his great-niece to sleep. Since he stood just outside her line of vision, he could regard her unnoticed, and Brenan couldn't help but feel a little envious of Chrissy, snuggled in close, the lilt of Shari's soprano voice soothing her into a deep sleep. In fact, Brenan's eyelids grew heavy, and he seriously contemplated making his excuses and retiring to his bedroom. But another tradition in the Sheppard family was reading the Christmas story from the Gospel of St. Luke. Brenan's brother-in-law had been awarded the privilege tonight, much to Brenan's relief. He felt so tired he could barely see straight, let alone read from the Bible.

Brenan blinked, seeing his mom's orange tabby, Sunkissed, hop up on the couch. The animal nestled himself next to Shari, and Brenan realized she had that way about her, attracting both people and pets. Greg was daft to risk his marriage for what Shari had termed "a fling." And Shari—she was one remarkable woman to take him back, and all to God's glory. Brenan couldn't get over it. He kept thinking about it, much to his irritation.

Before he had a chance to consider his actions, he walked to the couch and scooped up Sunkissed, setting him on the carpeted floor. The cat meowed, but Brenan ignored the protests as he seated himself beside Shari.

"Hey, that wasn't nice, Uncle Bren. Sunkissed was dozing."

He glanced at his niece, who held gold garland in her hands. "Would it have been better if I sat on the thing?"

"The *thing?*" Laura gave him a look of admonishment. "Sunkissed isn't a *thing.*"

"My apologies for the offense, Laura," he said with a smirk, "but I've always believed that furniture is for people, and obscure corners—preferably outside—are for cats."

Laura rolled her eyes, Miriam chuckled, and Karan grinned before muttering, "Typical Bren."

Beside him, Shari grinned. "You never did like cats, did you?"

Turning to his right, he met her blue-eyed stare. "Nope. Never did."

Her smile widened at his admission before she glanced down at the sleeping baby in her arms.

Bren stretched his arm out along the top of the sofa and reached across Shari's lap with the other to caress Chrissy's soft cheek. "Babies look so angelic when they're sleeping."

"Yes, they do."

"And this girl is a very healthy little angel." He grinned and straightened. "But each time I look at her, I feel this inexplicable burden for an orphanage in Cambodia." Brenan didn't know why he was telling Shari all this, but it seemed the thing to do. "I heard about the place from a fellow missionary. Children, some as young as newborn babies, are left at the doorstep. Many are sick and need medical attention, but the ailments are usually curable."

Shari looked aghast. "They're left at the doorstep of the orphanage? Abandoned?"

Brenan nodded. "Usually it's a family member—a grandmother or distant relative—who has been left with the responsibility of caring for the child for one reason or another. Due to the extreme poverty in that country, many can't afford to pay for healthcare. Even if they could, qualified physicians are hard to find."

Shari's gaze turned misty. "That breaks my heart."

"Mine, too."

"You and Elena *have* to go."

Brenan chuckled at Shari's determination. "Well, we'll see." The truth was, Elena didn't want to leave Brazil and her people. Many of them were in as much need as the poorest of Cambodians.

"What's to see, Bren? Those children need you. God didn't put that burden on your heart for nothing."

He couldn't quell the smirk tugging at his mouth. Shari had always been something of an advocate for the underprivileged. In high school she befriended the kids others picked on.

Like himself. Brenan had always been the guy who wasn't good at sports, a little awkward and clumsy until he'd grown into his feet.

At that moment, Dan and Ian sauntered into the living

room and sat down. Dan set his large, black Bible on the coffee table, an indication he was ready to read the Christmas story whenever Miriam spoke the word.

Brenan sat back and relaxed as light chitchat ensued. Meanwhile, his mother, Karan, and Laura finished decorating the tree. A good while later, Laura took Chrissy upstairs to the portable crib.

"Remind me. Do you and Karan have other children?" Shari asked Dan as she smoothed out her black dress over her knees.

"Two sons. Both in the army." Dan's expression was a mix of pride and remorse.

"Broke their mother's heart," Karan said from across the room. "I cried for a week after they went off to boot camp. That's where they are now. But they should be here with us."

"Now, Karan. . ." Dan shot his wife an understanding glance. "They'll be back."

"How old are they?" Shari wanted to know.

"Eighteen and twenty." Dan shifted his weight in the armchair.

Moments of silence passed before Shari turned to Brenan. "Hey, Bren, tell me about Brazil. As I said before, I've read your quarterly newsletters, but tell me the inside scoop."

He grinned. "What inside scoop?"

"Well, what's your apartment or house like? What are the people like?" She arched a conspiratorial brow. "How'd you meet Elena?"

Everyone hooted.

"That's what she really wants to know, Bren." Dan laughed again.

Shari's face turned the color of her red sweater. "Okay, so

I'm nosy. Everybody already knows that about me."

Brenan's smile grew, and Dan and Ian chuckled. "Elena is a nurse at the hospital where I work."

"And?" Shari prompted.

"And. . .what?"

"How did you meet? Was Elena walking down the hallway, taking care of somebody, what?"

"Actually, she was angry with an uncooperative patient and hurled an empty bedpan across the room. I happened to be entering at that precise moment to see what all the yelling was about. Fortunately, I ducked before getting clunked upside the head."

Shari burst out laughing, causing Brenan to chuckle.

Standing near the tree, Karan whirled around and strode toward him. "How come you never told Mom and me that story?"

"I don't know." He laughed again, mostly because Shari was still cackling next to him.

"Guess you just have to ask the right questions," Ian said with a toss of his blond head and a wry grin.

"So she got your attention, eh?" Shari's shoulders shook with amusement.

"I suppose you could say I got her attention. Elena felt so ashamed for losing her temper that she apologized about five times. Finally, she asked if she could make me dinner in recompense for her deplorable behavior. I agreed. Things progressed from there."

"Smart woman," Shari said. "She knows the way to a man's heart is through his stomach."

While others found the remark amusing, Brenan didn't. He studied the hem on his trousers. The truth was, Elena hadn't found her way to his heart. He thought she had, but it seemed someone else still occupied that special place.

He looked at Shari. Her blue eyes sparkled back at him.

"Did she do the whole soft music and candlelight thing?"

Feeling oddly mesmerized, Brenan found it hard to even muster a smile. "Candlelight? Yeah."

"You should have sensed trouble right there, buddy," Dan quipped.

Positioned directly behind him, Karan smacked the top of her husband's head. "Marriage is blissful, remember?"

"Oh, yeah. Glad you reminded me."

More chuckles filled the room.

"All right, everyone, I think it's time for the Christmas story." Miriam reentered the living room, and her announcement put a cap on further merriment. "Just as soon as Laura returns from putting the baby to bed, we'll begin."

Dan slid his Bible onto his lap and flipped it open.

Shari leaned closer to Brenan. "I'm sorry if I embarrassed you. Sometimes I get carried away."

"No harm done." He gave her a smile and moved his hand from the back of the couch to her shoulder. He gave it a squeeze—an effort to assure her. But seconds later, he brought his arm back to his side. He shouldn't touch her. He shouldn't even sit next to her. Even the same room was too close a proximity, and yet he couldn't get himself to budge.

"I'm really happy for you, Bren."

Her words crimped his heart, and he realized that somewhere in the deepest recesses of his being he didn't want Shari to feel happy about his impending engagement to Elena.

He wanted Shari to love him.

Chapter 5

And so it was, that, while they were there, the days were accomplished that she should be delivered. And she brought forth her firstborn son, and wrapped him in swaddling clothes, and laid him in a manger; because there was no room for them in the inn.' "

As Shari listened to Dan Strang read from Luke, chapter two, she tamped down anguished thoughts of those poor children being left on the orphanage's doorstep in Cambodia. She tried to pay attention to the Christmas story but found herself asking Jesus to protect those helpless kids on the other side of the world. Wouldn't Shari love to tell *them* the Christmas story and about how much Jesus loves them! She would probably want to adopt every single child she met.

Maybe I could adopt one of those orphans. Would it be allowed, since I'd be a single mother?

Shari decided to ask Brenan about it later. Perhaps he could put her in touch with that missionary friend he'd mentioned.

She forced herself to relax and pay attention to the Bible reading.

" 'And, lo, the angel of the Lord came upon them, and the glory of the Lord shone round about them; and they were sore afraid. And the angel said unto them, Fear not: for, behold, I bring you good tidings of great joy, which shall be to all people. For unto you is born this day in the city of David a Saviour, which is Christ the Lord.' "

Shari marveled as she always did whenever the reality hit her. The Word was indeed God and became flesh in order to save mankind from sin and eternal death.

What a wonderful Savior to leave His heavenly home and become a human by the lowliest of births.

Shari felt her eyes grow misty as Dan finished reading. She glanced at Brenan, only to find his brown eyes regarding her with interest. Giving him a tentative smile, she wondered why he was staring at her.

She looked back at the others, thinking Brenan was still very much that quiet, introspective man she'd known so long ago. It gave her an odd sense of gratification to know that, in spite of the years of distance separating them, she could still draw him out of his shell.

When the reading was finished, Brenan touched her shoulder. Again, Shari turned to face him.

"Are you still a coffee drinker?"

She nodded.

"If I make a pot of decaf, will you have a cup or two?"

"I'd love it."

She smiled, and Brenan stood. She watched him leave the living room then wondered if now wouldn't be a perfect time to ask him about the orphans and his missionary friend.

Following him into the kitchen, Shari paused at the doorway while Brenan scooped coffee grounds into the filter. She took a moment to collect her thoughts, until Brenan saw her and grinned.

"Can I get you anything?"

"Um, no, but I wanted to ask you about that orphanage."

"Oh? What about it?" Brenan walked to the sink and filled the carafe with purified water.

"I wondered if I could get more information about it, specifically about the possibility of adopting a child. I've wanted kids for so long, and it just never worked out before. But I'd be a single mother. Do you think this orphanage would consider me qualified and. . .first things first, does Cambodia even allow adoptions?"

"I think they do." Brenan poured the water into the automatic coffeemaker then flipped the ON switch. "Tom and his wife have already adopted two kids."

Shari tried not to feel too optimistic. How many times in the past years had her hopes been dashed when it came to having a child of her own?

Too many to count.

Brenan's smile suddenly widened, and he strode toward her. Without warning, he leaned forward and pressed his lips to hers. Shari felt his soft beard brush lightly against her face as the moment lingered. To her surprise, the kiss warmed her insides more than a cup of hot coffee.

"Merry Christmas," he whispered, straightening.

"Merry Christmas," she murmured back, feeling stunned by what just occurred.

As if in explanation, Brenan flicked his gaze above her head. "Mistletoe."

She looked up and gave a nervous little laugh. "Oh!"

He chuckled.

"Okay, you got me. I never saw it coming, and I never noticed the mistletoe up there."

She glanced up again, and in that time, she felt Brenan's arms encircle her waist. Wide-eyed, she stared back at him. His dark brown eyes peered down at her, warm and rich with a hint of longing.

Shari put her hands on his chest, pushing him back. "No, Bren. We shouldn't."

He sobered then released her. "I know. You're right."

She saw a flash of hurt in his eyes and caught the sleeve of his sweater before he could turn away.

"Bren?" She frowned. What could he possibly be thinking by kissing her?

He swallowed before replying. "I guess it's seeing you again, Shari."

She felt heartsick at the idea she might have ruined more than just his Christmas Eve. "I'm sorry."

Brenan rubbed the backs of his fingers over her cheek. "And that's the problem—I'm not."

"But—"

Before she could ask him about his fiancée waiting for him back in Brazil, Karan burst into the room.

Brenan took a step back, and Shari suddenly felt like they were mischievous teenagers again, kissing on the sneak like they did at age fifteen.

"Mom made chocolate mint pie. It'll go great with the coffee." Karan smiled at Shari. "Want to help me slice and serve?"

"Absolutely."

Shari cast a glance at Brenan, but he was already making his way back into the living room. She wasn't certain of all that had just happened between them, but one thing she knew for sure—Shari wasn't about to stand in the way of Brenan's happiness a second time.

What in the world possessed me to kiss Shari?

Brenan sat on the sofa while conversation droned on around him. He didn't hear a word anyone said as he berated himself for being so impulsive. It wasn't his nature, and yet he couldn't seem to help himself. Shari standing in his mother's kitchen, under the mistletoe, her pink lips puckered in thought... She'd simply looked too good to resist.

Brenan glanced at the entryway as Karan strode into the living room carrying a large tray. He stood to help, but Ian beat him to it.

"Shari went up to her room," Karan announced while handing out coffee and cake. "She has a headache, and I can understand why. The poor dear drove all the way from Ohio today, and she's beat."

Brenan wasn't surprised at the news, but he would bet it was his kiss, and not a headache, that caused Shari to retire for the night. He'd be lucky if she ever spoke to him again.

"Ian, would you be a sweetheart and bring in Shari's luggage?" Karan placed a set of keys in her son-in-law's palm. "She needs the blue suitcase that's in the trunk."

"Will do." The younger man grinned and reached for his wife. "I never pass up a chance to play in the snow."

Laura smiled and took his hand. Together they walked off.

"Bring the luggage in first," Dan hollered after them. He shook his head. "Kids."

Brenan felt a tad envious of his niece and Ian just as he'd felt envious of Karan and Dan over the years. *Lord, it seems everyone has someone, except for me.*

"Do you think Elena would like the snow?"

His mother's question yanked Brenan from his self-pity.

"I—I don't know."

"Hmm." Miriam furrowed her brows. "Something bothering you, Bren?"

"Yeah." He set his untouched slice of cake onto the tray. "But maybe I'll have a new perspective on things tomorrow. I'm exhausted." He stood. "I think I'll turn in for the night."

"We're not far behind you," Karan said, sipping her cup of decaf. "I feel pretty whipped myself."

Brenan forced a smile then kissed his mother and sister before wishing Dan a good night's sleep.

As he climbed the steps, he rued his foolish heart. Talk about perverse human nature! Beautiful Elena awaited him in Brazil. But, no, she wouldn't do. Instead, his heart longed for a woman who didn't return his feelings—Shari, a woman who would never love him back.

Chapter 6

S hari lay in the darkened bedroom listening to the wind howl outside. She kept reliving Brenan's kiss. Odd, how his kisses hadn't affected her when they were teens. But tonight's surprise smooch left her reeling.

Even so, Shari was determined not to give in to her feelings. What's more, the realization that her premonition had been right all these years caused a swell of guilt in her chest. Brenan hadn't married because she'd hurt him so badly.

Oh, God, please heal his heart. Isn't he in love with Elena? If he is, then why did Bren say he wasn't sorry after he kissed me?

A gust of wind whistled around the Open Door Inn, and Shari snuggled deeper into the pile of quilts on her bed. Once more, she thought of Brenan, and it pained her to think her very presence wounded him all over again. As for herself, Brenan's kiss had awaked her senses. She couldn't recall the last time she'd been in a man's arms for a sweet, romantic interlude—and her last date with "Mr. Octopus" didn't count. What a sick twist of fate that now, when she felt attracted to Brenan, he wasn't available.

But, maybe he could be. . . .

No! No! No!

Shari reined in her foolish thoughts. If she came between Brenan and Elena, the Sheppards would regard her as that same selfish, rebellious woman she'd been twenty-three years ago. Karan would tell Abby, and then Shari's Christian testimony would be at stake. How would she prove to her siblings that Jesus was as real as Greg's illness had been if Christ couldn't be seen in her life?

On that thought, Shari closed her eyes and allowed the exhaustion from driving all day to overtake her. Minutes later, she slept.

The next morning, Brenan awoke early. He showered, dressed, and then phoned Elena. He hoped that hearing her voice would alleviate his doubts about them as a couple. But instead of Elena, her roommate Dori answered the phone. At twenty-two years old, Dori was the youngest on the team. Spunky and like-able, she taught school for all the missionaries' kids.

"Elena's not around. She left for the weekend with a group of the others. They're celebrating Christmas by skydiving over Rio de Janeiro and then hiking into the Amazon."

Brenan sat forward and frowned. "Elena's doing *what*?"

"Skydiving. Tomorrow they trek through the jungle." Dori giggled. "You know them, Dr. Sheppard. They're crazy."

Yes, he knew. That is, he was aware of the five daredevils on the team, but he hadn't thought Elena was one of them.

"You couldn't pay me enough to jump out of an airplane, unless it was about to crash or something."

Brenan grinned at Dori's remark. "Thank you for the information. Please tell Elena I called to wish her a Merry Christmas."

"Will do. But, um, is that all you want me to tell her?" Dori's voice suddenly took on a teasing, singsong tone.

He knew what she was fishing for; however, the only three little words Brenan could manage to say were, "Yeah, that's all."

He disconnected the call and sat back in the armchair in the corner of the bedroom. He thought about how well Elena and Dori got along and then struggled again with age difference between Elena and himself. And it wasn't her daring that troubled him. Skydiving actually sounded fun, and he'd already hiked through parts of the Amazon with a tour guide. It was Elena's apparent footloose spirit that caused Brenan to rethink his marriage proposal. He suddenly realized he didn't want to spend the rest of his life trying to tame an energetic and overzealous wife. What if he didn't succeed?

Lord, I sense that Elena is beautiful in more ways than just her physical appearance. She loves You. That should be enough for me, but it isn't. I'll admit my attraction, but I'm not sure I could live with the rest of her.

His heart suddenly reminded him that he was attracted to Shari Flannering, too.

I'm one hopeless mess.

❧

"You can't leave without breakfast!"

Shari blinked at her hostess's exclamation. Standing in the kitchen near the back hall, her suitcase in tow, Shari had been all set to trudge out to her car, clean off the snow, and drive to her parents' house. She'd said good-bye to Karan, Dan, Laura, and Ian, thankful that Brenan wasn't around. But when she entered the kitchen to thank Miriam for allowing her to stay overnight, the older woman halted Shari in her tracks.

"I'm baking cranberry muffins. Karan made a delicious egg, cheese, and sausage bake. Please stay." Miriam wore a beseeching expression.

Shari's resolve crumbled. She didn't want to appear ungrateful, after all. "Well, it does smell awfully good in here."

Miriam beamed. "Let me get you a cup of coffee."

Minutes later, cup and saucer in hand, Shari was escorted back into the dining room where Laura was feeding baby Chrissy.

"I didn't think you'd get away that easily," Karan teased. "Mom has this thing about feeding people."

Shari laughed. "So I've discovered."

"And she won't let anyone help her cook, either, although she did grant me the privilege of creating my Italian egg bake."

"It sounds scrumptious."

"You'll love it, Shari," Dan piped in.

Karan relayed the recipe, and Shari listened with a smile while she sipped her coffee. The egg dish sounded easy enough to put together, and the fact that it could be prepared the night before only added to the beauty of it.

At last, Miriam brought out warm cranberry muffins. A short time later, she carried in the rectangular glass baking dish containing Karan's masterpiece. Then Brenan followed his mother into the dining room, and Shari felt a nervous little flutter fill her insides.

"Merry Christmas, everyone." Wearing black jeans and a forest-green cotton pullover, he glanced around the table until finally his gaze met hers. "Morning, Shari."

"Morning, Bren." Her face began to warm under his scrutiny.

"Merry Christmas, bro."

He grinned at Karan, and Shari almost sighed in relief when

he removed the weight of his stare. But then, to her discomfort, Brenan took the chair beside her. As he sat, his shower-fresh, spicy scent wafted to her nostrils. She found it most appealing, and suddenly Shari felt doomed.

I'm going to eat to appease Miriam, and then I'm out of here!

"Let's all hold hands and ask the Lord's blessing," Miriam said from the head of the table.

No! Shari's mind screamed. But out of a sense of propriety, she smiled at Brenan and offered her hand.

He took it in a firm, but gentle, grip.

"Ian, will you pray for us?"

"Sure."

Please be quick about it. Shari bowed her head, closed her eyes, and tried to concentrate.

"Thank You, Lord, for this food and for family and friends. Thank You for coming to earth two thousand years ago and taking on the frailties of human form in order to save our souls. Thank You for. . ."

Shari wanted to groan as the younger man's prayer seemed to go on forever while her hand was held captive in Bren's.

Finally, Ian wrapped it up. "We ask Your blessing on this food and on this Christmas Day as we remember Your birth. Amen."

A chorus of amens rang out from around the table. Brenan gave Shari's hand a small squeeze before releasing it. His gesture seemed to zing up her arm and go straight to her heart.

Moments later, plates were passed as Miriam served everyone a healthy portion of the egg bake. Shari began to eat, forcing herself not to gobble so she could high-tail it out of the Open Door Inn and Brenan's disturbing presence.

"So, Shari. . ."

She glanced at the object of her tumultuous thoughts. "Yes?"

"What made you decide to become a dental hygienist?"

She swallowed the food before it stuck in her throat. "Um, well, I was working at a dentist's office as a receptionist and realized that with some additional training I could just about triple my wages. So I went back to school, got my license, and that's how it happened."

"Do you enjoy it?"

"It's okay." Shari sipped her coffee, hoping it would wash down her emotions. "Pays the bills."

"Bet you have a lot of them, what with Greg being so ill and all."

Shari looked across the table at Karan who'd made the remark. "Actually, I don't have a lot of medical bills. I'm blessed to have premium health insurance through my job, and Greg was awarded disability coverage through the State of Florida. Of course, I don't own a house. That was the first to go shortly after Greg got sick."

"That's right. Abby said you have a two-bedroom apartment." Karan wiped her mouth with a red paper napkin. "She told me it's in a nice complex with a pool and a clubhouse."

Shari nodded. "I'm very comfortable there, and somehow I squeeze my family into my place when they visit." She laughed, recalling last Christmas, when her two brothers slept in sleeping bags on the living room floor. Two nieces and Luke's wife crowded into Shari's queen-sized bed. Shari and Abby slept on the floor nearby so their aging parents could occupy the guest room. The next morning, however, none of the adults except Shari's mom and dad could move—although it was a great excuse for jumping into the hot tub.

"You've been through so much, Shari. I sense your trials have made you a strong woman." Miriam smiled while spreading butter on half of her muffin.

"Oh, I don't know how strong I am." She thought of how weak-kneed and nervous she felt at the moment, just sitting beside Brenan. She tried not to look for his reaction, but out of the corner of her eye, she saw him give her a smile.

Finally, Shari couldn't stand it any longer. She scooted her chair back. "I need to get going. Thank you for breakfast. Thanks for everything."

"You're welcome, dear." Miriam smiled. "So good to see you again."

"Likewise."

Brenan turned in his chair. "Before you go, Shari, why don't you follow me upstairs to Mom's computer? I'm sure she won't mind if I use it to print off information on the Cambodia ministry I told you about last night."

The adoption possibility. How could she possibly forget about those poor children on the other side of the world?

"Bren, of course you can use my computer." Miriam sipped her coffee. "Just watch that printer. It's been giving me fits lately. Jams up every so often."

"Thanks for the warning." Brenan slid his chair back and stood. Placing his palm beneath Shari's elbow, he helped her to her feet and guided her toward the steps. "Tom built a pretty elaborate Web site. I think you'll find it extremely informative."

"I'm sure I will."

Together, they climbed the steps and entered Miriam's large bedroom. In one corner was a nook in which a computer desk fit almost perfectly. Brenan booted up the machine then pulled over a second chair. Shari sat down, forgetting all about her anxious, fluttery feelings. Instead, she felt hopeful. God obviously had a reason for allowing her to stop here last night in the middle of a blizzard. Perhaps that reason had something to do with adopting a Cambodian orphan. Maybe the Lord would finally bless her with that one thing she'd never been able to have, no matter how hard she'd prayed. . .

A child.

Chapter 7

Engrossed, Shari explored the Web site. She learned Hollia's House, the Cambodian orphanage, was named after a little girl who had died of leukemia. Hollia's parents were part of the American mission team that began the work there a little more than five years ago. After seeing the smiling faces of some of the youngsters and then reading their stories of how they came to live at the Hollia's House, Shari wanted to adopt them all.

"Bren, you have to go. It says many of the children at the orphanage are in need of medical care—like Hollia who died of cancer."

"I know what the site says." He sat back and stretched his arm out along the top of Shari's chair. "Tom's been after me to join his ministry for the past three months."

Shari sat back, too. "Why the hesitation?"

"Well, for one, I want to be sure it's God's will for me. There are a lot of worthwhile causes in the world. I can't take on all of them."

"True." Shari glanced down at her dark brown corduroy slacks and began to fidget with a piece of lint.

"Reason number two, Elena doesn't want to leave Brazil."

Shari looked up. "Ah. Yes, well, I see where that might pose a problem."

"And that's not the only problem."

Shari watched Brenan stare at the computer monitor. His profile was so familiar to her, yet so strange, especially with the addition of that well-groomed, inky black beard. She imagined it would feel more soft than scratchy beneath her fingertips.

She gave herself a mental shake. What was she thinking?

Refocusing on their conversation, Shari's common sense told her to leave the subject of Elena alone, but she couldn't seem to do it.

"What problem are you referring to, Bren, if I'm not being too nosy?"

He turned and regarded her, then leaned closer, as if about to divulge a very personal secret. "For some time now, Elena has been talking marriage. Each time she broached the subject, I'd get what I can only describe as a check in my heart. I discussed the matter with my pastor who told me I've just been single too long. I'll get over it." Brenan took a deep breath. "I've been trying, but that check doesn't go away."

"Did you mention this to Elena?"

Brenan shook his head.

"That might be a good place to start."

"You're probably right."

"So what's the problem?"

Brenan expelled a weary sounding breath. "Talking won't fix one of my biggest concerns. It's the difference in our ages."

Shari felt an odd twinge of jealousy. "How young is she?"

"Just turned thirty."

"Thirty isn't that young, Bren." Shari quelled her envy. "But she's still got many childbearing years ahead of her."

She can give him a family, and I can't. Shari shook off her wayward thoughts. *Why am I even thinking about me? I have no part in this equation.*

"I'm not so concerned about the childbearing part of Elena's age," Brenan said, recapturing Shari's attention. "What makes me wary is her rather irresponsible behavior. Elena acts more like she's twenty. I don't want to become some sort of father figure to my wife. If I marry, I want a partnership. Camaraderie. I think a husband and wife should be on the same emotional and spiritual plane."

"Well, yeah, that's the way it's supposed to work." Shari laughed and tore her gaze from Brenan's earnest eyes. "But I'm afraid I'm no expert in that area. For half my marriage, I was blissfully ignorant of reality, believing Greg loved me the way I loved him. But then, one day, I got this phone call—"

Shari halted.

"Go on," he urged. "Tell me."

Brenan's tone was filled with such compassion, that Shari didn't think twice about continuing. "One day I received a phone call from a woman named Annette Jenkins. She had just discovered Greg had a wife and, as a way of getting even, she decided to contact me and divulge the whole ugly truth about her fling with my husband. Actually, it was more than a fling."

Brenan winced.

"And here I thought he was away on business, working hard, missing me while he slept alone in his hotel room. The truth was he'd been staying with her. They even had an apartment together! Greg had lied to Annette, too, saying he was on business when he'd come home to me." Shari smacked her palm against her forehead. "Stupid me, I never suspected a thing."

"Aw, Shari, I'm so sorry."

"Thanks." She ran her thumbnail up and down the crease in her slacks. "But maybe I got my comeuppance, huh?"

After throwing out the challenge, she looked up and studied Brenan's face, gauging his reaction. All she saw in his expression was sympathy.

"I wouldn't wish that kind of heartache on my worst enemy." He slipped his arm around her shoulders and gave her a hug. In a soft voice, he added, "And I never thought of you as my enemy, Shari."

His gentle words, his nearness, and embrace seemed to penetrate her very soul. Lifting her hand, she touched his cheek, and then her fingers found their way to his silky beard. Their gazes locked, and Shari thought she could drown in his brown eyes.

But suddenly reality hit. *What am I doing?*

She shot up off her chair. "I have to go."

"Shari, wait."

She didn't, but instead hurried across the room and out the door. Running down the steps, she prayed Brenan wouldn't follow. She found her coat in the closet, grabbed her purse, and called a good-bye as she hustled passed the dining room.

"Thanks for everything!"

"Whoa, Shari, wait up a sec."

She ignored Karan's request and grabbed the handle of her suitcase, still in the back hall.

"Good seeing you, Karan."

"But I want to ask you about New Year's Eve." She jogged through the kitchen to catch up. "Good grief, where's the fire?"

Shari's face flamed. "Don't ask!"

With that, she bolted out the door and to her car.

From his mother's second-story bedroom window, Brenan folded his arms and watched Shari unbury her car. Snowflakes swirled in the winter air, and he prayed she'd safely make it to her folks' place before the next storm hit. As disappointed as he felt watching her go, a swell of hope plumed inside of him. He recognized the longing in her eyes. It had mirrored his own.

Shari's fighting the same battle I am. But why? Does she think all men are untrustworthy—like Flannering?

Brenan considered various scenarios and concluded he could spend all day guessing. He'd have to pray. Only God could change Shari's heart—and his, too.

Lord, I think I still love her. Is that possible? Most of all, is it Your will?

"Bren, what did you do to Shari?"

Hearing the reprimand in his sister's voice, he pivoted toward the door and faced her. "I don't know what you mean."

"Yes, you do. You scared her. What did you say?"

"Karan, I think. . ." Brenan stroked his beard and pursed his lips. ". . .I think we scared ourselves. Maybe we scared each other."

She narrowed her gaze and stepped toward him. "I don't get it."

He shrugged. "I don't either, but I'd like to pursue the matter." He headed for the door, skirting his sister.

"Pursue the matter? As in you and Shari?"

Brenan glanced over his shoulder and grinned. "Me and Shari. Kind of has a nice ring to it, don't you think?"

At Karan's wide-eyed, gaping expression, he chuckled all the way downstairs. Even as a kid, Brenan enjoyed riling his older sister. He especially liked to get in the last word.

Ah, yes, some things never changed.

≈≈≈

"Merry Christmas!"

Shari threw her arms around her mom and dad, then her brothers and Abby and Abby's husband. Next, she hugged her sister-in-law, Rebecca, and nieces and nephews, Elizabeth, Crystal, Madeline, Andrew, and Johnny.

Shari expelled a sigh of relief. "I'm so glad to finally be here."

"Ditto. Your mother worried you'd get stuck in another snowstorm," Walt Kretlow said with a wide grin. At age sixty-nine, his hair had turned to silver, but Shari's father was still as tall and willowy as ever. The sound of his voice hadn't changed much either. It still rang with authority, although his features had softened. "Glad to see that wasn't the case."

"Me, too, but those last few miles were difficult. Roads are pretty slick."

Sylvia shooed everyone out of the delicious-smelling kitchen. Bread was rising in the automatic bread maker, and a roast cooked in the oven.

"When can we open presents?" four-year-old Madeline wanted to know. She had inherited Luke's blond hair and blue eyes.

"Soon," Sylvia promised her granddaughter. She smiled at Shari. "The kids are so impatient."

"That's to be expected. It's Christmas." Shari hugged her slender mother again. "It's good to be home."

"It's good to have you home."

Arm-in-arm, they made their way through the small house and into the living room. Shari drank in the sight of her family, noticing two were missing.

"Where are Ashly and Simon?" she asked, referring to her brother Mark's kids.

"Deidre's got 'em," he groused.

Shari's heart did a nosedive, not so much because the kids weren't here, but at her brother's tone. Mark and Deidre were in the process of a nasty divorce and, judging from the last few times she'd talked to him, Mark was growing angry and bitter.

Lowering herself into one of the overstuffed armchairs with its red and green throw, Shari considered her younger brother as he sat on the couch. Remote in hand, he surfed the TV channels. He stopped when the kids squealed over a program they wanted to watch.

The phone rang, and Sylvia left the room to answer the call.

"So how was your drive, other than hitting snow north of Milwaukee?"

Shari turned to her lovely sister-in-law Rebecca and smiled. "Other than that, I made good time."

"How was your stay at the Sheppards' bed-and-breakfast?" Abby wanted to know. "Kinda boring, I imagine, with just Miriam there."

"Well, actually, Karan and Dan were there along with Laura and Ian and their sweet little girl Chrissy, and, um. . ." Shari turned and scratched the back of her head. "Brenan was there too."

"Get out of town!" Abby leaned forward, and under the lamplight, her hair had a purplish hue. Being a beautician, she was always doing something trendy to her short hair. "Brenan was there? Was it like World War III or something?"

"No, not at all. We got along great." *Maybe a little too great,* Shari added silently.

"You mean he didn't even make mention of how you dumped him?"

"Abby, that was a lifetime ago. Bren and I got along fine. Everything was fine." Shari hoped her no-big-deal tone belied the tumult raging inside her.

"Fine?" Mark pinned her with an incredulous stare. He sat forward and dangled his hands over his knees. "Shari, if I was Brenan I'd never want to see your face again, and if I did, there'd be trouble."

"Mark!" Shari blinked, shocked by his vehemence.

"I'm just being honest."

The minister in Walt Kretlow suddenly emerged. "Brenan is a Christian, Mark, and Christians forgive those who trespass against them."

"Yeah, whatever." He sat back on the sofa and crossed his legs. Shari thought her brother, wearing faded jeans and a gray sweatshirt, appeared rather disheveled. His light brown hair had outgrown its last cut, and his chin was bristly, as though he'd forgotten to shave this morning.

Mild trepidation gripped her. *He's letting himself go. He doesn't care anymore.*

"So, Shari, how is Bren these days? My, my, it's been a good number of years since I saw him last."

At her father's inquiry, she pushed out a smile. "Oh, he's doing just fine."

"There's that word again," Abby remarked. Sitting beside her husband, Bill, she arched a brow. "Somehow I don't think things were as *fine* last night as you say."

Shari waved a hand at her. "Oh, I'm tired, Abby, that's all."

Sylvia appeared at the doorway. She was all smiles. "Guess who just phoned? Brenan Sheppard. It was like old times, hearing his voice just like when he used to call for Shari."

She wanted to groan, but she kept a rein on her emotions.

Her mother looked right at her. "Bren wanted to make sure you arrived safely. He said he was worried about you. Isn't that sweet?"

Shari just grinned, willing her cheeks not to redden with embarrassment.

"He also said to tell you that he printed the information you wanted off the Internet, and he'll give it to you tomorrow at church." Sylvia clasped her hands with glee and peered across the room at her husband. "Isn't that marvelous? Bren and Miriam are coming to church tomorrow."

"Wonderful." Walt sported a pleased expression.

"I invited them here for lunch afterwards."

"You did?" Shari tried not to visibly grimace.

"Oh." Sylvia frowned, obviously sensing Shari's discomfort. "Shouldn't I have done that? I'm sorry. I thought by the way Bren talked that you were friends."

"We are." Shari groaned inwardly. "Listen, don't mind me. I'm exhausted and not thinking straight. Of course it's all right that Bren and Miriam come for lunch tomorrow. Miriam was the perfect hostess last night."

"Was Bren a good host?" Abby smirked.

Shari tossed her a withering look.

"Can we open presents now?" Andrew asked, leaning against his dad. The boy was Abby and Bill's eldest son, and Shari decided he was growing more handsome each year.

"Walt, what do you think?" Bill asked. "Can the kids rip and tear?"

Shari grinned as her father chuckled and nodded. "Have at it, kids." His gaze spanned the room, and he smiled. "Now that Shari's here safe 'n' sound, it's really Christmas!"

Chapter 8

The following morning, sunshine streamed into the room Shari shared with her niece Elizabeth. She figured it was just her bad luck that another snowstorm couldn't have been blowing through Door County right now, keeping Brenan and his mother at home.

Rising from the bed, she padded across the cold wooden floor and down the hall to the bathroom. She showered and dressed, changing clothes three times before deciding on a black skirt, white turtleneck, and a colorful coordinating button-down sweater. As she took care in applying her cosmetics, she tried to convince herself she wasn't out to impress Bren.

Yeah? Then why didn't I tell my family that he's got a woman waiting for him back in Brazil?

Shari stared at her reflection, hating the turmoil in her heart. She felt a stab of jealousy each time she thought of Elena. She had no idea what the lady looked like or who she was. However, Shari found herself secretly hoping things wouldn't work out for her and Bren. Then, she despised her wayward emotions all the more.

Oh, God. Shari closed her eyes. *I prayed for a wife for Bren, and now You've answered that prayer. Please let me be happy for Bren and Elena—and work in Bren's heart so that the doubts he told me about are alleviated once and for all.*

After a quick breakfast, Shari rode to church with her parents. Luke and Rebecca followed in their SUV, loaded with the three kids. Once they arrived, Shari helped her mother prepare two large urns of coffee for the brief fellowship to be held in the basement of the quaint country church following the service. Shari had forgotten how small the structure was. It seemed miniscule compared to the church she attended in Florida.

Sylvia wiped her hands on a nearby towel. "Well, that ought to do it. Shall we head upstairs?"

Shari nodded, but dread filled her being at the thought of coming face-to-face with Brenan.

"What's wrong, dear?"

Shari gave herself a mental kick before sending her mother a smile. "Nothing's wrong. Nothing at all."

"Sharon Rose, I know you too well." Sylvia's blond brows knitted together in a frown. "Something's bothering you. What is it?"

For about five seconds, she considered confiding in her mom, but then realized Sylvia would fret throughout the service and worry all afternoon. *No, best to keep things to yourself.*

Shari laughed. "I'm being silly, that's what it is. It's been eons since I've seen a lot of the people who'll be here today. I guess I'm feeling a bit nervous."

Immediate relief washed over Sylvia's features. "Oh, don't worry about anything. Folks wonder how you're doing all the time. Dad and I stay busy trying to keep 'em up-to-date."

Still smiling, Shari followed her mother up the narrow steps and into the tiny vestibule. Several individuals whom Shari didn't recognize were hanging up their winter wraps.

While Sylvia stopped to chat, Shari wandered into the sanctuary. Already, her brother Mark had arrived and sat next to Luke, Rebecca, and their kids. Abby would show up soon with her husband, Bill, and their brood. While the minister's offspring rarely darkened this church's door, they had decided to gather together today out of respect for the Christmas holiday and their father.

Lord, You don't have to prove Yourself to anyone, but I ask that You would reveal Yourself to my sister and brothers. Please let them see that Christianity is real—that You are real!

On that thought, Shari traipsed across the quaint, country church. She chatted with several of her parents' friends, and then a gentleman whom Shari had never met started playing the organ so loudly it drowned out their discussion. Wishing folks a good day, she made her way to the front pew on the left side. It was the one her family had occupied ever since Shari was in grade school. Noticing that Abby had arrived and was busily seating her children, Shari looked for a place to squeeze in and still leave room for Mom.

At that moment, Shari glimpsed Brenan and Miriam strolling up the aisle. She hated the way her heart leapt at the sight of him, although he was a head-turner in his charcoal pattern suit coat, gray band-collar shirt, and black trousers. But she managed to smile a greeting.

Brenan nodded. "G'morning, Shari."

"Morning."

He grinned when she continued to stare at him, until Shari realized how stupid she must look and tore her gaze from his bearded face.

"Bren!" Abby's exclamation rivaled the organ. "My long-lost big brother!"

He chuckled as she gave him a hug. Then, she pulled him forward and introduced Bill. Meanwhile, Mark and Luke stood and clasped hands with Brenan. Miriam was sucked into the throng minutes later.

Suddenly the organ quieted, but the welcome committee did not. Shari's father appeared at the pulpit and cleared his throat. Next, he grinned out over his congregation. "As you can see— and hear—my children are in attendance today."

Everyone chuckled, and Shari could tell her father was thrilled that everyone showed up. Tossing a smile at him, she turned to take her seat but realized there wasn't a space left for her beside Abby. *Of course, if Abby would kindly move her purse and scoot in closer to Bill. . .*

"No room here, sis. You'll have to sit back there." Abby indicated the pew behind her by thumbing over her shoulder.

Shari's gaze bounced to Miriam and Bren, then back to her younger sister's smug expression. "No problem, Abb." She wasn't about to let on that sitting beside Bren was the last thing she wanted to do. She wasn't about to appear rude either.

Stepping alongside the end of the pew in which Brenan sat, she forced a smile. "Mind if I sit here?"

"Course not, Shari." Bren slid over, forcing his mother to do the same.

Shari took her place. But the instant her arm brushed his, she felt doomed.

Abby twisted around and handed back Shari's Bible, still in its leather carrying case. Brenan politely reached for it and gave it to Shari.

"Thanks."

He smiled.

Shari's heart skipped a beat.

"It's also nice to have Miriam Sheppard here, along with her son Brenan. For those who don't know or may have forgotten, Bren's a doctor, and he's serving the Lord in Brazil as a medical missionary." Walt waved him to the platform. "Why don't you c'mon up and say a few words, Bren?"

Shari rose and stepped aside to let him out. Then, she claimed the spot next to Miriam so she wouldn't have to get up again.

"The Lord is really doing a great work in Brazil," Brenan began. "I've felt privileged to serve with the team over there. They primarily help the impoverished folks who live in *favelas*, or the slums. There's a real need in that part of the country." He paused. "But lately I've sensed God's call to a different part of the world, and I'd appreciate your prayers on this matter."

Shari saw him flick his glance in her direction, and something of a thrill spiraled up her spine.

"There is an orphanage in Cambodia that I'm burdened for. I'm acquainted with the man who runs it, and he's been pleading with me to come and help with his ministry. The children at the orphanage are in dire need of medical care. Here are some specifics."

Shari watched as he pulled something from the inner pocket of his suit coat. Was it the information he'd printed off the Internet for her?

"The orphanage cares for some one hundred and fifty children, but that number is growing by the day. An estimated one hundred and forty *thousand* children in Cambodia are orphans, having lost their parents to suicide, AIDS, and any number of illnesses and infections plaguing the malnourished and extremely poor in that region. Some children are disabled, like the twelve-year-old girl I was told about. She had been helping her mother harvest rice and stepped on a mine that was left over from the Khmer Rouge days. Consequently, she lost a leg. Other children live with hunger and severe malnutrition. They don't have homes, families, and education, nor do they have healthcare. They appear on the doorstep of the orphanage dirty and many times suffering with any number of tropical diseases."

Shari felt tears welling in her eyes. Her heart constricted as she listened to the plights of the orphans.

"A good number of the children come with behavioral problems due to the years they lived with abuse or neglect or both. In short, these children need Jesus Christ. They need to hear about salvation through Him. They need hope. Ministry goes well beyond helping to heal diseases and repair wounds. There is a spiritual aspect to it that I don't take lightly. But the question is, does God want me in Cambodia?" Brenan's gaze scanned the congregation. "That's why I ask you to pray—and please remember Hollia's House in your petitions also." He inclined his dark head ever so slightly in a show of thanks.

Shari sniffed and wiped the moisture from her tear-stained cheeks. Miriam handed her a Kleenex, extracting one from her purse for herself, too. Then Brenan sat down in the pew. He glanced over at Shari and sent her a rueful grin.

She dabbed her eyes. "You did a wonderful job up there—really conveyed the need of the hour."

He answered with a diminutive nod.

"I'm glad you and Elena are thinking about helping that orphanage."

Brenan leaned over and whispered, "Elena won't be coming."

"Oh?" Curious, Shari tipped her head. But, before she could inquire further, her father's voice filled the sanctuary.

73

"Thank you, Brenan. Now let's stand and sing our first hymn "Angels We Have Heard on High.""

Shari stood, as did Brenan and Miriam and the rest of the congregation. From her vantage point, Shari caught sight of her brother Mark. His gaze lingered on her face before moving to Bren. Finally, he glanced at his hymnal and sang with everyone else, but Shari found the nonverbal exchange rather odd. What was Mark thinking?

It was then Shari recalled his struggle with forgiveness in lieu of the ugly divorce proceedings he faced. Perhaps he wondered how Bren could forgive her after she'd run off with Greg a lifetime ago. As she sang, Shari closed her eyes and prayed her brother and sister-in-law would reconcile. But first and foremost, she prayed they would become Christians. She also brought Abby and Bill, Luke and Rebecca, and her nieces and nephews before the Lord. Her desire was to see her entire family come to a saving knowledge of Jesus Christ.

But now, as the words of the familiar Christmas carol tumbled from her lips, she couldn't stop thinking about the orphans in Cambodia. Her heart crimped with a longing to help them all.

". . .in excelsis De–e–o."

The song ended, and Shari lowered herself into the pew that suddenly seemed to have shrunk. Glancing to her right, she saw that Karan and Dan Strang, along with another family, now occupied the space on the other side of Miriam, forcing her to move over, which in turn caused Shari to sit even closer to Brenan.

To Shari's dismay it felt *way* too comfortable.

Chapter 9

After the service, Shari and Abby ducked out of church as the fellowship downstairs began. Brenan had been preoccupied by folks who wanted to hear more about the orphanage, and Shari had to admit she would like to have learned additional details. However, she had promised her sister they'd help their mom by preparing lunch before the Sheppards arrived. Now that Karan and Dan were coming to lunch as well, she and Abby would have to set two extra places at the dining room table.

"You know, I think Bren still has feelings for you."

Shari glanced at Abby, who placed silverware around the table. Following her with a stack of plates, Shari digested the remark and wondered how to reply. She had feelings for Brenan, too. But what about Elena? She suddenly felt awful if she'd come between him and the woman God wanted him to marry. What would her family and Bren's family think of her now?

Except Bren did say he had a "check in his heart" about marrying her. . . .

"Shari?"

She looked up at Abby.

"You know what? If you and Bren got back together, I

might even believe there's a God."

Shari was momentarily dumbfounded. "Why do you say that?"

Abby shrugged and set down the last of the silverware. "I always thought Brenan Sheppard was the perfect Christian—if there could be such a thing. I idolized him when I was a kid. He was like the big brother I adored when my real big brothers picked on me and teased me."

Shari smiled. "I never knew you thought of Bren that way."

"I did. And when you ran off with Greg, I hated you for a long time."

Shari winced.

"But I got over it," Abby continued. "I grew up. I learned Christians were more like our dad than Bren, and I learned that most romances ended like Romeo and Juliet's and not like the ones in fairy tales. Then I met Bill. He's a great guy, trustworthy, honesty, makes a decent living. I figured he was the best I'd find out there—and, don't get me wrong, I love him. But it's like I keep waiting for the day to come when he doesn't want to be married anymore, or, like Deidre, he decides he's got more important things to do in life than be a spouse and parent."

Shari wasn't sure what to say. She wanted to alleviate Abby's fears, but she didn't know Bill that well—and look what happened with Greg!

Abby walked around the table and came to stand right in front of her.

"I can tell that Bren's faith is real. I know Dad's is, too, even though he's made a lot of mistakes. But it's different with Bren. His faith shows on his face, and it's heard in his voice. I mean, when he was talking today about those kids in Cambodia, I felt like hopping a plane and adopting the whole orphanage."

Shari chuckled again. "Yeah, me, too."

Abby smiled. "And seeing you and Bren together today gave me some hope that maybe there is such a thing as everlasting love. I mean, he obviously still loves you. I saw it in his eyes when he looked at you. And you've been distracted ever since coming home yesterday saying everything was 'fine.'" Abby snorted. "Fine, yeah, right. I think you've got feelings for Bren, too."

"You're right. I do." Shari all but whispered the reply, fearing the fallout such an admission might bring.

But before she and Abby could discuss the matter further, the backdoor banged, and children's voices echoed through the otherwise quiet little house. The hungry troupe had arrived.

In the kitchen, Shari helped her mother ready the meal. She felt relieved that Brenan seemed to be giving her some space. He was hanging out with Mark and Luke in the living room and, judging from the chuckles emanating from that area of the house, they were enjoying themselves.

When at last they sat down for the noon meal, Mark was seated between her and Brenan. Once more, Shari was glad for the buffer. She felt herself relax and began to enjoy the company.

After they finished eating, there was talk of snowmobiling. Shari heard Brenan say that he'd brought along a change of clothes, suspecting "the Kretlow boys" would engage him in some sort of outdoor activity. Dan Strang opted to watch the football game on TV with Walt and Bill, and Shari decided she'd make herself useful in the kitchen again. But on her way in, she encountered her brother and niece.

"Daddy, you promised," Elizabeth said as large tears rolled down her cheeks.

"Oh, stop it. You go ice-skating all the time."

Shari couldn't suppress a chuckle. "Luke, how can you not be persuaded by that sweet face pleading with you?"

He smirked. "Those are crocodile tears. She turns 'em on and off like the bathroom faucet."

"Daddy!" Elizabeth cried all the harder.

"Oh, you poor thing." Shari gathered her niece in her arms and hugged her close. "You're so mean, Luke," she teased her brother. "You broke your daughter's heart."

"She'll get over it." He narrowed his gaze at her. "Shari, for your information, all these kids know you're a big pushover."

"Well, of course." She stroked Elizabeth's blondish-brown hair. "What are aunties for? Now, what do you want, sweetheart?"

Shaking his blond head, Luke walked away, and Elizabeth sniffed. "I want to go ice-skating this afternoon. My friends'll be at the rink, and Daddy said he'd take me and Crystal."

"I'll take you."

"Goody!" The nine-year-old's tears vanished so quickly, it amazed even Shari. Pushing out of her embrace, the girl ran through the house rounding up her sister and two cousins.

Luke appeared, dangling the keys to his truck. "Four kids won't fit in your car."

Even though there were five kids in the house, little Madeline was too young to partake of this outing, but Luke was right. Four children couldn't safely ride in her compact car.

Shari accepted the proffered keys, wondering if maybe she'd really been had by her niece this time.

Climbing the steps, Shari exchanged her black skirt and heels for black jeans and insulated hiking boots. When she returned downstairs, Bren was waiting for her.

"Want some company?"

The offer caught her off guard. "You don't want to snow-mobile?"

He shrugged. "I thought maybe we could talk while the kids skate."

Shari's heart suddenly hammered inside her chest. Staring into Brenan's gingerbread-colored eyes didn't calm her in the least. She felt so torn, wanting to spend time with him, yet wondering if the idea was wise. Was a relationship between them God's will? Everything was happening so fast.

But, then, gazing into her palm at Luke's keys, she figured it was foolish to forestall the inevitable. They had to talk. Their attraction to each other was obvious—so much so that even Abby noticed. Perhaps discussing things would help set them both in the right direction.

"Okay, come along." She smiled. "I'd love company and. . ." Feeling spry, she tossed the keys at him. "You can drive."

Brenan knew the way to the ice rink. He'd skated there himself as a kid, although now, according to Luke, a brand-new warm-ing house had been erected, complete with a snack bar that served coffee and hot chocolate.

Driving through Forest Ridge, the town in which he'd grown up, Brenan noted the changes, some subtle, some not so subtle—like the movie theater. That building went up in the last decade or so, but the restaurant he and all his buddies used to hang out at in their high school days was still there, although its name was different.

"Do you have fond memories of this town, Shari?" he asked over the din of the chattering kids in the back of the SUV.

"Yes, for the most part." She smiled at him, and Brenan

thought it lit up this cloudy afternoon like a ray of sunshine.

So how did he go about telling her what he wanted to say? He knew there was a chance Shari would reject him a second time, and he did his best to prepare himself for that worst-case scenario.

They arrived at the ice rink, and the kids ran for the warming house. In a flash, they had their skates on and were headed back outside.

Brenan purchased two cups of coffee and walked over to where Shari had found seats on the bleachers, which faced a large plate glass window in order for parents and spectators to observe and/or supervise the skaters. He handed her the steaming brew then sat beside her. He wondered, again, how he might begin to voice his innermost thoughts.

"Bren?"

"Hmm?" He glanced her way.

"You said this morning in church that Elena wouldn't be going to Cambodia with you—that is, if you even go. Can you tell me why?"

He almost breathed a sigh of relief. *Leave it to Shari to get the ball rolling.* "Sure, I can tell you. She phoned me last night from the hotel where she and some others on our team were staying. We wished each other a Merry Christmas, and then I told her in the nicest way I knew how that I wasn't returning to Brazil."

"What?"

He grinned at Shari's look of incredulity. "I'm not going back. Even if God closes the door on the ministry in Cambodia, I feel certain I'm not to return to Brazil."

"But what about your belongings? Don't you have to pack your stuff?"

"I don't have all that much, and what little I do own, the team will pack and ship it to me."

"Are you. . .well, are you afraid of seeing Elena again? Maybe seeing her again will stir up your feelings and—"

"No, that's not the case. I'm not afraid to see Elena." Brenan thought his "once-bitten, twice-shy" theory might be correct after all. Shari didn't want to get hurt again, and who could blame her. "I respect Elena, and she's a beautiful person—a fine sister in Christ. Last night I told her she's an outstanding nurse, and I feel privileged to have worked with her."

Shari grew quiet and stared out the window.

Brenan leaned closer to her. "But, Shari, I've sensed all along something wasn't right between Elena and me. Now I know what it is. I don't love her."

She faced him, her expression bordering on curiosity and trepidation.

He locked his gaze with hers. "I'm still in love with you."

Before Shari could reply, a man burst into the warming house. He glanced around, wearing a wild-eyed look, and began shouting. "Someone call 9-1-1. My daughter's hurt. I think she stopped breathing!"

Chapter 10

"Here she comes. She's regaining consciousness."

Brenan knelt on one side of the child and Shari on the other. The little girl had taken a tumble on the ice, and someone behind her accidentally stepped on her fingers with their skates. Afterwards, she'd gotten to her feet but passed out, scaring the wits out of her father.

"Did she hit her head?" Brenan queried.

"I'm her mother—and no, she didn't," stated the woman who peered over them with a troubled look. "Angie was crying after she fell, but no sound was coming out of her mouth. Then her lips turned blue, and she collapsed."

"Could be that the pain from her injury caused your daughter to black out." Brenan gave the mother a little smile before looking back at the girl. He inspected her pupils before sitting back on his haunches. "Angie, can you hear me? I'm Dr. Sheppard."

She blinked and stared up at him with large brown eyes. At last, she nodded.

While Brenan continued his examination, Shari packed snow around the child's wounded hand. She guessed Angie's fingers were broken, although her thick mitten had provided a good amount of protection. The injury could have been worse.

A small crowd had gathered, and someone said the ambulance was on its way. Shari watched as Brenan interacted with the child. He assured her that everything would be okay. He asked what her favorite color was and if she had brothers and sisters. Answering his questions successfully distracted Angie, and she even smiled. When the paramedics arrived, Brenan and Shari moved out of the way.

"Thanks a lot, doc," the girl's father said, sticking out his right hand. A red ski hat with yellow trim covered his head, but his face was ruddy from the cold December wind. His expression, however, looked much calmer than minutes ago, when he'd entered the warming house.

Brenan shook the man's hand. "Glad I could help, although I really didn't do much."

Shari stood by, watching the exchange and thinking Brenan had done more than he realized. He had a soothing presence and an air of confidence about him, yet there wasn't an arrogant bone in his body. What's more, she noted that Brenan had a wonderful way with kids. It affirmed the idea in Shari's heart that he belonged in Cambodia.

Angie was taken off the rink and to the hospital. Normalcy returned, and the skating continued. Shari's nieces and nephews wanted to skate awhile longer, so she and Brenan headed for the warming house again. Several people inside approached them, asking what had happened, and Shari felt relieved she didn't have to reply to Brenan's earlier admission.

He's still in love with me.

Shari could hardly say she was surprised. She'd suspected it since Christmas Eve. But her mind was in a whir. She couldn't think straight.

When at last they returned to Shari's folks' house, they discovered Karan and Dan had left, and they'd taken Miriam with them.

"Looks like you're stuck here for dinner," Walt told Brenan with a chuckle.

He replied with a good-natured shrug. "If dinner is as tasty as lunch, I'm a happy man."

Shari watched her mother's cheeks turn pink from the compliment.

"Shari can drive you home later," Walt said.

"Well," Brenan hesitated and flicked a glance in her direction. "Only if she doesn't mind."

"Of course I don't mind, silly." She rapped him on the upper arm before sauntering off to the kitchen. But her easy reply belied the knot in the pit of her stomach. What on earth was the matter with her?

Dinnertime arrived, they ate, and afterward, Shari carried a tray of iced and decorated Christmas cookies into the dining room. She spotted Brenan outdoors on the patio talking with Mark, who smoked a cigarette. She noticed her brother appeared very attentive to whatever Bren was saying.

"Shari, did you just hear me?"

She shook herself. "What?"

Luke chuckled. "I said Bren's a great guy."

Her heart did a flip, but she managed to set down the dessert tray without knocking something over. "Yeah, he is."

Abby's words from earlier in the day came back to Shari. *Seeing you and Bren together today gave me some hope that maybe there is such a thing as everlasting love.*

Her family would approve of the match. Shari felt certain of that now. She turned back to where Brenan and Mark still stood outside. Could it be God was answering her prayers with regard to family members. . .and He was using Bren?

⚜

Sometime later, Shari stuck her key in the ignition of her car and fired up the engine. She didn't even reach the highway before the words poured from the depth of her soul.

"Bren, I don't know what's happening."

"What do you mean?"

"I mean about us. You said you still love me, but—"

"Shari, I realize I put you in a bad position, and I'm sorry. But I can't help how I feel, and I thought you needed to know."

She mulled it over as she drove to the Sheppard's bed-and-breakfast. They rode for miles in silence.

At last they reached the Open Door Inn. Shari parked and, before she could say another thing, Brenan reached over and set his hand on top of hers.

"Thanks for the lift home. Maybe we'll talk sometime this week." He opened the car door and hopped out so fast, it jarred Shari's senses. She didn't want to part on such an uncertain note.

"Brenan, wait." She killed the motor and climbed from behind the wheel. She watched as he backtracked until he stood just a foot away, his hands stuffed into the pockets of his navy blue down jacket.

"You didn't put me in any sort of bad position. I'm just confused, I guess. You're a wonderful guy, and we have so much in common. We're both burdened for the same ministry, and we love children, but. . ." She wracked her brain, searching for the right words to express all the tumult inside of her. "Oh, Bren, I think I'm falling in love with you, but I'm just like. . .well, I. . ."

Brenan stepped closer, pulled his hands from his pockets,

and cupped her face. His palms felt warm against her cold cheeks. "Shari, I would never hurt you. I'd die before I would ever break your heart. You don't ever have to worry about that from me, okay?"

She nodded as tears clouded her vision. She knew he spoke the truth. "But what about your mom and sister? Will they think I'm the same selfish woman who hurt you once and am now ruining your chances of happiness with Elena?"

"What?" Brenan brought his chin back, looking shocked. "My mother and Karan love you, Shari. They always have. I talked to my family last night after getting off the phone with Elena. Mom said she'd known all along that I still loved you."

His words were like a healing salve on her wounded spirit. "Bren, I think I love you, too."

Beneath the glow of the outdoor light Shari watched him grin. "I know. You said that already."

He kissed her and folded her into an embrace. Shari felt more cherished and secure than she could ever remember.

"I swear I'll never hurt you again, Bren."

"I'm not worried." He rested his temple against the side of her head. "And I'm not in any hurry either. I've waited this long for you, Shari. . .I can wait a little longer until you're sure you love me, and you don't just *think* you do."

She smiled, deciding Brenan Sheppard was a rare gem, a golden nugget along a stony pathway.

Suddenly, Shari felt moisture on her lashes and cheeks. She blinked and looked up. Fat snowflakes swirled in the frosty night air and landed on her nose and in her eyes.

"What is it with this stuff?" Shari stepped back and gazed into Brenan's bearded face. "It's snowing again!"

"Yeah, looks like you're stranded here."

Shari laughed. The light snowfall was hardly a major winter storm.

Brenan nodded, indicating the bed-and-breakfast behind them. "Plenty of room at this inn."

Realizing there was nowhere else she'd rather be than curled up beside Brenan while a fire blazed in the hearth, she hooked her arm through his. "You know, I think you're right. I'd better not drive in this *blizzard*."

"Right. Smart move."

Arm-in-arm, they walked to the house, and Shari thought of the tune she'd heard on the radio a few nights ago. She hummed a few bars and then, together, she and Brenan sang, "Let it snow, let it snow, let it snow!"

SYLVIA'S CHOCOLATE MINT CHRISTMAS PIE

Crust
   1¼ c. all-purpose flour
   ½ t. salt
   ½ c. (1 stick) chilled butter, cut into small pieces
   2–3 t. ice water

1. Mix together flour and salt. Cut butter into flour mixture until crumbly.
2. Add water, one tablespoon at a time, tossing with a fork until a soft dough forms. Shape dough into a flat disk, wrap in plastic, and chill for one hour.
3. After an hour, roll dough and fit into 9-inch pie pan. Trim edges, leaving 1-inch overhang. Make a fluted edge. Chill again, this time for thirty minutes.
4. Preheat oven to 375°F. Bake crust for approximately twenty-five minutes, until very light golden brown. Cool slightly. Reduce oven temperature to 325°F for filling.

Filling
   1½ c. sugar
   ½ c. (1 stick) butter
   2 oz. (2 squares) semisweet chocolate, coarsely chopped
   3 large eggs
   1 t. white vinegar
   1 t. peppermint extract
   Dash of salt

1. Prepare filling by first mixing sugar and butter in medium saucepan, stirring until sugar has dissolved. Remove from

heat. Add chocolate. Stir until melted and mixture is smooth. Next add eggs, vinegar, peppermint, and salt. Stir well and pour filling evenly into prepared piecrust.

2. Bake for 35–40 minutes at 325°F. When done, allow pie to cool and serve it topped with a dollop of whipped cream.

ANDREA BOESHAAR

Andrea has been married for over twenty-five years. She and her husband, Daniel, have three valiant adult sons and two precious daughters-in-law. Andrea has written articles, devotionals, and over a dozen novels for **Heartsong Presents** as well as numerous novellas for Barbour Publishing. She is the author of the highly acclaimed Faded Photographs series, which includes the following three women's fiction titles: *Broken Things, Hidden Things,* and *Precious Things.* For more about Andrea and for a listing of all her books, log onto her Web site at: www.andreaboeshaar.com.

Orange Blossom Christmas

by Kristy Dykes

Chapter 1

The phone rang just as Landon Michael popped a cold capsule in his mouth and washed it down with a glass of juice squeezed from oranges picked from his own grove. He decided to let the voice mail catch the phone call. He felt too wretched to talk to anybody. All he felt like doing was getting back to his recliner and spraying down with a medicated throat spray.

Ring-g-g-g-g.

"Atchoo!" He reached for a tissue. What if it was someone from the high school? Principals couldn't get sick. At least that's what his staff told him yesterday when he left, coughing up a storm. They said they couldn't do without him, especially with Christmas vacation coming up next week. There was simply too much work to be done, they told him. Was this his secretary calling? Did she need something important?

Ring-g-g-g-g.

He smiled. Was it somebody offering to bring him some homemade chicken soup? But if it was Miss Available-with-a-capital-A home ec teacher Pamela Perkins, well, he'd pass, thank you very much. . . .

Ring-g-g-g-g, ring-g-g-g-g.

His sense of duty got the best of him, and he grabbed the phone, determined to squeak out a greeting, raspy though it would be. "Hello?"

"Howdy, there. My name's Pastor Rodney Ellerson callin' from north Georgie. Is this the Orange Blossom Bed and Breakfast Inn?"

Landon coughed.

"I must've dialed the wrong number—"

More coughing.

"Could you tell me if I reached Lake Wallace, Floridy?"

"Yes. Sorry. I've. . .got a. . .terrible head cold."

"What a bad time of year—winter—to get yourself a cold. A cold in cold weather. Why, that's turrible."

Landon looked out the kitchen window and saw the bright-as-summer sun shining down on the clear-as-day lake. He smiled, knowing the thermometer read eighty-eight. "Any time of year is bad to get a cold. *Atchoo.*"

"Yer right about that, pardner. So, this *is* the Orange Blossom Bed and Breakfast Inn?"

"Yes." What did this caller with the Georgia twang want? Landon glanced out the bank of windows in the great room. Nestled among gigantic orange trees, he saw the little brown wooden house across the road, the Orange Blossom Bed and Breakfast Inn. Nobody had stayed in it since his wife died a year ago. The B and B had been her brainchild. As far as he was concerned, it wasn't a B and B any longer. It was back to its original status—a cracker gothic cottage from Old Florida—what some historians called the early days of Florida. Eons ago, his forebears had built it and lived in it. These days, it was as vacant as a classroom in summer.

"Well," drawled the preacher from north Georgia, "the

reason I'm calling is my wife saw an article about the Orange Blossom B and B in her favorite magazine, and she got this idear to book a room for our church secretary as a gift from us and the church. I think it's a right good idear myself. . .I'd even venture to say it's inspired by God, you know, providential, because, you see, our church secretary is the most deservin' person in the whole wide world of a little R & R. . . ."

Wonder if he's long-winded in the pulpit, too?

"Why, our church secretary—Lois is her name—just like Lois in the Bible—why, she directs our children's church program, and last Sunday night, she put on the kids' Christmas play with twenty-three wriggly, writhing kids. Ever since she's been our secretary—six months now—our church has grown by leaps and bounds. . .why, she's got as many idears as a doctor's got pills. . .and besides that, she's the most dedicated secretary in church history, I do believe. . . ."

Bingo. A long-winded talker is a long-winded preacher. Landon smiled, remembering what his minister-father liked to jokingly say about long-winded visiting preachers. *If they don't strike oil after twenty minutes, they ought to quit boring.*

"And so, we're a-wantin' to book a room. Please say there's room at the inn." He let out a belly laugh. "Get it? Room at the inn? Like in Jerusalem two thousand years ago when Joseph and Mary came a-knockin' on the door of an inn. Please say ya got an empty room at yer B and B. My wife's got her heart set on yer place for Lois. . .it's a little piece of heaven smack dab in the middle of a Florida orange grove, is what she said. Please don't say you're full."

No, we're not full, that's for certain. Landon smiled again.

"My wife loved them pictures of the Orange Blossom B and B—that funny-lookin' house a-settin' near a little lake in central Florida, and that was that. There's no other B and B to be had for Lois's R & R, as far as my wife's concerned."

Landon was surprised. The preacher's wife had *just* seen that article? Why, the Orange Blossom B and B had been featured in the magazine over two years ago.

"My wife buys all her magazines at the library for a quarter. 'Course they're a little out of date when she gets them, and sometimes the coupons are ripped out, but that don't bother her none a-tall. We'd like to book a full ten days for Lois"—he paused, and a fumbling noise came across the phone lines—"no, make that eleven days—I just checked my calendar. She'll get there December 15, and she'll leave December 26, the day after Christmas. She'll be arriving next Friday. You take Visa?"

Landon had a coughing fit.

"I knew I hadn't lost ya. I heard ya breathin' the whole time I been a-rattlin' on. Try using nasal spray. Then you won't have to breathe through yer mouth. When ya have to breathe through yer mouth, yer throat gets dried out, ya know? And besides, it sounds turrible. Yep. I knew I hadn't lost ya."

"It. . .hurts. . .to talk."

"I can empy-thize. I had a cold last month. Like I said, I'm real sorry yer sick."

"Thanks."

"My grandpappy always said, 'Take cold medicine, and in seven days you'll be well. Don't take cold medicine, and in seven days you'll be well.' In other words, you'll be as good as new in a week, medicine or not."

"I hope so."

"My credit card number is. . ." The preacher rattled off some numbers.

Landon jotted them down hurriedly.

"Can you send me a brochure?" The preacher rattled off an address. "My name's Pastor Rodney Ellerson. Did I say that already? E-l-l-i-s-o-n," he spelled. "Ellerson."

A few minutes later, as Landon plopped in his leather recliner in the great room, he realized with a full-blown case of worry that he now had a guest coming to the long-closed Orange Blossom Bed and Breakfast Inn.

In one week's time!

He glanced out the windows. The cottage across the road needed a thorough cleaning. It was probably covered in dust bunnies and cobwebs. And he was as sick as a dog.

"*Atchoo.*" Why had he taken this booking? Maybe it had something to do with the reverend. He liked his down-home flavor. This preacher reminded him of his own father—a minister, too. This preacher had the same quaint Southern drawl and the same penny-pinching-by-necessity ways. His father would be amused when Landon told him about this preacher from north Georgia wanting a room for his secretary.

Maybe it had something to do with what the preacher said. *My wife's got her heart set on yer place. . .she loved them pictures of your funny-lookin' house a-settin' near a little lake in central Florida.*

Landon sprayed his throat with the vile-tasting green stuff, reflecting on the way the preacher's wife described the Orange Blossom Inn.

A little piece of heaven in a Florida orange grove?

I may just donate the church secretary's stay. I may not charge the preacher a penny.

The booking, though, and why he'd done it. . .maybe it had something to do with that poor church secretary. Into his mind popped a picture of his father's church secretary at the church he presently served in North Carolina. . . . Fiftyish.

Spinsterish. . .or was it widowish?

Overworked for sure. . . And definitely underpaid.

This Lois lady with the children's program on her shoulders, as well as a host of other things at her church, will probably enjoy the solitude of the Orange Blossom, he decided. *She's sure to be refreshed during her stay. It's quiet around here, that's for certain.*

He unwrapped a honey-and-lemon throat lozenge, popped it into his mouth, leaned back, and closed his eyes.

Somehow I'll manage to get the place cleaned up before she arrives.

❧

Through a deluge of rain, Lois Delaney drove down the dark, lonely road in the midst of Florida orange groves, hunting the sign the proprietor said to look for: Orange Blossom Bed and Breakfast Inn.

For long minutes now, she had slowed at every sign, then accelerated past them. Where was that sign? He said to go six miles past the main highway. Hadn't she gone six miles by now? Rats. She should've noted the mileage when she turned off the highway.

Now, she looked carefully at the odometer and decided to go exactly two more miles, then turn back and begin hunting again.

What a time to be arriving at a B and B—and one set in such a remote place. She checked her watch by the light of the dashboard. Five past eleven. But she couldn't help the lateness of the hour. First, she'd gotten a late start. Too many duties in the church office before Christmas. Then, of all things, her windshield wiper motor had broken in south Georgia, and she spent hours in the Toyota dealership while they fixed it.

Whoever heard of a windshield wiper motor breaking? And on a new car, at that? If it'd been her old car, she could've understood. She'd driven that thing for nearly seven years, and its windshield wiper motor had *never* given her a problem.

What more could go wrong? Nothing, she assured herself. All would be well shortly. She would soon arrive at the Orange Blossom B and B, fall into a freshly made bed, perhaps a canopied four-poster. And then she would sleep late the next morning, at least past her usual 6:30. Then she would head for the wide front porch for a leisurely and delicious breakfast that included, according to the brochure, freshly squeezed orange juice and orange blossom honey.

At the Orange Blossom B and B, she would meet interesting people from all walks of life. The magazine article showed several guests eating breakfast together on the plank porch. Perhaps she would form lasting friendships with some of the guests. Outgoing and gregarious, she was always making new friends.

During the week, she planned to take walks in the orange grove and around the lake for quiet reflection, something she rarely had time for.

"One thing's for sure," she said aloud as she continued driving at a snail's pace so she could look for the sign through the rain, "I need some quiet reflection. And rejuvenation, too."

She thought about her recent breakup with Phil. Oh, how that had hurt. She was ecstatic when they started a relationship four months ago. After all, the playing field was narrow for a thirty-two-year-old single Christian woman.

Evangelist Phil A. Pullman had held a revival at their church, and from the first, she'd been impressed with—and attracted to—this dashing, debonair minister, charisma dripping off him like the rain now falling from the sky.

But that wasn't why she came to care for him during their four months of e-mails, phone calls, and occasional visits. It was because he truly seemed to care for her. And he was so dedicated to the ministry. And he made her laugh—he was as zany as she was. She recalled the times they belted out hymns together, him singing in his beautiful baritone, her as off-key as the day was long, both of them ending the songs laughing like hyenas.

She remembered the funny name he called himself, a play on words, his eyebrows going up and down every time he said it, her laughing in her usual way, loud and boisterous.

I'm Evangelist Phil A. Pulpit. Get it? Fill a pulpit. That's what I do.

Two weeks ago, he wrote her a succinct e-mail that *hadn't* made her laugh. In fact, it made her cry.

> *Hi, Lois. I don't know how to say this. This is hard. I enjoyed our times together. I thought we had a future. Two weeks ago, I met Nicole Wilson. She's a preacher's daughter. She sings like an angel, and she even plays the harp! Can you believe that? We've already sung a duet together. "Father, Make Us One" was the song. She's a high soprano, and oh, did we sound good, if I do say so myself. Although she's only eighteen, she'll be a great asset to my ministry. I hope you can understand this. I want you to know, I'll always consider you a friend. Phil*

Lois blinked back a tear, recalling the hurtful e-mail. Just what did her future hold in the man department? "God, are You ever going to send me a man, the right man? If so, when?" Her voice was whiny, but she couldn't help it.

From the time she was a little girl, she'd wanted to be a wife and mother, the best in the world, just like her own mother had been and still was. But so far, life hadn't led her that way. Instead, she became a publicist who was now working as a church secretary temporarily.

"Lord, are You listening?" She wasn't embarrassed about talking to the Lord like this. She and the Lord were on a first-name basis. She had loved the Lord with all her heart, as the scriptures instructed, for her entire life. She and the Lord had had many conversations.

Now, though, she was doing all the talking. The Lord was mute.

She smiled, remembering a poem she'd recently come across, and she said it now.

Now I lay me down to sleep,
Lord, give me a man for keeps!
If there's a man beneath my bed,
I hope he heard each word I said!

She laughed uproariously. "Lord, *please* give me a man, a good Christian man. Think how much we can accomplish for Your kingdom as a team." She paused, contrite. "Okay, Lord. I admit it. That's just a side benefit. The real reason I want a man is because I want someone to care for me, someone I can share my life with, and vice versa."

She slowed for yet another road sign, then proceeded. "Okay, Lord, I'll be quiet so You can speak."

Nothing.

For a couple of minutes, nothing.

"All right, Lord, I've been in this journey of faith long

enough to know that when You don't speak I'm supposed to rely on the last word You gave me. And that's this. I'm to continue to draw close to You and believe that You are working things out for my good."

She drove on, the odometer clocking off yet another mile. "There it is," she exclaimed as she made a sharp left turn off the paved road and onto a dirt one. "Orange Blossom B and B, here I come. R & R at the rescue for this heart-weary woman."

She made her way slowly down the dirt road—a quagmire in the rain—as she searched for the B and B.

"Look for a stone-and-stucco home on the left—that's where I live," the proprietor had said. "Then pull into the driveway directly across from it. That's the B and B."

She spotted the stone-and-stucco home—just barely—in the darkness. Her enthusiasm dampened. No lights on the road? The porch? From inside the proprietor's house? The B and B? She wheeled into the driveway of the B and B, just as the proprietor had instructed.

Her headlights flashed on a small wooden structure, the charming wooden cottage pictured in the brochure, and she felt heartened somewhat.

"Orange Blossom B and B," she called out cheerily. "I'm here at last."

She turned off the ignition. Momentarily her automatic headlights went off. What now? It was still drizzling, and besides, no one was about. No people. No cars. No proprietor.

Should she get out and knock on the door? She knew it was 11:30 at night, but she also knew that the proprietor was expecting her. The last time they talked on her cell phone—three hours ago—she told him about her windshield wiper motor mishap. She also told him she would be late. So where was he?

She tooted her horn.

A dog barked at her car window, and her heart leapt to her throat. She looked sideways and saw the biggest dog she'd ever laid eyes on—or so it seemed given the circumstances. He was standing—*standing?*—at her window, his paws on her car door.

"Down, Marmaduke," came a man's gruff voice in the darkness. Then a flashlight came on.

She cranked up the engine and threw the car in reverse.

"Miss Delaney?" The man thumped on her window.

Through the tinted glass she made out a man standing there holding an umbrella, although she couldn't make out his features.

"I thought you weren't coming." He thrust his hand backward, toward the cottage. "This is the Orange Blossom B and B. If you'll get out, I'll show you to your room. And I promise to corral Marmaduke. Don't be afraid of him. He's a great big baby."

Marmaduke let out a howl.

"Hush, Marmaduke." The man petted the dog. "I promise you, his bark is bigger than his bite."

She didn't care to test the man's last statement as the dog let out another ferocious bark. What should she do now? She felt like driving away.

"Miss Delaney?"

She looked straight ahead where her headlights shone, to the little cracker gothic cottage in front of her, saw the wide front porch, noted its charm, and thought about its unique history.

"Your pastor, Reverend Ellison, booked this room for you.

I talked with him last week."

Ever the frugal one, she remembered her pastor's hard-earned money that he'd invested in her Christmas vacation.

"It's not luxurious by any means, but I think you'll find it pleasant."

She turned off the ignition. She would at least look things over. "We'll see," she said under her breath.

Chapter 2

Landon held the umbrella over Miss Delaney as they walked toward the front porch. He'd already tied Marmaduke firmly to a newel post.

He was surprised at Miss Delaney's appearance. When the reverend from north Georgia had said the words "church secretary" on the phone, Landon thought fiftyish and spinsterish—or was it widowish?—simply because of his father's church secretary.

This church secretary was nothing of the sort. Oh, she wasn't a beauty queen, but she was certainly attractive. Her short blond hair had a bounce to it, and he was almost certain her eyes were light blue, a fitting complement, if so. It was too dark to get a good look at them. And her jeans-clad figure was pleasing—not too thin like so many young women. And she seemed friendly, not to mention her mannerliness and politeness.

Once on the porch, he stood the open umbrella at a precise angle to let the raindrops fall down, then shined his flashlight at the door as he unlocked it and pushed it open. "Come on in."

"It's locked?"

"Well. . .yes."

"There aren't any guests staying here? Besides me?"

"Well. . .no."

She didn't say anything.

He felt bad. But he could at least be cheery. "This house is called a cracker gothic cottage."

"I read about it in the brochure. Groovy."

He stepped inside, fumbled for the light switch, and clicked it on. "This is the central hallway. When my ancestors lived here—"

"Your ancestors lived in this house?"

"That's right. Back then, there were no front or back doors to this hall. But we added doors to keep in the AC. The construction is called a—"

"Shotgun?"

"No. A dogtrot. A shotgun is where you can look through the front room and see all the way to the back. In a dogtrot, all the rooms open off of a central hall, kind of like a breezeway. The early settlers were called Florida crackers because many of them had cattle, and when they popped their whips, a *crack* sounded. Anyway, they built their homes this way to catch the breezes."

She clasped her hands to her heart. "Can't you just envision some of your relatives standing right here in this hall?" Enthusiasm dripped off her. "Maybe with a broom in their hands, sweeping? Or the paddle of a churn, making butter? Your great-great-grandmother, perhaps?"

He shrugged. "Never had anybody ask me that. Here's the parlor." He walked into a room on his left, and she followed him in. He made his way to a lamp, turned it on, then another. His wife always said lamplight created a pleasing ambience.

"Welcome to the. . ." He swallowed hard as he glanced around. The place was a mess. Thick dust was everywhere—on the furniture, the whatnots, and the dark-stained pine floors.

And a strong musty smell permeated the air. He found his voice. "Welcome to the Orange Blossom Bed and Breakfast Inn."

"Thank you." She wore a shocked expression on her face.

He felt terrible. Miss Available-with-a-capital-A home ec teacher Pamela Perkins had offered to clean up the place for him when she heard about his guest, and he'd gladly taken her up on her offer. He'd been sick with this wretched cold, and the workload at school had been heavy due to the approaching Christmas holidays. For the first time, he'd been glad for Miss Perky Pamela's wily ways. Had she gotten her dates mixed up? For sure. Phooey.

"This is where I'm supposed to get some R & R?" A drop of water hit Miss Delaney on the head, and she gasped, then wiped it off and looked up. A big black mildew stain dotted the tongue-and-groove pine board ceiling.

"The place appears to be a little run-down. . . ."

"I'll say." Another drop of water hit her on the head, and she took two steps forward, away from the steady leak.

"I haven't had the time to devote to the B and B." He looked down at the pine floors, noting the discoloration—apparently from the water dripping from the ceiling. "It's been closed for a year—since my wife passed away. She ran it. I'm a high school principal, and I keep a small herd of cattle, and besides that, I have a ten-acre orange grove. There aren't enough hours in the day to do all that *and* run the B and B." He coughed. All this talking was making his throat act up. Was he getting a relapse? Phooey.

She didn't say a word, but now her expression read "tired."

"Look. I have some explaining to do. I apologize. Big time. A friend was supposed to come clean for me today. I don't know what happened. But town is eighteen miles down the road. You can follow me, and I'll get you a motel room—at my expense. I'm really embarrassed."

She yawned, stifled it, then extended her hand toward him. "At least let's introduce ourselves first. I'm Lois Delaney. And you? You're Mr. Michael, right?"

"That's right." He reached for her hand, shook it, released it. "Landon Michael."

Sparkles danced in her eyes. "Landon Michael?" she blurted. "As in, Michael Landon?" She laughed uproariously.

Landon didn't know what to think. The woman was standing there laughing at him. Like a hyena? Yes, definitely. If he wasn't a church man and if she wasn't a church secretary, he'd vow she had imbibed.

"Sorry." She looked subdued again, though the sparkles were still in her eyes. "It's just that your name. . ." She laughed—hooted actually. "Landon Michael. . .why, it's the reverse of the late actor's, and you look exactly like him. People ever tell you that?"

"A few."

She hummed the *Bonanza* theme song as her hands strummed an imaginary guitar, a goofy look on her face. "Dum-duh-duh-duh-duh-duh-duh-duh-duh-dum-dah. . .dum-duh-duh-duh-duh-duh-duh-duh-duh-dum-duh-duh-duh-dah." Only she was off-key, way off.

"My grandmother was a fan of *Bonanza* when it was popular. When I was born, she suggested it to my parents." He spoke deadpan-fashion on purpose.

She looked like she was about to cackle again but suddenly regained her composure. "I was only kidding."

He stood there with his arms folded across his chest. He had thought she was mannerly and polite? Ha!

"I'm just being silly—"

Words well spoken, Miss Zany Delaney. "So, are you ready to head for town?" His arms were still folded, and he was sure he wore a stern expression. Good. The sooner he got rid of this crazy woman, the better.

"Look." She took a step toward him. "I have some explaining to do. I apologize. Big time."

He had said those very words earlier. In that exact order. He was somewhat amused. And curious about her.

"I'm really embarrassed."

He dropped his arms. *There she goes again. Repeating me.* He smiled.

"I didn't mean to be so silly. I've been told I'm zany. . . ."

Bingo.

"But I've also been told I'm smart. And it wasn't too smart of me to laugh about your name. It's just that I'm so tired. . . ." She let out a long sigh. "And I had such a bad day, what with the late start, and then the rain, and then my windshield wiper motor breaking—whoever heard of a windshield wiper motor breaking, and on a new car, at that? And then the long delay to get it fixed, and then more rain, and then I couldn't find your place, and it got later and later, and finally I arrived and found this"—she gestured all around her—"a defunct bed-and-breakfast, and I. . .I—"

"I understand." He threw up his hand, traffic cop style, chuckling. "Tell you what. If you'll forgive me for this," he said, pointing to the room, "I'll forgive you for laughing at my name. Agreed?" He thrust out his palm. "Let's shake on it, okay?"

"Okay." She held out her hand.

The moment he touched her, something happened to him.

He couldn't hang words on it, so he tucked it inside to contemplate later. "Come on. Let's get this place locked up, and then we'll be on our way."

"I've decided to stay."

"You have?"

"Y—yes, I. . .I have."

He heard the catch in her voice. Was something going on with her, too? He looked long and hard at her. "If you're sure, then?"

"I'm s—sure."

In her plaid shorty pajamas, Lois put the sheets on the iron bedstead in the charming little room, looking forward to crawling into bed after such a long day. Why had she suddenly decided to stay? Especially after Mr. Michael offered to get her a motel room in town? She wasn't sure.

When she told him her decision, he had shown her about the place, opening and closing the doors of the bedrooms, the kitchen, the large pantry, and the two bathrooms.

"These aren't original to the house, of course," he'd told her. "People used privies out back in the old days."

Then he insisted on bringing in her luggage in the drizzle without her help. She was a little embarrassed. She tended to pack things in small bags, and some of them had items spilling out of them, like her hair dryer and curling iron and other stuff. But he managed to get her things in without dropping anything in the wet grass.

Then he vaulted across the dirt road to his house and returned with bedding—sheets, pillows, towels, and even a new-looking comforter.

"The bed's made," he'd told her when he got back, "but it's been a whole a year. Needs changing. Even the comforter."

He offered to help her make it, but she said she would do it herself.

"Be sure to open some windows," he said. "This place needs airing out. Tomorrow I'll see about getting it cleaned." Then he apologized again for the inconvenience and left.

"Inconvenience?" She pulled the comforter over the sheets, thinking about the leaky ceiling and stained floors in the parlor. "It doesn't matter about the inconvenience, Mr. Michael Landon, I mean, Landon Michael. What matters is that you're letting a piece of living history disintegrate right before your eyes."

She dug in one of her bags for her facial cleanser, then trudged to the bathroom. "How unique, to own a cracker gothic cottage. Don't you realize how valuable this place is? Maybe not in monetary terms, but certainly in the historic sense."

She washed her face and dried it on a towel he'd brought over. "Haven't you ever heard the saying 'A stitch in time saves nine'? The longer you let this cottage go, the more it'll cost you to bring it back up to par. Oh, well. It's none of my business. What *is* my business is to get some rest."

She walked to the window, raised the shade a few inches, and opened the window just as high. A pitter-patter of rain greeted her, an inviting sound to her now. Across the room, she raised the other window the same few inches.

"The raindrops'll sing me to sleep." She smiled as she pulled down the bedding and crawled in.

As her head hit the pillow, her mind turned to the question that had been gnawing at her. Why did she decide to stay? After her disappointment of seeing the place dirty and in disrepair? Not to mention the lack of interesting guests?

She yawned. She was sure she'd stayed because of her fatigue. Yes, that was it, wasn't it? Tomorrow she would probably leave. This was no place for a vacation.

Like a vapor, the face of Michael Landon—correction, Landon Michael—appeared before her eyes. Was she dreaming? She didn't think so. She saw him with that charming grin, then with that stern expression which only intrigued her more.

She thought about his comical name. What was his mother thinking when she named him? She recalled his handsome good looks, just like the late actor's. Dark bushy hair. Sun-burnished skin. Taut, well-formed muscles. She thought about his interesting life. High school principal. Cattleman. Grove owner.

She thought about the spark that passed between them when they shook hands that second time. For some reason, across her mind now flitted the face of Phil. Then Landon. Then Phil. Then Landon. Then Phil. Then Landon. She was so tired. Was her mind playing tricks on her?

"The Orange Blossom B and B." She was as wide awake as all get-out. "An R & R retreat? Looks like S & W to me—stress and worry."

Chapter 3

L ois awoke the next morning in the strange surroundings with a start. What time was it? She glanced at her
wristwatch. Nine thirty-five! She hadn't slept this late
for eons, even on Saturdays like it was today.

She breathed in deeply. Was she smelling some kind of air
freshener? She recalled the proprietor's promise. *Tomorrow I'll
see about getting this place cleaned.*

She sat up in bed, refreshed in her spirit. Had a cleaning
lady already been here—in this very room as she slept—swish-
ing fragrant spray around? Had the cleaning lady used flower-
scented furniture polish, perhaps? But a quick glance at the
dusty bedside table told her that no cleaning lady had been on
these premises today.

A movement at the window caught her eye, and she looked
that way. The curtains were swaying in a gentle morning breeze.
She pushed back the covers, jumped up, and was across the
room in a flash. She raised the shade all the way up and was met
with a dose of sunshine that warmed her soul. She raised the
window as far as it would go and saw a sight to behold.

Orange trees thick with orange blossoms—and as fragrant
as the perfume counter at the mall.

"Well, what do you know. So that's what I'm smelling." She couldn't get over it. Everywhere she looked, she saw orange trees dotted with fragrant white flowers. She was itching to get outside and explore the surroundings.

She ran to the other side of the room, threw up the shade, then the window. She saw a shimmering lake, as clear as crystal. Tied to a dock was a dinghy. To her far left, across the dirt road, she saw Mr. Michael's sprawling stucco home. Beyond that was a barn and a few head of cattle grazing in a field. She even heard a distinctive moo in the distance. She was touched by the idyllic scene, her heart encouraged.

Sure, there were no interesting guests here. Sure, the place needed a deep cleaning and some repairs. But the orange groves. . .and the lake. . .and the charm of the cracker gothic cottage and its grounds. . .they wooed her like a beau to a girl.

She heard the front door open. *Click*. She heard it close. *Click*.

She froze in her steps. Who was in the house? Mr. Landon—correction, Mr. Michael?

"Oops," she whispered. "I've got to get his name right." Was Mr. Michael in the wide front hall? As far as she knew, he was the only one on the premises. She looked down at her shorty pajamas. She dashed to her suitcase and rummaged for her robe, but couldn't find it.

She remembered throwing it in a small satchel at the last minute. She scrounged the satchel's contents, found her robe, and threw it on, her stomach growling fiercely. She walked back to the door.

"Mr. Michael?" she said through the door. No answer. She cracked the door a peep and called his name again, with the same result. She opened the door six inches and stuck her head out. "Mr. Michael?" Still no answer. But a new scent assailed her. Food.

She saw an open door at the end of the wide hallway—the kitchen she remembered from last night's brief tour. She left her room, walked to the kitchen, and on the table, she saw a luscious sight. Breakfast—and a note propped up.

Please enjoy your breakfast. And make yourself at home. When you're ready to venture out, come look me up. I'm across the road doing paperwork. The cleaning lady is on standby. While she's here, I'd like to show you around the place, if that's okay with you.

Landon

"Yum, yum." She sat down at the table and partook. Sausage-in-biscuits, flaky and hot. Orange blossom honey and various jams. Chunks of fresh fruit. Orange juice. A choice of hot tea or coffee in tiny carafes.

All were pleasingly arranged on a large silver tray. She noted that the cloth napkins matched the dishes, both dotted with tiny white flowers in the midst of green leaves. Orange blossoms? Amazing. The crystal vase in the middle of the tray held. . .an orange blossom bouquet? Wonderful. She leaned forward and buried her nose in the flowers, drawing in a deep lungful of fragrance. She hadn't felt this carefree in a long time.

She stood up and did a joy jig, let out a victory yell, though a subdued "Yee-haw!" then sat back down and took a sip of her hot tea.

"As I said last night, Orange Blossom B and B"—she glanced around the room—"I'm here at last."

She smiled, a chant-poem forming in her mind, and she said it aloud.

I'm here at last
I'm here to stay.
I'm ready for adventures
To come my way!

With Miss Delaney's breakfast delivered, Landon came out of the cottage, made his way down the front steps, and headed toward the backyard. He needed to get some logs from the wood stack. Moments later, his arms laden, he walked down the side of the cottage on his way to his house across the road.

"Yee-haw," came Miss Delaney's voice from somewhere inside the cottage.

He rolled his eyes then chuckled. "Miss Zany Delaney, you're at it again." He crossed the dirt road, went inside his house, and deposited the logs on the hearth. Would they get some chilly weather in time for Christmas so he could light a fire?

He smiled, thinking about his usual procedure during Florida winters—a brightly burning fire in the hearth with the AC cranked up on high. That was about the only way Floridians could enjoy a fire, at least the ones in central and south Florida.

He crossed the hardwood floors of the great room and entered the French doors that led into his book-lined study. As he said in his note to Miss Delaney, he intended to do some paperwork this morning.

He sat down at his desk and in moments was engrossed.

Knock-knock.

He heard the brass knocker on the front door, looked up from his work, glanced at the clock. More than an hour had passed since he'd sat down. He strode out of the study and made his way to the door. He swung it open and saw Miss Delaney standing there.

"Mr. Michael, your note said to come find you." She was on the sidewalk leading up to the covered front entry. Apparently, she'd knocked on the door, then stepped back out in the sunshine.

Landon stood in the open doorway, his hand on the knob. The sun caught her blond hair at just the right angle, and it looked like the proverbial spun gold. She made a movement and her hair bounced just as it had last night. Indeed, her eyes were light blue. Azure? Yes. She was in jeans again, but this time she wore a red knit top that played up the vivid color in her complexion. Another proverbial saying came to mind: peaches and cream.

"Mr. Michael?" She was cupping her eyebrows against the sun.

"Uh, yes. Come in, Miss Delaney."

"It's Lois."

"And call me Landon, please."

"Sure, Landon." She stepped inside then paused and looked around. "Thank you for the delicious breakfast. I appreciate it."

"You're welcome." He stood there with his hand still on the knob. As she passed him, her scent smelled better than the orange blossoms outside or the Christmas tree inside. His sense of smell had finally returned after his dreadful cold, and he breathed her scent in deeply. Was it her shampoo? Her cologne? Those body sprays women used?

"What a beautiful home you have." Her gaze roamed the room.

"Thanks." His gaze followed hers. Gleaming hardwood floors. Elegant though comfortable furniture. Soaring ceilings. Oversized windows that framed the magnificent outdoors. The adjacent kitchen with its long inviting bar and stools, a big French country table beyond.

"Did your wife do the decorating or you?"

"She did. That's not my forte."

"She was talented, I'll say." She let out a low whistle. "This looks like something from those decorating shows on TV. The only shows I like are the ones that feature remodels of old houses. Just like you, decorating's not my forte, either. Ever watch those shows?"

He shrugged and shook his head. His TV stayed tuned to sports and the political commentary shows. And the news, of course.

"That's about all the TV I watch. I recently saw one on Willa Cather's refurbished Nebraska family home. Groovy, huh?"

He was amused by her use of the word "groovy." That was as passé as tie-dye. The teenagers that attended his high school certainly didn't say *groovy*.

"Oh, and I love old-timey movies. And reruns, too. I can't stand those shows where all they do is argue about politics. I don't watch too much of the news, either. It's so depressing. And I hate all those incessant sports programs. When I was growing up, when my father wasn't doing remodeling jobs, he ate, drank, and slept sports. I guess that's why I can't stand them now."

He smiled a wry smile.

"Would you like me to sit down?" She sank down on one of the two leather sofas flanking the fireplace and looked over at him, sparkles dancing in her eyes again, like she was baiting him.

He shut the door and came toward her. "Of course." *I would've asked if you'd given me the chance.* He rubbed his temples. "Sorry. It's just that I've been so absorbed this morning." He sat down in his recliner.

She leaned forward, her brows arched. "You said you'd show me about?"

"Yes."

"The Orange Blossom B and B is just like my pastor's wife described. A little piece of heaven. Of course she's more than my pastor's wife. She's my aunt. And my pastor is my uncle—"

"Reverend Ellison?"

She nodded. "I was working in Atlanta. I'm a publicist. When my firm downsized, Uncle Rodney and Aunt Clovis begged me to come work with them in their church in Milton, Georgia, for a little while before I took another position."

Absently, she toyed with her hair. "I'm not sure why I took them up on it. Big-city girl versus small-town ingénue." She let out a gentle laugh.

Landon settled back in his recliner. Was she as long-winded as Reverend Ellison?

"The town, Milton, is quaint, and so are the church and the people. Quaint means 'pleasingly old-fashioned.' Never thought I'd like that lifestyle, but I do. In fact, I love Milton." She laughed her bright hyena-like laughter. "I've always had a love for antiques and historical things. I guess that's why I like living there so much."

Bingo. I was right. You're as long-winded as good old Uncle Rodney.

"Ever visit Atlanta?" Again, she didn't wait for a response. "There's a restaurant named after a character out of *Gone with the Wind*." She clasped her hands together. "I love that story. I've visited the Margaret Mitchell house several times. It's where she actually wrote *Gone with the Wind*. And I've read two biographies of her. What's that title I just finished?" Her brows drew together, and she tapped on her chin.

You are one dramatic lady, he thought as she rattled on.

"Can't say I like everything about Scarlett O'Hara. Basically, she was a self-centered girl who lacked a sense of humor. But there's one thing I *do* like about her. She always had an optimistic bent. I'd like to think that I have that quality, too. Remember what she said when Rhett left her?" She fluttered her eyelashes, then threw her hand across her heart. " 'I'll think about it tomorrow. After all, tomorrow is another day.' " She gave Landon a saucy smile. "Don't you love positive, upbeat people? But I've gone on and on. I tend to do that when I'm real excited."

Landon stared at her. *This woman could talk the hind legs off a billy goat. Why, she zips from one subject to the next. I've never seen anything like it. She started out with her aunt and uncle and ends up impersonating Scarlett O'Hara. Talk about drama?*

"In my little town—"

Ring-g-g-g-g. . .

Landon looked heavenward. *Thank You, Jesus.* He edged forward. *I'm saved by the bell.*

Ring-g-g-g-g. . .

"Excuse me while I get the phone." *Miss Zany Delaney.*

"Sure. Take your time."

He made his way into the study. It was probably his cleaning lady calling. Early this morning he'd gotten ahold of her, and it just so happened that she had a cancellation today. That worked perfectly for him. Forget Miss Perky Pamela. He should've booked his cleaning lady from the beginning, but Pamela'd been so insistent about helping him.

A minute or two later, he emerged from his study and walked toward Lois. "Are you ready for your tour? That was the cleaning lady. She's on her way over."

"Ready." Lois rose to her feet.

Knock-knock.

"Wonder who that is?" Landon headed for the front door, puzzled. "The cleaning lady couldn't've gotten here that quick, and we don't have solicitors this far out." He threw open the door. There stood Pamela.

"Hi, Landon."

He tried not to stare. Tall, dark-haired, and tanned, with model-perfect features, Pamela was dressed in gym shorts that showed off her shapely legs and a tiny tank top that revealed— oh, never mind. He couldn't help noticing that her shorts hung below her waist and her top ended just above. A gentleman, he looked beyond her to the orange grove across the way. What did women think these days? Didn't they have any idea what their clothing did to a man? Or, rather, lack of clothing? And Pamela was a Christian, to boot!

"I came to clean the cottage like I promised." Pamela put her foot on the planter beside the door, leaned over, and tied her shoe, looking up at him the whole time. "May I have the key?"

Landon squirmed at the distressing view Pamela was displaying. What cottage? What key? Was her tank top getting tinier? Or was her skin growing in circumference? Bingo on both. Where was a man supposed to look? He focused on the grove again. *Keep me true, Lord Jesus, keep me true,* he silently sang—no, belted out—inside. *Keep me true, Lord Jesus, keep me true. . . .*

"Earth to Landon, as we're always saying at school. Are you reading me? I'm reading you loud and clear, Landon, and you're in la-la land. Par for the course." Pamela smiled brilliantly, which only made her beauty more striking.

He finally found his voice. "Come in, Pamela." He gestured inside. "I'd like you to meet someone." For some reason, he couldn't remember his guest's name. Lois Lane?

Lois was at his side in a flash. She thrust out her hand as Pamela took a step into the great room. "Hi, I'm Lois Delaney, and I'm a guest at the Orange Blossom. It's a pleasure to meet you. Pamela, isn't it?"

⁂

Landon waited in the yard for Lois to come out of the cottage. She'd run inside to get something after Pamela left. He was going to show Lois around his acreage, take her to the groves, the lake, and the barn as he promised.

You'd think they were long-lost friends, those two, the way they carried on when I introduced them.

Lois had a sanguine personality, for sure. Just knowing her for one day, he was fairly certain she never met a stranger.

He guessed that was a good thing—to be so outgoing. She must have tons of friends because she certainly showed herself friendly.

And she was definitely optimistic, something she referred to when she talked about Scarlett O'Hara. He had to admit her cheerfulness—loud though it was at times—was. . .was. . . endearing.

Endearing? He'd have to think about that, but it had a nice ring.

Chapter 4

Lois sat in Landon's church the next day, though not on the same pew, of course. Yesterday afternoon, when he'd finished showing her around his place, he mentioned that she could follow him to church on Sunday if she wanted to. She decided to take him up on it. Then she called Pamela and asked if she could sit with her. Now, in church, Pamela sat at her side. It was nice having a new friend.

Lois looked down at her hands, saw the rosy glow coming from the stained glass windows, glanced up at the beamed ceiling, and admired the beauty of the sanctuary. She liked the style of this church service. Though it wasn't as countrified as Uncle Rodney's church in north Georgia, it had a pleasant, homey feel. The friendliness of the people, the mixture of choruses and hymns, and the emphasis on children—as evidenced by a musical number by a kids' choir—all appealed to her.

Late yesterday afternoon, after she had freshened up following Landon's tour of his acreage, she headed for the café in town for supper, the one he'd told her about.

Funny. He was there, too, eating. He was almost finished with his meal when she arrived, but he asked her to join him. Out of obligation? After all, she was a paying guest in his B and B, and he'd spent half the day trying to make his guest feel at home. Out of courtesy? He was certainly a gentleman, she knew, though she'd only known him a short while.

"Please stand for the reading of God's Word," the minister said from the oak pulpit. "Brothers and sisters, turn to Psalm thirty-seven, verses four through six."

Lois and Pamela stood, their Bibles in hand, the pages turned to the verses.

" 'Delight yourself in the Lord and he will give you the desires of your heart,' " the minister read. " 'Commit your way to the Lord; trust in him and he will do this: He will make your righteousness shine like the dawn, the justice of your cause like the noonday sun.' " Then he prayed. "You may be seated."

The congregation took their seats.

Lois couldn't help noticing a little old lady on the front pew still standing, even after everyone sat down.

"That's Sister Gladys." Pamela leaned in close with her whispered comment. "She's a dear. Someone faithfully picks her up from the nursing home every Sunday. Sadly, she's suffering from senile dementia." She pointed to her temple, a compassionate look on her face.

Lois nodded in understanding. In their church in north Georgia, it was Miss Mavene. Similar lady. Similar circumstances. So sad.

Lois focused on Sister Gladys's clothing. Similar attire to Miss Mavene's. Sister Gladys was wearing a stained yellow pantsuit and green and white tennis shoes. Perched precariously atop her head was a black velvet pillbox hat, and on her arm hung a white oversized purse that bore jagged lines of blue ballpoint ink.

"Dear ones," the minister intoned, "today we are going to

look at three short scriptures. But they pack a powerful punch. The key words are delight, commit, and trust."

Sister Gladys leaned down and picked up a magazine from her pew, then stood upright and held the magazine out at arm's length. She bent yet again, pulled a saucer-sized magnifying glass out of her purse, and peered through it, studying the magazine.

Lois couldn't help smiling. Sister Gladys was holding a tabloid paper. Only it was upside down.

"If we delight in the Lord," the minister said, "the Bible says He will give us the desires of our hearts. It goes on to say that if we commit our way to Him and trust in Him, He will make our righteousness shine like the dawn and the justice of our cause like the noonday sun. What does all of that mean for us?"

He adjusted the gooseneck of his microphone on the pulpit. "It means, among other things, that the Lord will answer our prayers, vindicate us, and give us guidance."

Sister Gladys shouted "Amen, Brother Ben!" and muttered something nonsensical as she sat down with a thud.

Lois heard tittering among the crowd, saw people squelching chuckles, and smothered her own. Poor Sister Gladys. Miss Mavene in north Georgia never hollered out in a church service, though her oddities included walking around the altar during Uncle Rodney's sermons—until Uncle Rodney appointed one of the women to sit by her. He would never bar the door of the church to people like that. They needed Christian love and compassion even more, was his reasoning, and Lois's, too.

Lois glanced across the aisle and spotted Landon. *Wonder what he is thinking about Miss Gladys's antics?* Yesterday she'd detected that he had a slight sense of humor, but it was so. . . so. . .wry. Then another question loomed in her mind. Why was she even thinking about what Landon was thinking?

It's only natural, she told herself. *He's a Christian, he's unattached, and he's good-looking.* She squelched a chuckle that threatened to gurgle up her throat and reveal her thoughts. . . .

I'm saved. . .

I'm single. . .

And I'm searching!

Psalm 37? Where are you? She bowed her head. *Lord, forgive me for letting my mind wander. But sometimes a girl just can't help herself!*

Late that afternoon on the way home, Landon couldn't quit thinking about Lois. At the close of the church service, the pastor's wife had walked to the platform and invited all singles to the pastor's home for Sunday dinner.

For over two hours, the dozen or so singles—from college-aged to senior citizens—all of them women except him—had enjoyed good fellowship. After the lunch of delicious meat loaf and scalloped potatoes and all the trimmings, they went outside to the backyard and sat in lawn furniture in the pleasant December sunshine.

Landon had spent that time with the pastor, talking sports and politics. The women had chattered like magpies, Lois at the center of the bunch, making them laugh with her stories and antics. He could clearly see and hear her the entire time he chatted with the pastor.

He remembered more of her antics, when they were leaving and she was on her way down the front steps of the pastor's home and dropped her purse, its contents tumbling to the ground. She had laughed in her crazy way. He had never seen such an array of stuff in all his life. She had everything but the kitchen sink. Talk about a pack rat. Talk about disorganized.

Driving along now, he retrieved a napkin from the glove compartment, cleaned a spot on the windshield, swiped the dashboard, then dropped it into the little waste bag hanging from the radio knob. Into his mind popped a ditty from his childhood.

He likes me. He likes me not. He likes me. He likes me not.

He remembered how the girls would pull petals off buttercups as they chanted those two lines. Whichever line they ended up with on the last petal was supposed to be the truth of the matter. Only, in his mind the chant came out a different way.

I like her. I like her not. I like her. I like her not.

Yes, he liked Lois's dedication to the Lord. No, he didn't like her loud boisterousness. Yes, he liked her kindness, especially to people like Sister Gladys. At the close of the service this morning, he had seen her chatting with the elderly lady, then hugging her.

"Phooey," he said aloud as he turned onto his dirt road. "I don't have to like or dislike Lois Delaney. She's only a guest at the Orange Blossom. In a week, she'll be history."

Somehow, that thought didn't bring him comfort.

<hr />

Lois spent Sunday evening in quiet reflection, what she promised herself she would do at the Orange Blossom, though it was totally out of character for her. Give her people to surround her. Give her fun times. That was what refreshed her. But she determined to keep her promise to herself.

All evening, she read a little—from the stack of books she brought along. She also thought a little. But mostly, she rested.

Around eight o'clock, she went to the fridge and took out the meat loaf sandwich and iced tea the pastor's wife had insisted she bring home.

She sat down on the divan in the parlor of the quaint cracker gothic cottage, enjoying the delicious supper. Her eye caught and held the big black mildew spot on the ceiling. It had leaked so long, there was a hole that needed patching.

Tomorrow morning she would go into town and buy some lunch meat for a picnic down by the lake. She might even find a hardware store and see if they sold tongue-and-groove pine for the ceiling repair. If they did, she could tell Landon about it. Maybe she could help him fix it. Of course, that would necessitate a roof repair. You couldn't fix a damaged ceiling without addressing the problem behind it. But that was okay. With her expertise, she could help him fix the roof, too.

"Thank you, Uncle Rodney and Aunt Clovis, for this wonderful vacation." She put her feet on the ottoman in front of her. "It's just what I needed."

Chapter 5

B right and early, Lois was up, and she found breakfast on the kitchen table as usual. This morning she noticed it was crisply fried bacon, buttery croissants, and watermelon wedges. And of course the orange blossom honey, orange juice, and hot tea.

She crossed to the kitchen windows, opened them, breathed in the luscious scent of orange blossoms, walked back to the table, and sat down. "I'll never forget that smell. It's heaven on earth."

She drew in another lungful of orange blossoms. "Maybe someone sells an orange blossom body spray. I'll have to check out the mall in Atlanta on my way home." Another wave of the tantalizing scent wafted into the room borne on a morning breeze. "That would be fabulous, to smell like orange blossoms all year 'round."

She put a dollop of honey on her croissant, then bowed her head. "Lord, I thank You for this day. I thank You for Your goodness. Oh, Father, You are such a good God. You saved me, You kept me, and You take such loving care of me all the time. You said You would supply my needs, and You have. You said You would be a friend who sticks closer than a brother, and You are. You said You would never leave me nor forsake me, and You haven't."

She paused, thinking about her recent heartache with Phil. The Lord had been there with her, had seen her through. She jumped to her feet, did a little joy jig. "Yee-haw." She sat back down. *Thank You, Father, thank You, thank You, thank You. Help me to praise You always. In Jesus' name, I pray. Amen.*

You are delighting in Me, daughter, the Lord seemed to whisper.

She kept her eyes closed, enjoying the feeling of oneness with the Lord. She remembered the minister's sermon yesterday. She'd read Psalm 37:4–6 many times. But today, just now, it became real to her as she meditated on the tender voice of the Lord she was hearing.

"Lord," she prayed, "I truly want to be used for Your kingdom and Your glory. . . ."

That's more delighting. . . .

"Let my life count for You. . . ."

I am delighted that you are delighting in Me.

She opened her eyes, feeling spiritually refreshed, feeling better than last evening when she'd felt physically refreshed. She looked down, saw the honey in one hand and the croissant in the other hand. They were both speaking to her.

Eat me.

She smiled as she snapped her eyes shut. "P.S., Lord. Thank You for this food which I am about to eat. Bless the hands that prepared it."

She laughed out loud, a vision of Landon appearing before her eyes. . . . He was wearing a big white chef's apron as he fried bacon in his spacious granite-and-cherry kitchen.

"Oops. Forgive me, Lord, for my wandering mind. I really

do thank You for this food. Bless it to the nourishment of my body. In Jesus' name, I pray. Amen."

She took a bite of the delicious honey-dotted croissant—surely heavenly ambrosia. She chewed slowly, thinking about Landon again. Only this time, he wasn't frying bacon. . . .

He was holding her close. . . .

She dropped her utensil, a glob of gooey honey puddling by her plate, but she didn't wipe it up. Instead, she sat there absently running her finger around the rim of her teacup.

The vision appeared again. . . . She and Landon were standing in the orange grove beneath the blossoms, his arms around her, her head on his shoulder. . . .

Then the vision faded. She didn't know what to think, what to say. So she said what popped in her mind.

"Amen, Brother Ben!"

<hr />

Landon glanced up from his supper in the town café and saw Lois stepping through the doorway. He stood, gesturing at the empty chair across from him. "Hi, Lois. Won't you have a seat?"

She hesitated, her cheeks pinker than usual.

Hmm. Why was she hesitating? Was she blushing? If he didn't know better, he'd say she was acting shy. And that wasn't the way of Miss Zany Delaney. But he liked it, this uncharacteristic shyness.

Absently, she fiddled with the clasp on her purse.

He wondered. Why was she acting so awkward? "Won't you join me?" He gestured at the empty chair for the second time.

"I wouldn't want to interrupt you again. You were so kind to invite me to sit with you Saturday night. There are plenty of tables in here." She looked about.

He took a step forward, napkin in hand. "No, really. I'd like for you to sit with me."

She smiled at last, walked to his table, and situated herself in the chair as he tucked it in from behind her.

"Alberta's serving fried chicken and peach cobbler tonight." He sat down opposite her, gesturing at his heaping plate.

"Alberta?"

"The cook. Every Monday night, it's fried chicken."

"Yum, yum. Sounds good to me."

The waitress appeared, took her order, and sauntered off.

"So, what did you do last night and all day today?" He took a swallow of iced tea, set it down, then pushed his plate back an inch or so.

"Please. Go ahead and eat. Yours'll be cold if you wait on mine."

"That's okay."

"No, it's not. I told you I didn't want to discombobulate you, as my great-grandmother would've said."

"Discombobulate?"

She giggled. "Upset. Confuse. Please. Go ahead and eat."

He smiled, picked up his fork and knife, and cut into his chicken. "So, how have you whiled away your time at the Orange Blossom B and B thus far?" He took a bite.

"I'm relaxed, refreshed, and recharged. That says it all."

"Sounds like advertising copy." He threw her a wry smile.

She laughed, her eyes dancing. "I've used my thesaurus a million times in my publicist work. Like you said, at times, colorful descriptions are advertising copy and nothing else. But relaxed, refreshed, and recharged is really true about the Orange Blossom B and B. I could even add revitalized."

"How about refueled?"

"Definitely."

"Let's do some more synonymizing."

"Synonymizing?" She wiggled her eyebrows, looking mischievous.

He fixed his eyes on her, intrigued. "Yes, synonymizing." He was baiting her, what she'd done to him in his great room. He was enjoying this interchange with her, and he wanted to prolong it.

"Hmm." She smiled. "So, you want more synonyms. Let's see. . ."

The waitress set a plate in front of her, then a glass of iced tea.

Lois picked up her fork. "You already pray?"

He nodded. "But I'll do it again." He closed his eyes. "Lord, bless Lois's food. And bless her. In Jesus' name. Amen."

She took a bite of mashed potatoes swimming in gravy.

He didn't know why he'd added "And bless her." It just came out. "Getting back to our synonymizing, how about regenerated?"

She nodded and dabbed at her lips with her napkin. "Renewed."

"How about rejuvenated?"

"Well said. That's what happens in this little piece of heaven. Rejuvenation."

He chuckled. "I like that description of the Orange Blossom. A little piece of heaven. Your pastor's wife said that."

She nodded. "Aunt Clovis. That's where I got it from. And just think. She hasn't even been here. She's only seen those pictures in the magazine and the brochure. They don't do justice to this place."

He finished eating and put his napkin on the table. "How about rapturous?"

She nodded.

"Transported."

Her eyes sparkled. "To heaven."

They both laughed.

"Heaven?" He drummed his fingers on the table. "Eden."

"New Jerusalem."

"Celestial bliss."

"Celestial bliss? You're good." Her eyes were fairly dancing. "Let's see. The inheritance of the saints in light."

"Wow, you're good, too. Holy City."

"Island of the blessed."

"Happy hunting ground."

"Happy hunting ground?" Her eyebrows arched. Then they drew together, like she was contemplating something. "Hunting, did you say?"

He nodded. "Are you hunting something?"

"You could say that." She threw him one of his own wry grins and a shrug of her shoulders.

"Well, you know what they say." He leaned toward her.

"What?"

"The wish is the father to the thought."

Chapter 6

For several days, Landon's path seemed to cross with Lois's constantly, though it was entirely unplanned. He couldn't help comparing her with Miss Perky Pamela. Pamela was blatant in her manner. Lois was unpretentious. Pamela was a schemer, it seemed. Lois was more *que sera sera*. Whatever will be, will be.

Pamela dressed like a fashion model and complained about getting dirty. Lois dressed casually, though she was as pretty as a fresh-peeled carrot, as his grandfather would've said about her. She was always in jeans, except for last Sunday's church service. And she never complained about getting dirty. In fact, Monday evening at the town café, she'd asked if she could help him repair the roof and ceiling of the cottage.

On Tuesday morning, they'd tackled the job. Though he wasn't adept at that type of work, under her expert guidance—she said she'd learned under her father's tutelage—Landon found that the task wasn't too difficult. Maybe he would take her advice and keep the cottage running as a B and B. At the least, he decided he would keep it clean and in good repair.

Each evening—Tuesday, Wednesday, and Thursday—he had asked her to ride into town with him to eat at the café.

"It's only reasonable," he'd said. "No need for two cars to be going to the same place."

"And no need to waste the gas," she'd added, after accepting his invitations.

That didn't matter to him. That wasn't the reason why he invited her to ride in his car. He couldn't really say what the reason was, exactly, except that he liked her company.

One morning, she asked him about the newborn calf he'd mentioned, and he took her to see it in his motorized horse—his pickup truck. She'd peppered him with questions about his orange grove, and they had a picnic there, him explaining the orange-growing process, which she said was fascinating.

She inquired about the high school where he worked, and he took her on a tour of the empty building, since the students were on Christmas break. He told her about the calling he felt from God to work with young people in the role of principal.

"As a high school principal, I feel like I'm a missionary to students," he told her.

"How wonderful," she'd responded, admiration clearly in her eyes.

She'd asked him about the dinghy tied to his dock, and he took her out in it several times. Once, they wore swimsuits and he took her to the sandy beach on the far bank where he'd swum as a child when his grandparents owned the property. They took a refreshing swim that day, and she said she couldn't get over swimming at Christmastime. He told her that he learned to ski on this very lake on a Christmas Day. He was just past toddlerhood, he said. His grandfather had patiently taught him even though it took about a dozen attempts. Every time after that, though, he stood up immediately on those tiny skis, flying across the lake. He told her he was looking for another ski boat right now. His last one he'd recently sold, he said.

During those several days, she told him a lot about herself, about her work in public relations, and about the awards she'd won in the field, all to the glory of God, she said. When she talked about her desire to put the Lord first in her life, he found himself marveling.

In turn, she told him how much she admired him for his dedication as a high school principal. It was like they had a mutual admiration society going, but he felt they were both sincere in their kind comments to each other.

Enter Miss Pamela Perkins. Somehow, she'd managed to get in on some of his and Lois's times together. The three of them ate together one evening at the café, and the day he showed Lois the high school where he worked, they bumped into Pamela. She was coming out of her home ec classroom carrying boxes of Christmas ornaments.

"I'm going to put these on my tree at home." She tipped her head at the boxes. "I'm putting the finishing touches on it today. I chose a real tree this year instead of an artificial one. Why don't you two join me for Christmas Eve dinner so you can see my tree, and I'll cook us something good to eat?"

So, plans were made for Christmas Eve at Pamela's.

"Pamela *is* a good cook," he told Lois later. "Beats the town café. And that's saying a lot, because Alberta's cooking is the best—as you can attest." He laughed when he rhymed the words.

She laughed, too, at his little rhyme. "I wish I could cook a decent meal. Cooking's not my strong suit."

"But you've got other strong suits." He was thinking of her expertise on the roof and in the field of public relations. He also thought about her devotion to God and church work. He didn't believe he had ever run across a young woman like her, one who seemed to. . .to. . .commune with God. That was a good way of putting it.

Being a minister's son, he liked that quality most of all.

Chapter 7

Fresh from the shower, with her plaid robe on, Lois stood in front of the pine dresser in her room and blow-dried her hair, then put on her usual light application of makeup. Mascara, blush, and lipstick.

Today, Saturday, she was going to a Christmas party at a church member's house. Tonight, back at the B and B, it would be time for quiet reflection again, something she was looking forward to. Tomorrow morning was a Christmas Eve service at church, tomorrow evening the dinner at Pamela's, and Monday was Christmas Day. She would eat Christmas Day lunch at the café in town, and time would tell as to how she would spend the rest of the day. On Tuesday morning, she would be leaving the Orange Blossom B and B Inn, bright and early.

That last thought made her sad. This little piece of heaven had grown on her. It had such drawing power. It was beautiful—picturesque in a quaint sort of way. Idyllic was another way to describe it. She smiled as she thought about hers and Landon's synonymizing Monday night at the town café. What a hoot. What fun.

She looked about the room. Tongue-and-groove boards were on the walls as well as the ceiling, just like the rest of the interior of the little cracker gothic cottage. Pegs hung on the back of the door, and her jeans and shirts covered every one of them, and some of her clothes puddled on the floor. The floorboards attested to foot traffic through a ribbon of years, and the old-fashioned furniture was probably very near to what had been in the home originally.

What were the people like who lived here all those years ago? Landon's relatives? Ancestors, really. What were their thoughts, their feelings, their aspirations, and their goals?

She knew what her goals in life were. Her mind flitted to Phil. Funny. She hadn't thought about him all week. No, when it came to men, the only man she'd thought about was Landon. Was that bad?

"It's only natural," she said to herself, since they had spent so much time together this week. "What *is* our future? Is there even a future for us?"

She pulled on her clothing, jeans again, sleek black ones this time, her top a bright blue crisscrossed knit. It had caught her eye in the mall, and she purchased it because of the color. She put in red, blue, and gold earrings shaped like Christmas ornaments and a matching pin on her left shoulder that played "I Saw Mommy Kissing Santa Claus" when she pressed it. It was a gift from one of the kids at church. She pressed on it now, smiling at the tinny tune. It would be sure to garner a laugh or two at the party today.

Dressed now and ready to go, she picked up her purse and dug for her keys. Landon had told her this morning when he'd brought over breakfast that he most likely wouldn't be able to make the mid-afternoon Christmas party. Another calf was about to make its entrance into the world, he'd told her.

Outside the cottage, she glanced across the road and saw

no movement. That meant he wasn't going. A low feeling hit her in the gut. Her? The most upbeat of anyone around? The party person? The constantly jazzed belle of the ball? Why this sadness all of a sudden?

She got in her car, cranked up the engine, and turned on the radio. She knew the answer, as clear as the Christmas bells that jangled on the wreath on Landon's truck hood when he'd driven her around in it all week.

"A wreath on your truck?" she asked when she saw it, incredulous.

He only gave her one of his wry grins she'd come to know and like. Then he said, "Maybe some of your zaniness is rubbing off on me, Miss Zany Delaney."

She'd cackled at his nickname for her.

Then he added, "I saw another truck decorated like this, and I thought if I put a wreath on mine, I'd get a rise out of you."

"A rise?" She made her eyebrows go up and down. "This is the zaniest thing I've ever seen in my life, Mr. Bonanza." She hummed the theme song. "Dum-duh-duh-duh-duh-duh-duh-duh-duh-dum-dah. . .dum-duh-duh-duh-duh-duh-duh-duh-duh-dum-duh-duh-duh-dah." Only she was off-key, way off, and they had laughed together.

Now, as she put her car in reverse, she was immersed in her thoughts. In a few days, she would be pulling out of here, out of this enchanting man's life. That was the reason for her melancholy today. She knew it as sure as she was sitting there.

She turned the radio louder, backed up, and took off down the dirt road, her tires spinning in the ruts.

"You're just being melodramatic," she chastened herself. "Like a character in a novel." Just because she was leaving soon didn't mean that she and Landon couldn't have a relationship. A long-distance relationship was no big obstacle. In fact, she'd be willing to move to Florida in a heartbeat if there was a future for them.

She was really attracted to Landon. He seemed to be everything she was hunting for. Hunting? She smiled, thinking of their synonymizing again. When he had said "happy hunting ground," she was thinking about the fact that she was saved, single, and searching. It wasn't every day that you ran across a good man the right age who shared your faith and values, and besides that, he was as handsome as all get-out.

She remembered Uncle Rodney's and Aunt Clovis's pleas for her to graciously accept their gift of a stay at the Orange Blossom B and B.

"I believe it's providential for you to go there," Uncle Rodney had said.

"Yes," Aunt Clovis had chimed in. "I feel it in my bones that God's got something good ahead for you, Lois."

Providential? Something good ahead? Lois turned onto the paved road and floored it as she sped down the blacktop.

Landon in her life. Landon as her. . .husband?

"That's what I want. That's what I desire."

There. She admitted it.

Would Landon become these things? Would her stay at the Orange Blossom B and B prove to be providential, as Uncle Rodney thought? Would it be the "something good ahead" Aunt Clovis felt in her bones?

Only time would tell.

And Lois was one hurry-up woman who didn't like to wait on the proverbial Father Time.

But in this case, she had no say in the matter.

"Phooey," Landon screeched, still waving his arms like a windmill as Lois sped off down the dirt road. "You must be doing some deep thinking, woman. You never even heard me, and I was yelling like a loon."

He dropped his arms and looked down at his white shirt that was now covered in gray dirt. He tasted grit in his mouth, felt grit in his eyes. "Phooey. I've got to go take another shower, compliments of Miss Zany Delaney." But he was smiling.

Earlier today, he'd told her he didn't think he would be able to make it to the church Christmas party. But then the calf decided to cooperate. After the birthing, Landon had rushed inside, showered, dressed, and ran out when he saw Lois get in her car. He had intended to drive them in his truck. Only it hadn't worked out that way.

He failed to get her attention, even though he'd yelled. It was a good thing he hadn't walked up behind her car, rapped on the back windshield, and barked like Marmaduke, as he first thought to do. He figured that would be a little joke on her. But she would've run right over him. Thankfully, he hadn't done that.

Now, he headed back inside his house. He would jump in the shower again, press another shirt. . . He would be late for the party, but at least he would get to attend.

Chapter 8

Ever the cheerful one, Lois threw off her sadness like water off a duck's back as she drove down the highway. After all, tomorrow was another day. She couldn't help smiling as she thought about Scarlett O'Hara and her eternal optimism.

Within twenty minutes, she arrived at the Larsons' home. Today's party was for whomever from the church wanted to come. Pamela said there would be adults, teenagers, and children attending. It was to be a big barbecue, and she said there would be horses and ponies to ride and games for the young and old alike. She said people loved coming to the Larsons' home because they made you feel so welcome.

Rightly so. Mrs. Larson greeted Lois like she was a daughter as she stepped inside the foyer.

Pamela came across the foyer not long after Lois entered the house, carrying a silver platter of fruit. "Nice top, Lois. Looks like you dyed it to match your eyes. My friend, you're looking good today."

"Thanks. Coming from you, I consider that a compliment." Lois could see that Pamela's outfit was to die for, and besides, it revealed her womanly curves.

Pamela shrugged. "You're as cute as a button in everything you wear. Me? I'm as tall as the Tower of Babel. Want some?" She held out the fruit platter. "I'm taking this outside for Mrs. Larson, to the tables out there. That's where she's serving the food."

"Sure. I'll take a piece." Lois stabbed a wedge of fresh pineapple with a colorful toothpick.

Moments later, she greeted the pastor and his wife, then thanked them again for the lovely time she'd had at their home the past Sunday afternoon. They asked her some public relations questions, and she doled out advice freely. She was glad to help. It seemed this church was about to celebrate a major anniversary, like her church in north Georgia would soon be doing, and the pastor and his wife wanted some tips.

"When I first moved to Milton six months ago, I found out that the church would be fifty years old in one year from then. The first thing I did was form a committee to plan a month's worth of events for the anniversary month. I also planned one event for each month leading up to it. Next, I made the newspaper aware of our plans. They're doing an article a month on us. That's pretty groovy. Free advertising."

She was sure her eyes were showing her excitement. She always got excited talking about PR, especially when it furthered the kingdom of God. "Then, I started a children's program on Sunday mornings. If you want to reach young families, you'd better have a hopping kids' program. Our church was considered an older congregation—"

"The congregation got older through the years," the pastor said, "and no young families were added, right?"

"Right. When our community suddenly realized that Christ Church was on the map via the newspaper articles, and, coupling that with the new kids' program, well, our attendance started growing by leaps and bounds. I'm training workers now so that when I leave, they can take over." She had already explained to the pastor and his wife that her church secretary stint was temporary.

"Why don't you come work for us?" the pastor asked. "We can't pay you what a big firm in Atlanta could. But we'd make it worth your while—eventually. We're a small church, but we have big dreams."

Lois was dumbfounded. Just this very morning, she had decided that if there was a future for her and Landon, she would move to Florida in a heartbeat.

"Think about it, okay?"

"Okay."

For an hour, Lois wandered inside and out. She watched the children riding the horses and ponies. She stopped at the booths and tried her hand, taking her turn standing in line with kids and adults alike.

The beanbag throw. The ball roll across the lawn. The bean drop in three different sized cans. The Ping-Pong ball toss. The red-and-green-candy-in-the-jar guess. The puzzle puzzler.

The seed-spitting contest?

"Step right up, Miss," said the elderly man at the booth. "See how far you can spit a seed."

Lois laughed, imagining herself taking aim with her mouth and hurling a seed through the air. She might be silly but she wasn't crazy. Spitting seeds the farthest? No thanks.

"Can you make it two feet?" he said. "Three feet? Four?"

She smiled. "I'll pass, thank you."

Pamela came to her side, as well as a few other singles, from the college-aged to senior citizens, the same ones who'd been at the pastor's house last week. "Lois, Lois," they chanted over and over. "Lois, Lois, she's our man, if she can't do it, nobody can." They said the cheerleader cheer until a crowd gathered.

After much coaxing and amidst much laughter, Lois stepped up to the line.

"Get yerself a seed," the elderly man said.

On a small table, Lois saw a plastic butter tub filled with some sort of seeds. "Are these recycled seeds?" she joked.

"Not that I know of." His eyes twinkled. "I was told they're pumpkin seeds. Mrs. Larson carved the pumpkin herself, and she's got the pies to prove it."

Warily, Lois reached down, retrieved one of the seeds from the tub, and took a runner's stance, her right toe on the line.

The singles around her chanted her name again. "Lois-Lois-Lois-Lois."

Lois put the seed in her mouth. "Shoo-wee." She scrunched up her nose. "These things are salty." She pursed her lips, taking aim.

"Get ready," the elderly man said. "Get set. Go."

She thrust her head forward, spit the seed with all her might, and didn't even see where it landed because the grass was sparse and the seed was the color of the dirt.

The elderly man found her seed on the ground, marked it with a tall stick, and congratulated her for her distance, as did the others gathered around.

I sure am glad Landon isn't here. She didn't mind being the instigator of silliness, but this took the cake.

❧

Landon spotted Lois in the food line and made his way to her. "Nice spitting, Lois," he whispered, grinning.

She whipped around, her plate of food nearly toppling out of her hands. "You startled me." She looked shy, embarrassed even. "I thought you weren't going to come? I thought you said you wouldn't be able to make it? Uh. How long have you been here?" Her questions tumbled out staccato-like as she clutched at her throat.

"Long enough. I saw the contest." He wouldn't tell her that he had also entered it after she walked away. "The calf made her debut earlier than I expected, and so I was able to come. Why? Are you sorry?" He chuckled, envisioning her in the seed-spitting contest.

She smiled at him, genuine warmth in her eyes this time. "Oh, no. I—I'm glad you came. It's just that as I was. . .spitting that. . .that stupid seed, I was saying to myself that I sure was glad you weren't around. Now, I'm finding out you were there watching."

"Like I said, nice spitting, Lois. Your lips must have some strong pucker power."

Her face turned as red as the barbecue sauce on her plate. "I—I. . ."

"No need to get flustered." He patted her arm, grinning, amused as all get-out. And attracted, too, very attracted to her. He felt that spark again, what he'd felt the first night they met.

"I—I. . ." Her voice trailed off. It was so unlike her to be at a loss for words.

Liking what he felt about her, getting flustered himself, he turned quickly, toward the food line. "I'm going to get some barbecue. Save me a seat at your table, okay?"

～☙～

Late that afternoon at the Larsons' home, everyone—adults

and children alike—gathered their lawn chairs in a wide-spreading cluster. Lois found herself sandwiched between Landon and Pamela.

The pastor led in singing Christmas carols. That was followed by testimonies offered spontaneously by people who attested to God's goodness in their lives in the past year. Then the pastor brought a Christmas devotional.

Lois enjoyed the warm camaraderie, her heart touched by everyone's kindness and friendship.

The woman who was in charge of the games stood and came to the front of the group. "I'd like to announce the winners of the various contests. We have some prizes to hand out. Drumroll, please."

Everybody beat on the armrests of their lawn chairs, the palm-to-aluminum *thwacks* making everyone laugh as the woman set prizes on a card table in front of her.

Landon seemed to be in a playful mood. He leaned over and thwacked Lois's armrest a few times, and she did the same thing to his.

The woman picked up a prize off the table. "The children's winner of the beanbag throw is Chase Miller."

The crowd clapped as little Chase came forward to claim her prize, a red net Christmas stocking filled to the brim with Christmas candy.

"The adult winner of the beanbag throw is Marta Johnson."

The crowd clapped as Marta came forward and received an identical prize.

"The children's winner of the Ping-Pong ball toss is Cassidy Kelly."

The crowd clapped as little Cassidy came forward and received her prize.

On and on the woman went, calling out the winners in both the children's and adult categories, awarding the prizes, the crowd clapping.

"And now, for the seed-spitting contest, we'll announce the adult category first. We've divided it into two parts. Men and women. Ladies first. The winner for the women's division is"—she thrust out her hand dramatically—"drumroll, please"—everybody thwacked on their armrests—"Lois Delaney."

The crowd cheered uproariously.

Lois, feeling the heat rise to her face, got up and made her way to the front.

"And the winner of the men's division"—the woman thrust out her hand dramatically—"again, drumroll, please"—everybody thwacked on their armrests—"is Landon Michael."

Landon made his way to the front and grinned his disarming grin at Lois, which made her heart beat all the harder. He took his place by her side as the crowd made playful catcalls and clapped loudly.

"The prize for this important contest is, tah-dah—a pumpkin." From under the table, the woman drew out two orange pillows in the shape of pumpkins. "Well, they're pumpkin pillows. I'm sure they'll remind you of this day for a long time." She held them out in front of her. "Lois and Landon, we hereby proclaim you the champion seed-spitters of our entire congregation. Congratulations!"

Applause broke out again.

Landon leaned close to Lois. "The secret's in the lips." Then he winked at her.

Lois couldn't think of a thing to whisper back, not a thing.

On her way home from the Christmas party, Lois pressed her Christmas pin on her left shoulder, the tinny tune filling the car. "I Saw Mommy Kissing Santa Claus." She sang along.

Then she pressed it again and sang along, only she changed the words.

"I *felt Landon* kissing *Loi–is*," she sang softly over and over.

Chapter 9

Standing on the church steps after Christmas Eve service, Landon asked Lois to ride with him to Pamela's home for Christmas Eve dinner that evening.

"Thanks, it'll save gas," she told him.

He rolled his eyes out of her view. Sometimes her thriftiness annoyed him. Oh, it wasn't that he was loaded. He gave reasonable attention to his finances. He just didn't squeeze the dollars as much as she did. He'd had a lifetime doing that as a minister's son, and that was enough.

That evening, as they rode down the highway, he wasn't thinking about her penny-pinching ways that sort of irked him. He was thinking about how good she smelled, and how energized she was, and how nice she looked. Tonight, it was crisply pressed black jeans, high-heeled black boots, and another top that matched those mesmerizing blue eyes of hers. She chattered about this and that, apparently content to let him sit quietly not saying much, just enjoying her company. That was a nice feeling, not to be pressured to join in a conversation, and it pleased him that she allowed him to do this.

He marveled at her. She was as smart as a whip, always coming up with ideas. Right now, she was talking about how he could promote the Orange Blossom B and B as a place for brides to bring their bridesmaids the weekend before their weddings for a bride's slumber party. Nifty idea, if he said so himself.

"You could even have weddings in the orange grove." She turned toward him, her face awash with excitement. "You could advertise them as 'A Wedding Beneath the Blossoms.' The bride and her bridesmaids could get dressed in the cracker cottage. The receptions could be held under big white tents, or in town somewhere."

He smiled and nodded as she continued talking, suggesting that he also promote the B and B as a place for small family reunions. Small tents could be put up in the backyard for the kids to sleep in, she said. Kids would love that, she went on, cousins camping out with cousins.

"Groovy." He laughed as he said the old-fashioned word she was always using. "I can see why you won awards in the public relations field. You're very clever."

"Thanks."

He leaned forward and tuned the radio to Christmas carols. "Silent Night" wafted through the car. "The Christmas Eve service this morning was meaningful, don't you think?"

She ran her hand through her bouncy blond hair and turned toward him. "Very touching. The children's number added a special touch, and then, when the choir sang the 'Hallelujah Chorus'—why I felt like shouting, 'Hallelujah!'"

"You mean you wouldn't have said 'yee-haw'?" He chuckled.

"I–I. . .when did you. . . ?" She clutched at her throat.

He loved it when the cat got her tongue. That had to be a mighty big cat, because she loved to talk. He smiled inwardly, envisioning a big, fat tabby. "When did I hear you say yee-haw?"

She nodded, still clutching her throat, looking like a kid with her hand caught in the cookie jar.

He loved it when she got shy. He didn't know why. But it attracted him to her like a bee to a blossom. He chuckled again. "It was the first morning you were here. I'd just put your breakfast in the kitchen. I went around back to get some logs, and I was coming down the side of the cottage when I heard you holler 'Yee-haw!' "

"I had no idea you were around. . . ."

"Just like when you were spitting seeds?"

She looked down, fiddled with her purse at her side, and didn't say anything.

With a sidelong glance her way, in the dimness of the dashboard lights he saw her thick eyelashes sweeping her cherry-red cheeks. He resisted the urge to reach over and caress those cherry-red cheeks. Innocence. That's why he liked her shyness. It showed her innocence, and he loved that about her. Loved? He bit his bottom lip, thinking hard.

Finally, she spoke, softly. "Yee-haw is a word I use when there's no other word to describe the joy I'm feeling. It's *really* zany, so I never say it in front of anyone."

After that, neither said a word for miles. They rode down the dark highway in the car that was lit up only by dashboard lights, both of them apparently lost in thought. When they approached town, he noticed the red and green reindeer-shaped lights that hung from tall light poles. On one street corner was a group singing Christmas carols.

"So you liked our choir's rendition of the 'Hallelujah Chorus' this morning?" Landon stopped at a traffic light, humming "We Wish You a Merry Christmas" along with the carolers on the corner.

"Oh, yes. I haven't seen a choir do that in a long time. I'll have to suggest that to Uncle Rodney for our church next year. I thought a choir had to have a lot more voices to pull that off, but I see now that even a smaller church can do justice to the 'Hallelujah Chorus.' When I lived in Atlanta, I went to a huge church, and we had a hundred-voice choir." She paused, like she was in deep contemplation. "That church was great, but there's something special about smaller congregations, don't you think? I never knew that until I started working with Uncle Rodney."

So much for her shyness, he thought with a wry grin.

"I have lots to tell Uncle Rodney when I get home. Suggestions to make, and all."

"Here we are." Landon turned into Pamela's driveway. Her house was nearly identical to every house lining the street, except that her Christmas decorations were tasteful.

"Groovy decorations." Lois picked up her purse.

He turned off the ignition. "Pamela decorated the inside of her home nicely, too."

"You've been here?" Her eyebrows arched.

"She—"

"I'm sorry. I shouldn't have asked that. It's none of my business."

"Pamela hosted a get-together for the church singles group."

"Oh."

He wouldn't tell her that Pamela had also had him for dinner twice during the first two weeks of December. When she invited him the third time, he was tied up. And the fourth time. And the fifth. She hadn't asked since then.

"I've only known Pamela a week, but I'm sure we'll be friends for life. Ever heard that song? It's old, I know. It was popular when I was a teenager." She clasped her hands together dramatically. "Friends are friends forever," she belted out, "if the Lord's the Lord of them. . ."

He winced. What an off-key voice she had, and apparently she didn't care.

She laughed her bright, hyena-like laugh. "I'm being silly, aren't I? I get this way when I'm excited." Her feet pitter-pattered on the floorboard. "Christmas Day is tomorrow!" She reached for her door handle.

"I'll get your door." He opened his door, climbed out of the car, shut the door behind him, and walked to the passenger side. He opened her door, held it while she climbed out. He touched her elbow, guiding her up the walk. The moment he had touched her, there was that spark again.

All the way to Pamela's front door, he hummed inwardly. But it wasn't "We Wish You a Merry Christmas." It was a golden oldie his grandfather used to sing.

"Let Me Call You Sweetheart."

When Lois and Landon stepped inside Pamela's home, she greeted them both warmly, Southern hospitality exuding from her.

Everywhere Lois looked, she saw Pamela's flair for entertaining, from the cinnamon scents that beckoned, to the tall Scotch pine that shimmered, to the Christmas carols that soothed, to the luscious hors d'oeuvres that set her taste buds watering.

"Oh, Pamela," she exclaimed, looking at the tree bedecked with gold and silver ornaments and hundreds of tiny white lights. "It's the most stunning Christmas tree I've ever seen."

"Thank you, Lois." Pamela stood looking at the tall tree.

"I love Christmas. It's my favorite time of all. The decorating and cooking and baking and gift buying. . .why, it's the most wonderful time of the year."

Lois sauntered to the mantel that was strung with greenery, spellbound. The greenery sported the same gold and silver decorations as the tree. "Everything is beautiful."

Pamela looked pleased.

Lois glanced around the room. Over a large archway were the same greenery and decorations. The coffee table had a similar floral arrangement. Through the archway, she saw the dining table adorned with yet another arrangement of like fashion. Everything coordinated. "What magic you work with your hands, Pamela."

"What a nice thing to say."

Lois grabbed Pamela in a sisterly hug, and they both laughed.

"Let's get started with some finger foods, shall we?" Pamela made her way across the room.

"Sounds good to me." Lois was close on Pamela's heels.

"I made some of Landon's favorites tonight." Pamela stopped at a marble-topped chest. Pointing at the small silver trays containing hors d'oeuvres, she motioned for Landon to come.

Lois smiled at Landon as he approached. "You're so quiet, I almost forgot you were here."

"I didn't." Pamela gave Landon a dazzling smile.

Landon joined them where they stood near the marble-topped chest.

"I made shrimp dip for you, Landon." Pamela seemed to have eyes only for Landon.

A twinge of jealousy hit Lois. It was now obvious to her that

Pamela had her dibs on Landon. Twenty minutes ago, in the car, she had told Landon what a great friend Pamela was. *So much for my talkativeness. Why couldn't I keep my big mouth shut for once?*

But then another thought hit her, one of contrition for feeling jealousy in the first place. Landon was an open playing field. She had no claim on him. And besides, Christians weren't supposed to be jealous.

"Here, Landon." Pamela held out a shrimp-dip-laden cracker on a napkin. "I know you love this stuff." She had a playful look about her, her eyes lighting up like the Christmas lights behind her.

He took the cracker from her. "One of my favorites, as you said, Pamela." He popped it in his mouth. "Delicious." He rubbed his midsection.

"Here, Lois." Pamela held out a cracker on a napkin to Lois.

"Thanks." Lois took it and nibbled it. "Yes, it's delicious." Her manner was stilted. She couldn't help it.

All through Pamela's exquisite dinner of stuffed Cornish hens, potatoes au gratin, and fresh asparagus with hollandaise sauce, Lois was quieter than usual. She could never hope to compare with Pamela. The woman was a wonder in all that mattered to a man.

After they ate their dessert—trifle in a footed glass bowl— the evening came to an end, and Lois was glad. Lois and Landon said their adieus and left.

As Landon drove toward home, Lois didn't say too much. She had a whole lot of thinking to do.

~~~

What's up with Lois? Landon couldn't help wondering as he

drove down the highway. *She chatters like a magpie all the way to Pamela's, and she's as quiet as a clam all the way home.*

Had he done something to offend her? He certainly had not. Did she think he had flirted with Pamela? He certainly had not. He couldn't help it that the woman was on the prowl. Oh, he didn't mean that like it sounded. Pamela was a nice enough young woman. And he knew Lois really liked her. She'd said so on the way there.

When they'd arrived, Lois was as friendly as all get-out. She went on and on about Pamela's decorating, even hugged her like a sister while she laughed like a hyena. Miss Zany Delaney. But after that, Lois grew quiet, and she was still acting that way now.

He thought about Pamela again. She'd come on strong all evening, like she was staking her claim on him. Had she been trying to get a subtle message across to Lois? Most decidedly so. In fact, there was nothing subtle about it. He knew what was going on. He wasn't born yesterday. Pamela was in pursuit. And Lois was in retreat.

He had quickly grown weary of the cutesy romantic triangle they had thrust upon him all evening. . .Miss Perky Pamela, overextending herself to him at every turn. . .

Miss Languid Lois, withdrawn and out of sorts. . .

And him? He was Mr. Lame Landon, ever the gentleman, trying to keep peace.

Women, he fumed inwardly. *All they think about is the M word.*

"Phooey." He thumped the steering wheel.

"Did you leave something at Pamela's?" Lois glanced his way. "Your jacket? You don't have it on."

"It's in the backseat."

"Oh."

He slowed for the turnoff to his road. Tomorrow was Christmas Day. Lois had told him she had enjoyed some times of quiet reflection while at the Orange Blossom. Well, tomorrow he would take all day for his own quiet reflection.

He would put the turkey in the oven. Though he wasn't a cook—a few breakfast foods were his limits—surely he could bake a turkey. He would follow the directions on the wrapper. It was that simple. And he would cook some rice—no, he couldn't make turkey gravy so it would have to be mashed potatoes. Mashed potatoes tasted better without gravy than rice did. And he would open a can of green beans.

All the while he was preparing his meal, and then during the eating of it, he would quietly reflect. Maybe he would find some of that refreshment Lois talked about. And revitalization. And rejuvenation.

He surely hoped so.

⁂

Lois didn't know what to think, so she tried not to. As the miles ticked off, she sat there just like Landon, not saying a word. It certainly wasn't like this on the way. She had been so excited that she talked up a storm. Now, she felt numb.

But her thoughts started whirling again, even though she was trying hard not to think.

She reflected on how quiet a guy Landon was. At times, she wished he would enter into conversations with her. And why had he acted that way all evening? Like a lame duck was how she would describe him.

And why had Pamela been like that? So solicitous of him that it made Lois want to scream. When Lois walked in, her first thought had been how gracious and hospitable Pamela was. Within five minutes, Lois knew Pamela for what she was. A woman with a mission. To get Landon Michael.

A cold chill hit Lois. Wasn't that what she was, too? A woman with a mission? To get Landon Michael? Just the other day she'd admitted to herself that she wanted Landon in her life, particularly as a husband. Then what was the difference between her and Pamela? They clearly wanted the same thing.

Lois shifted in her seat in Landon's car. She'd never felt so down. Though Landon was five inches from her, it felt like five miles. And it might as well be.

She glanced over at him. His eyes were narrowed, and his mouth was in a thin line. He looked contemplative—no, contemptuous was more like it.

He probably had her pegged—a woman just like Pamela. And he probably felt she was a loony toon with her loud, boisterous ways in comparison to his solemnity. Loony-toon Lois. A fitting name.

Well, one more day and she would be out of here. And that meant out of his life. Forever.

He would probably like that.

She pushed down the sob that threatened to gurgle up her throat.

Chapter 10

Christmas morning, Landon pulled the thawed turkey out of the refrigerator and set it in the sink. He studied the directions on the plastic packaging. If he got it in the oven now, he could eat Christmas dinner at one o'clock or so.

"I should invite Lois." He glanced out the windows at the cottage across the road. "She's all alone, and nobody should be alone for Christmas."

"I'm eating with Alberta on Christmas Day," she had told him when he dropped her off last night. "The café's open for the midday Christmas meal."

He thought of his own Christmas plans today, eating and quietly reflecting. Then he thought about his original plans, before he booked Lois at the B and B. It was his annual custom to drive to his parents' parsonage in North Carolina and spend a few days with them during the holiday season.

Tomorrow morning, as soon as Lois left, he would head up there. His parents had been understanding when he told them about his delay. His father, just as he expected, had been amused about the unusual booking by the preacher in north Georgia for his church secretary.

"Unusual booking? Unusual lady." Landon couldn't get his mind off Lois this morning. How did he feel about her? Was there a chance of a future for them? He thought about their differences.

Her, the talker; him, the quiet one.

Her, the disorganized; him, the neatnik.

Her, the spendthrift; him, the spender.

But then he thought about their commonalities.

Their faith.

Their values.

Their morals.

And he reflected on her little snippets of shyness that intrigued him. He remembered her lovingkindness to everyone she met.

"Yes, I'll invite her to eat Christmas dinner with me."

As he cut the packaging off the turkey, then scissored around the cooking directions and laid the small plastic square on the counter, his earlier questions gnawed at him. *How do I feel about her? Is there a chance of a future for us?*

He shrugged his shoulders. "I'll take her carefree, *que sera sera* attitude concerning our future. What will be, will be."

He put the turkey in the oven, walked across the road to the cottage, and knocked on the front door.

❧

After Lois ate the breakfast Landon laid out for her, she pulled out her Bible. She turned to Psalm 37:4–6, the passage she had reflected on all week.

"Delight yourself in the Lord and he will give you the desires of your heart," she read. "Commit your way to the Lord; trust in him and he will do this: He will make your righteousness shine like the dawn, the justice of your cause like the noonday sun."

She ran her hand across the sacrosanct words, then looked heavenward. "Okay, Lord, I've been delighting in You. Now, I'm going to commit my way to You. I desire Landon really bad. He's so groovy. I think the teenagers at church would say he's one awesome hottie. But if he's not the one You have for me, then. . .then close the door."

Her heart pounded. Those words were hard—no, torturous—to say. "I. . .I commit him. . .as well as the future of our relationship. . .into Your hands, dear Jesus."

Keep trusting in Me, the Lord seemed to whisper.

"Okay, Lord, I'll do that. I'll trust You. And I know You'll do Your part, as it says in the Word. You're going to make my righteousness shine like the dawn, and the justice of my cause like the noonday sun, whatever that means for me."

She drummed her fingers on the table. "What explanation did the pastor give for the last part of that passage? Hmm. Now I remember. He said it means that God will answer our prayers, He will vindicate us, and He will give us guidance."

She bowed her head. "Lord, first I'm asking You to answer my prayers, namely, to help me put You first in my life no matter what happens in my *love* life. Second, I'm asking You to vindicate me. I feel like such a goon around Landon. Sometimes I get excited, and I feel that he gets annoyed about it. Help him to see me as I truly am, a woman with a heart after You. Third, I'm asking You to give me guidance. I don't know what the future holds. But You do, Lord. You know my right hand from my left. You know the number of hairs on my head. So lead me now, dear Jesus. In Thy name I pray. Amen."

Knock-knock.

Lois looked up. Who could that be? Landon was the only likely caller. Why was he over here? She got up from the table and pulled the sash of her robe more tightly about her waist. She walked to the front door and opened it a crack, just enough to see out. After all, she was in her robe. There stood Landon, as she expected. But again, why was he here?

"Earth to Lois." He laughed. "You there?"

She smiled, feeling shy.

"Merry Christmas." He jangled a silver bell at her.

"Same to you."

"Can you come to my house for Christmas dinner?"

"Alberta's cooking dinner for me, in town—"

"I know Alberta's cooking. But I'm cooking, too. And I'd like you to join me, if you will. I can't cook like Alberta, but hopefully it'll be fit to eat."

"I wouldn't want to—"

"Discombobulate me?" He chuckled.

She laughed. "You remembered that funny, old-fashioned word my great-grandmother would've used?"

He nodded. "I just put the turkey in the oven. It should be ready by one o'clock. Say you'll come. There's no way I can eat a whole turkey by myself."

She stood there thinking. He really sounded like he wanted her to come. That made her feel good. Maybe he didn't think she was a complete ignoramus. Perhaps there was hope for them after all.

He held the silver bell higher, jangling it again. "Lois?"

"All right. I'll be there at one. And thanks for the invitation. I'm sure it'll be delicious."

Ten minutes later, she was in the shower, deep in thought. A poem formed in her mind, and she said it aloud.

*I hope I can act
Dignified today.
Maybe he'll like me
Better that way.*

She cackled at her silly little rhyme. But in her heart, she hoped it came true.

Chapter 11

L andon felt bad as he looked over the burnt part of the
turkey, toward Lois where she sat on the other side of
his dining room table. The top part of the bird was as
black as tar and smelled almost as bad.

"So much for reading directions. I thought sure I could
cook a turkey."

"You win some, you lose some." She smiled at him, empa-
thy in her eyes. "I'm sure it'll taste good."

He shrugged. "I shouldn't have run out to the barn when I
did. I thought I'd only be out there a few minutes, but then I got
dirty, and then I had to take another shower, and while I was in
the shower, the smoke started, and of course I couldn't see it, had
no idea the turkey was burning—"

"You sound like me." She looked up at him shyly.

"Talking so much and all?"

"No, I was thinking about our cooking skills. Or should I
say, lack thereof?"

He smiled at her. "Shall we pray?"

Throughout dinner, their conversation proceeded without
a hitch. Landon was glad. What with the burnt turkey and the
undercooked mashed potatoes, he needed something pleasant

167

going on. Lois talked in her usual bright, cheerful way, though he noticed she was somewhat subdued. He was his normal self. Quiet but with a listening ear.

She helped him clean the kitchen, which was nice. He wondered why he had cooked today—or attempted to, he should say. He should've gone to the café, like Lois had planned to do.

He scraped the plates. She loaded the dishes in the dishwasher. He washed the platters and the pots. She dried them. He put them away. He. She. He. She. He. She. They seemed to work well together. That was a pleasant thought to him as they finished in the kitchen.

"Will you excuse me for a moment while I call Aunt Clovis and Uncle Rodney and wish them a merry Christmas?" She picked up her purse from the sofa, reached inside it, and pulled out her cell phone.

"Sure."

She dialed a number.

"While you do that, I'm going to the barn. I'll be back in a few minutes, okay?"

The phone to her ear, she mouthed, "Okay."

Fifteen minutes later, when he came back inside, she was in the kitchen, looking in his cabinets.

She turned, her hand on a cabinet knob, her cheeks cherry red. "I–I. . ."

He smiled. There it was again. That shy, innocent look about her.

She found her voice. "Aunt Clovis said I should make you a dessert. I was looking for cookbooks. But I don't want to be presump—"

"Please proceed. A dessert sounds wonderful. Look in the cabinet over the phone. I think you'll find a few cookbooks in there." He walked toward his recliner in the adjacent great room and sat down. "While you do that, mind if I look at the sports channel for a few minutes?"

Lois opened the cabinet door over the phone, saw a shelf full of cookbooks. One caught her eye. *Delightfully Southern Recipes* by Lucy M. Clarke.

Excited, she pulled it out, read a little, found it was written by a Georgia author—yes!—turned to the index, and on a lark looked up the word "orange." To her delight, she saw eleven recipes. When she spotted Orange Blossoms, she almost did a joy jig. She flipped to the page and read the recipe. It looked easy enough.

"Do you have any cake mixes, Landon?" She projected her voice across the wide kitchen bar.

"You can look in the pantry, but I don't think so."

She opened the pantry door and scanned the shelves. "Rats." She whipped out her cell phone and dialed Aunt Clovis again. "Aunt Clovis, do you have an easy recipe for a yellow cake?"

"Why? Did you decide to make Mr. Landon Michael"—she cackled like Lois was always doing—"imagine a name like that." Her laughter trailed off. "Did you decide to make him a dessert, darlin'?"

"Yes, ma'am. I'm making Orange Blossoms. You pour yellow cake batter into miniature muffin tins, bake them, and then dip them in an orange glaze. Yum, yum. And it's so apropos, too." Lois smiled one of Landon's wry grins as she looked out the windows. "We're surrounded with orange blossoms, you know."

"Yes, darlin'," Aunt Clovis said in her Georgia twang. "I saw them pictures in the magazine, remember."

"This recipe I found looks luscious, Aunt Clovis. But it says you have to have a cake mix, and I don't have one. So I thought I'd use a substitute. An easy yellow cake recipe is what I was thinking."

"Have no fear, the chef is here. Hold on, darlin,' while I get my recipe box."

Lois heard fumbling on the end of the line as she waited.

"Here it is. It's called 1-2-3-4 cake. It's as easy as pie."

Lois jotted down the recipe as Aunt Clovis dictated it. Then she told her good-bye and hung up.

"Landon," she called across the wide bar, "I'm making you some orange blossoms."

"Orange blossoms?"

"They're little cake-like thingies with an orange glaze."

"Do I have the ingredients? I don't know of a store that's open on Christmas Day. Even the mini-mart."

"Hmm. Aunt Clovis's cake recipe is pretty basic. Butter, sugar, flour, eggs—that sort of thing. You have those?"

"I think so." He got to his feet, came in the kitchen, and helped her gather the ingredients onto the counter.

"I'm not much of a cook," she told him, "but both of these recipes—Aunt Clovis's and this Lucy M. Clarke's—look like a cinch. Any dimwit can make Orange Blossoms."

***

Landon stretched out in his recliner, the TV tuned to a sports channel, a fire going in the hearth, the AC cranked up to high, the pleasant sounds of a woman working in his kitchen sounding like music to his ears.

Lois's hands shook. She wanted these luscious little orange thingies to turn out well for Landon. She looked in a bottom cabinet for miniature muffin tins. Only round cake pans. Rats. She looked in the next cabinet, then the next. None anywhere. Oh well, who cared? She would make a two-layer cake and pour the luscious orange glaze all over it.

Butter, sugar, baking powder, eggs, flour, milk, vanilla flavoring. She sifted the dry stuff together, then combined the wet stuff, according to Aunt Clovis's recipe. *This is as simple as 1-2-3-4, just like the cake's name.*

She would've hummed, but she saw that Landon's eyes were closed where he lay in his recliner. *He must've dozed off.*

Carefully, she poured the batter into the two cake pans and set them in the preheated oven. *Tah-dah, I even remembered to turn the oven on, heh-heh-heh.* Then she turned the timer on.

She whipped up the orange glaze, set it aside, and joined Landon in the great room, delicious smells already scenting the air. A quick glance his way told her he was still dozing. She took a seat on the sofa, being careful not to awaken him, though she was itching to talk.

Nothing says lovin' like something from the oven, she hummed inwardly, the Pillsbury ditty filling her heart. She smiled, feeling like a kid finding a pony on Christmas morning.

Shortly, the timer dinged.

"I smell something good." Landon opened his eyes and pushed the recliner forward. "Yum, yum, as you're always saying."

"Yum, yum is right." She jumped up from the sofa and made her way into the kitchen. She pulled open the oven door, leaned down, and peered at the cake pans.

She let out a wail, couldn't help it.

"What's wrong?" Landon came running into the kitchen, alarm in his voice.

She let out another wail.

"Burn yourself?" He was behind her now.

She stood there, staring at the cake pans in the oven.

He bent down and looked at them. He stood up, laughing like she was always doing—like a hyena. He laughed so hard, tears watered his eyes.

She stood there in shock.

He finally quit laughing. "What did you do to that cake?"

She pulled out the two cake pans with oven mitts and set them on a protective mat.

He started laughing again.

She looked down at two little pancake-like cakes, one in each pan. The pans should've been filled with delicious yellow cake by now. "I guess I. . .I. . ." She went over a mental checklist of ingredients, remembering each one. "I guess I forgot to add something. . . ." She spotted the sack of flour by the sink and felt deflated—no, embarrassed beyond words.

His gaze followed hers, and he was laughing again, uproariously. "Lois, you forgot the flour."

❦

Landon watched Lois cross the road and enter the cottage.

He started laughing again and couldn't seem to quit. He'd never laughed this hard in all his life.

"To forget the flour? That takes the cake!"

He laughed at his pun.

"Any dimwit can make Orange Blossoms," she'd said.

As he scraped the orange glaze out of the mixing bowl and washed it down the sink drain—he'd insisted on cleaning up the kitchen—his burnt turkey came to mind.

"Well, Lois, we have another thing in common. Neither one of us can cook." He licked a dollop of orange glaze off the spoon, then chuckled. "No, we can't cook a lick."

Chapter 12

That evening, Landon looked outside the windows of his great room. Though there was no moon and the sky was as black as velvet, the night was young. He made his way outside, picked up a lantern on the porch, unleashed Marmaduke, and headed for the orange grove.

In a clearing, he sat on a bench, told Marmaduke to sit, set the lantern on the ground in front of him. He would do some of that quiet reflecting, what he hadn't had time to do all day. First, he had cooked Christmas dinner. Then he and Lois ate together. Then there was the cake mistake.

"Cake mistake? I'm pretty clever, if I do say so myself." He chuckled.

After the cake mistake, she had left, and the afternoon whiled away with him getting another leisurely, restful nap. "Now, for some quiet reflection."

Immediately, Lois popped into his mind. . . .

Lois with her cheerfulness.

Lois with her humor.

Lois with her kindness.

Lois with her devotion to God.

Lois, Lois, Lois.

It seemed he couldn't get his thoughts to focus elsewhere.

Lord, give me guidance concerning her.

Marmaduke growled.

"Easy, boy." He looked through the orange grove and saw a thin trail of light coming his way. A flashlight? Lois, perhaps? Of course. It couldn't be anyone else.

Marmaduke barked.

The thin trail of light went in the opposite direction.

"Lois? Is that you?"

The thin trail of light halted.

"Lois? If it's you, please come toward my lantern."

The thin trail of light proceeded toward him. In moments, she was in front of him. "I'm sorry. I didn't mean to disturb you."

He patted the spot beside him. "Have a seat?"

She hesitated.

"Please? I'd like to talk to you. Something I don't do much of, as you've probably noticed." He smiled up at her.

She took tentative steps toward him, then sat next to him.

He took the flashlight out of her hands and turned it off. The moment their hands touched, he felt the spark. In that instant, he knew that he knew.

She's the woman for me.

Thank You, Lord.

"You're sure quiet tonight, Lois." The lantern on the ground gave off the perfect amount of light, dim and romantic.

"Reflecting, that's all." Her voice was soft.

"Me, too. That's why I came out here. I was reflecting on our relationship."

She didn't respond.

He breathed in the night air, thick with the scent of orange blossoms all about them. He laughed, thinking about her Orange

Blossom recipe. Thingies, she'd called them. "I was laughing because I was thinking that you cook about as well as I do."

She let out a gentle laugh.

He wanted to put his arms around her, hug her to him and tell her what she meant to him. He would start slowly.

She breathed in deeply, like she was enjoying the scent of the orange blossoms, too.

"I'm a little old-fashioned, just like my cracker gothic cottage." He grinned. "So I'll ask you before I attempt it. May I hold your hand?"

She nodded as she looked down and fiddled with her bracelet.

He studied her. If the sun were shining, he was sure her cheeks would be cherry red, and the thought thrilled him. He reached out, found her hand, clasped it in his, and squeezed it.

She squeezed back.

"A few minutes ago, I was praying for guidance." *Concerning you.*

"I–I prayed for that, too, this morning," she whispered.

His heart rejoiced. There was that telltale catch in her voice. "And what did the Lord say to you?"

"He told me to keep trusting Him." Quietly and concisely, she explained the passage in the Bible she'd been reflecting on all week. "Those verses became my guidepost in matters that. . . well, that apply to. . .me."

He drew in a lungful of the scented air as he gathered her in his arms and hugged her to him. "You know what I think?"

"What?"

"I think that. . .love is a-bloom."

"I–I think. . .so, too."

Early the next morning, Lois loaded her car, her heart feeling as light as a feather after what happened last night.

She recalled how he had asked to hold her hand. "I'm a little old-fashioned," he'd said. She was, too, but she was so overjoyed at his romantic overture, she felt like saying, *Forget the old-fashioned stuff. Just take me in your arms, mister.* She smiled at the thought.

Now, Landon crossed the road and came toward her. "Since I'm heading for North Carolina, and you're heading for north Georgia, what about if I followed along behind you on I-75? We could stop for meals together, all day long."

"Sounds like a great idea." She flashed him a brilliant smile, her heart beating hard.

His eyebrows raised. "Not groovy?"

"Well, that, too."

He put his arms around her. "*This* sounds like a great idea. Groovy, too." He hugged her tightly.

She smiled, wanting to do a joy jig but restraining herself. Instead, she hugged him back warmly.

"Ahh, Lois. . ."

"Landon. . ."

He drew back and stared down into her eyes.

She thought her heart would melt.

"I'd like to conduct an experiment." His voice was husky.

"Experiment?" All she could think of were the test tubes she saw in his high school chemistry lab when he'd given her a tour of the building.

"I'd like to test your pucker power. . . ."

Feeling shy, she averted her eyes.

He cupped her chin and lifted her face. Their eyes met. He

came toward her, lips meeting lips. For a long moment, they stood in the sunshine surrounded by a heavenly fragrance, entwined in a sweet embrace.

He released her, seemingly out of breath. His eyes were playful as he looked into hers. "I'm at a loss for words. But that's not unusual. Do you have anything to say?" His chest heaved as he waited.

"Yee-haw!"

ORANGE BLOSSOMS
by Lucy M. Clarke

Duncan Hines Golden Butter Cake Mix

1) Set oven at 350° F.
2) Make cake mix according to directions but add 1 t. orange extract.
3) Spray miniature muffin tins with Pam and fill ⅔ full.
4) Bake until just barely browned. Tip: This takes very little time in the oven, so keep a close watch. The goal is for them to be moist.

Glaze
2 c. powdered sugar
1 t. finely shredded orange peel (optional)
enough orange juice to make a runny glaze

1) Mix ingredients together.
2) Dip each muffin in glaze and place on rack to harden.
3) Enjoy! Yum, yum!

ORANGE-PECAN CAKE
by Sharon Schuller Kiser

½ c. chopped pecans
⅔ c. butter, softened
1½ c. sugar
3 eggs, separated
¾ c. orange juice plus 2 T.
1 t. orange extract
1 t. grated orange peel (optional)
2½ c. flour
3 t. baking powder
¾ t. salt
¼ t. baking soda
½ t. cream of tartar

1) Set oven at 350° F.
2) Grease and flour tube pan. Sprinkle with pecans. Set aside.
3) In large mixing bowl, cream butter with electric mixer. Gradually add sugar, beating well. Add egg yolks one at a time, beating well.
4) In small bowl, combine orange juice, orange extract, and orange peel. Set aside.
5) In separate bowl, combine dry ingredients except cream of tartar. Then add dry ingredients to creamed mixture alternating with orange juice mixture.
6) In separate bowl, beat egg whites and cream of tartar until stiff peaks form. Fold into batter.

7) Pour into prepared pan. Bake at 350° for 50–55 minutes. Cool in pan 10 minutes.
8) Remove from pan, punch holes in cake with a fork, and pour glaze (below) all over cake.

Glaze

½ t. grated orange peel
½ c. orange juice
¼ c. sugar
1 T. butter

1) While cake is cooling for 10 minutes in the pan, combine all glaze ingredients in saucepan and cook over medium heat, stirring constantly until sugar dissolves.
2) Pour over cake.
3) Enjoy! Yum, yum!

KRISTY DYKES

Kristy lives in sunny Florida with her husband, Milton, a minister. An award-winning author and former newspaper columnist, she's had hundreds of articles published in many publications, including two *New York Times* subsidiaries, *Guideposts Angels*, etc. She's written novellas in three other Barbour anthologies. Kristy is a public speaker, and one of her favorite topics is "How to Love Your Husband," based on Titus 2:4. Her goal in writing and speaking is to "put a smile on your face, a tear in your eye, and a glow in your heart." Fun fact: Kristy is a native Floridian, as are generations of her forebears (blow on fingertips, rub on shoulder). She loves hearing from her readers. Write her at kristydykes@aol.com or c/o Author Relations—Barbour Publishing, P.O. Box 719, Uhrichsville, OH 44683.

Mustangs and Mistletoe

by Pamela Griffin

Chapter 1

"Just exactly what kind of favor do you want from me?"

Taylor Summerall hooked her hands on her hips and narrowly eyed her three brothers. Towering over her by a foot, Will and Robert stood to the side, clearly interested bystanders. Their oldest brother, Chad, leaned his forearm against the black banister near the bottom stair, putting him closer to a level with her modest height. He had that annoying, crooked smile on his face. The one Taylor always saw before he dropped the proverbial bomb.

Taylor tapped her satin pump against the parquet floor of the bed-and-breakfast's lobby. "I have a wedding to go to, and I have to be there, ready to walk down the aisle in half an hour. So you'd better make this snappy."

"Remember this past summer, when you wanted me to take that friend of yours sightseeing?" Chad asked, a speculative gleam in his eye. "The one visiting from Colorado?"

"Sandy—yeah. So what? It turned out well for you. You both hit it off."

"But a deal was involved. Before I agreed to take her, you said you'd do anything I wanted. That you owed me one."

Taylor gave an impatient nod. What was this leading up to?

Did he want her to wash his dirty laundry for a month? Clean his room? Do his chores? No, that was too juvenile and something he'd only made her do when they were both in high school.

"I have a friend from college who's coming to stay here through Christmas," Chad drawled. "He's an unmarried accountant from Chicago and will need someone to show him the ropes. Get him acquainted with ranch life—riding horseback, roping a calf, the whole nine yards. Show him around the place. Give him a good old Texas-sized welcome."

Unease crept up Taylor's spine. "Oh, no. No way, Chad. You do it."

He straightened from the staircase rail. "You owe me one. Remember?"

"He's right, Taylor," nineteen-year-old Will chimed in. "I'll be too busy helping Dad with chores needing done around the ranch, and Robert here has to study for finals. So we can't do it, either."

Robert nodded in silent assent, backing up both his older brothers.

Taylor bit back a groan. Why couldn't God have blessed her mother with all girls? Surely, three sisters wouldn't have been so demanding.

As though reading her mind, Chad softened. "I'm not asking you to marry the guy, Taylor. Only to do what you'd do for any other guest staying at the B and B. He'll be here longer than most since he's a buddy of mine."

"How long?" Taylor asked, frowning.

"Ten days—through Christmas, like I said. His mother just remarried and is on a cruise somewhere with her husband, so he doesn't have anywhere else to go for the holidays."

Wedding! At the reminder, Taylor glanced at the black

wrought iron clock on the stucco wall. "I have to leave right now if I'm going to make it to church in time. Hailey will never forgive me if I hold things up and she's not married on the dot of three."

"And what about Derrick?" Chad insisted.

Taylor grabbed her matching rose-satin evening bag from a nearby chair. She threw the gold chain strap over her shoulder. "Could we please talk about this some other time?"

"Not really. He's coming tonight."

"Tonight!" Taylor hadn't checked the reservations list yet this week. The days preceding Christmas usually didn't bring a lot of people to The Silver Spur Ranch. "Oh, okay, fine. Whatever. Just a word of warning, Chad. Do *not* try to pair us off together. I'm perfectly satisfied with my life just the way it is."

Whirling around, she headed out the door and into a blast of Texas sunshine, though the wind from the north chilled her. Thinking of Kevin, the man to whom she once was engaged, tears skimmed her eyes. She fumbled for her keys and headed to her car.

❧

Twilight clouded the acres of grassy land and the woods beyond with dusky purple as Derrick Freeborn paid the driver, stepped out of the taxi, and grabbed his one suitcase.

So this was The Silver Spur.

To his right, a life-sized nativity scene sat on the ground, illuminated with white spotlights. The drive was lit up with red luminaries, giving the appearance of candles in small paper sacks, though when he moved closer to inspect one, he saw a glowing bulb inside. Again he looked up at the three-story ranch house, a relic of a bygone era. Dimly lit red, blue, and white strings of lights curled in a spiral around each of the five white columns at the front and echoed over the straight balcony rail above. Below that, a circular stained glass window featured the double S at a slant—the bottom curve of the first S tucked into the top curve of the second. Massive double doors stood between him and what would be home for the next ten days. On either side, an electric-lit cowboy boot in green kicked up its heel in welcome. Above, a red-lit sign declared, "Merry Christmas, Y'all!"

Derrick felt as if he were in alien country. He'd never been south of Chicago and wasn't sure why he'd accepted Chad's invitation to spend Christmas with his family. He certainly was no cowboy.

One thing astonished him—no oil wells. He'd harbored a rather silly boyhood belief that everyone from Texas must have a geyser in their backyard, even a capped or defunct one. The weather was colder than he expected it would be, too. Not bitterly cold and windy like Chicago, but cold enough for his suede jacket with its sheep's wool collar.

Well, come good or bad, he was here now. And, according to his recent doctor's visit, in crucial need of rest and relaxation, though how much of that he'd get on a ranch B and B was debatable. The small business firm for which he was a new accountant was going under, and he'd spent many a night examining the records kept in computer files. When he found evidence of possible embezzlement, he'd alerted his boss. Now an investigation was under way, and everyone's job was on the line.

Derrick headed up the four stairs of the cement porch and went inside, assuming that since the gargantuan ranch house was open to the public he should just go on in and not look for a doorbell. From somewhere, instrumental Christmas music was playing "Silent Night" featuring acoustical guitars. He nodded in approval as he took inventory of the empty lobby. Black and white tile floor. Western décor on the walls and shelves of a ceiling-high cabinet next to what appeared to be a receiving desk. Furniture—Spanish-Colonial-looking. A black wrought iron railing wound along the stairway, which was placed in an unusual jerky curve, as if the stair-layer had had the hiccups when he built them. Ten white stairs with a black-and-white-swirled runner made a gradual slope upward then stopped. A set of three more stairs catty-cornered from that, stopped, and a level ledge went for about five feet. Then a set of six stairs went up and stopped, angling off to another set of stairs. . . .

The sound of the door opening behind him and a breath of cold wind chilling his neck cut short his perusal. He turned to see a vision in a pink strapless gown. Hair the color of cinnamon lay in soft curls atop her head. Eyes, so light blue they almost appeared without color, drew him in. Her cheeks were chapped pink from the outside cold. She held a large bunch of red and white roses in one hand, but with both hands she pulled the ends of her fuzzy shawl up to her neck and tightly around her bare shoulders, as if hoping to hide her slim form in the shiny dress. She didn't break eye contact, though her expression was one of unease.

Derrick blurted the first thing that came to mind, "No one's here to check us in right now. I was just counting the stairs." He winced at his foolish statement.

Her eyebrows lifted. "Counting the stairs?"

"An odd habit of mine. Counting things. I like numbers."

"Oh." Her expression settled into disfavor. "You must be the accountant Chad told me about."

"Yes. I'm Derrick Freeborn." He walked the few paces

between them and held out his hand. She gave it a reluctant halfhearted shake, then moved her arm to clutch her shawl tightly around herself again. Did she think he was going to jump her?

"How do you know Chad?" he asked.

"I'm his sister."

"Then you must be Taylor! I've heard a lot about you."

She pulled in her lips, as though exasperated. A faint dimple appeared in her left cheek. "I'll just see where Mother is. She's usually the one behind the desk."

Before he could answer, she was gone, her shoes rapidly clicking across the floor as she moved toward an opening on the left. No door blocked it and, curious, he moved to look into the next room. From his vantage point he could see a cozy fireplace, with the flames crackling inside, a mantel above it decorated with eight holiday knickknacks, and what must be a ten-foot Christmas tree nearby. A live one, if he could go by the smell of pine.

Suddenly she was back, the frown still on her face, the flowers missing. "Mother told me to tell you that she was sorry she wasn't here when you arrived. She had to take care of something that came up. I'll check you in."

He followed her back into the lobby, and she slipped around the waist-high counter, sitting down before a computer. She typed something on the keys, then stood and shoved a gold-embossed, red leather-bound book his way. "Please sign this. We like to keep a record of all our guests."

Her manner was polite but stiff, and Derrick sensed she'd rather be anywhere but with him. Once he set down the pen, she handed him a key with a plastic disk and the number 204.

"How many rooms do you have here?" he asked.

"Ten for the guests, not counting the private family rooms

in another wing. You have the Lone Cowboy Room." She smiled, though it didn't reach her eyes. "Second door on the left at the end of the stairs. Enjoy your stay."

"Thanks." Picking up his one suitcase, he moved to go, then snapped his fingers and turned to face her again. "One more thing. Chad mentioned something about the B and B offering lessons in horseback riding and other ranch-style activities?"

She visibly stiffened. "Yes. Though it's not mandatory. If you'd rather just stay in your room during your time here, that's fine, too."

Derrick hid a smile at her obvious effort to get rid of him. He didn't need two guesses as to who his teacher might be. "As long as I'm here, I'd like to give it a whirl. I've always wanted to learn how to ride a horse and rope a calf."

"Great," she said in a flat voice. "Your lesson will take place at seven-thirty—in the morning—so you'll need to eat breakfast early. In other words, no sleeping late."

"I think I can manage that. How many others are taking the course?"

She dropped her gaze to the open book. "Um, actually, it's just you."

This time he couldn't shield his grin. "Then I guess I'll be seeing you bright and early tomorrow morning, teacher."

❧

Taylor watched Derrick climb the stairs. So, he'd figured out that she would be teaching him. Or had Chad relayed that information?

For a Chicago accountant, Derrick looked different than she'd imagined. She had pictured a meticulously neat, skinny man with a buzz haircut, pen sticking out of a shirt pocket, and wire-frame glasses. But that didn't describe the tall, strapping man taking the stairs. His dark hair grew a little long and fell in an easygoing wave over his forehead. His physique, under the casual, patterned block sweater and brown slacks, looked as if it was accustomed to regular workouts, and his mink-colored eyes yielded a wide range of emotions. From curious, to amused, to gentle. . .

At the stairs' ledge, he turned—and caught her staring up at him. He smiled and used one hand to lean against the banister.

"One last thing. When you see Chad, could you tell him I'm here? I'll be in my room if he wants to come up or phone me."

"Sure, I'll tell him." Taylor began busying herself with closing the guest book and replacing it and the pen on the counter beside the computer. She jotted a note to Chad and put it where he was sure to see it. When she felt it was safe, she looked up. Relief swept through her to find that the new guest had gone.

Taylor grabbed her purse and headed straight for her room to shimmy out of the embarrassing dress. Of all the outfits for Chad's friend to see her in! Hailey had insisted on strapless gowns for her bridesmaids, sure when she'd ordered them that the weather would cooperate. It hadn't. And though the neckline was modest compared to some of today's fashions, Taylor still thought it too low. Despite the heated banquet room and large crowd, she'd kept her mother's shawl tied around her shoulders throughout the reception, ignoring the smirks and lifted brows from the five other bridesmaids. Worse, though she'd tried to avoid it, she somehow had been the one to catch the bridal bouquet. Immediately she'd tossed it in another direction, as though she were playing Hot Potato. But her ploy hadn't worked, and she'd ended up with the roses. Then had come the teasing remarks about how "Mr. Right must be waiting just around the corner," the mild jokes, and the light but probing questions inquiring if there really was anyone in the wings.

Taylor let herself into her room, closed the door, and removed the offensive dress, pulling it over a hanger. She slid into her comfortable, toasty warm flannel pajamas and breathed a sigh of relief. Grabbing her Bible, she settled into bed, pulling the petal-soft sheets and thick quilt around her, and prepared to spend a few minutes soaking up God's Word. She was almost to the end of the chapter before she was cut short by the shrill ring of her bedside phone. Seeing it was an inside call by the blinking button, she nabbed the receiver.

"Yes?"

"You sent him to bed without supper?" Chad's question came back. "At six o'clock in the evening?"

She rolled her eyes toward the ceiling. "And how was I supposed to know he hadn't already eaten?" She squirmed, feeling a tinge of remorse when she remembered her cool treatment toward the new guest and her objective to rid herself of his presence quickly. "He could've said something if he was hungry."

"True, but to my knowledge most B and Bs don't offer dinner, so he probably didn't know he was invited. He's my guest, Taylor, and he's spending time with our family—that means all the meals and private parties. Get used to it. And telling him he had to eat breakfast before seven-thirty or he couldn't have his riding lesson was pretty lame, too."

Taylor muttered something not fit to be aired, then silently repented. "I didn't say it like that. Is that what he told you?"

"He didn't tell me anything. But when I rang his room to invite him to dinner and he said that he had to get to bed early or he'd miss his riding lesson, I figured you were up to something."

"I am. I have to help Mom plan for this Friday. The Graystones are coming for their annual visit and are renewing their wedding vows—it's their fiftieth anniversary. A morning lesson works best for me."

"Yeah, but seven-thirty? Since when do you give lessons that early? Most guests like to sleep in their first night here. And they don't go to bed hungry."

Taylor frowned. "If you're so concerned about his eating and sleeping habits, then why didn't *you* stick around to check him in?"

"I had to run to the store. Anyway, Mom wants to know if you're coming down to eat."

She sank back against her pillow. "No. I ate plenty at the wedding reception. I think I'll just go to bed early. I have a busy morning ahead teaching your college chum how to play cowboy." She couldn't keep the bite out of her words. How had she ever let him rope her into such a situation?

There was an uncomfortable pause. "Listen, Taylor, I'm sorry if I came across heavy-handed this afternoon and pushed you into this. It's just that when I was in Chicago, Derrick showed me a really good time, and I want to return the favor."

"Okay, so remind me again why you're not the one hanging out with him and I'm stuck with the job?"

"Besides my usual chores, I've got other things around the ranch that I need to help Dad with. Things that won't wait 'til after Christmas."

Taylor understood, though she didn't have to like it. She was generally the one who taught the guests to ride. She and her younger two brothers, and they had their own convenient excuses.

"Anyhow, I'm sorry," Chad said again.

"You're forgiven." Taylor was accustomed to her brother's phone apologies. He didn't like face-to-face meetings that involved an admission of guilt on his part, and since all the phones in the ranch house were connected to the main desk, including the family's bedroom phones, Chad had developed this method of communicating when he wanted forgiveness.

"See you in the morning."

"Yeah, good night." Taylor replaced the phone and stared at it.

Ten days. Hopefully the time would fly past and the Yankee from the Windy City would blow back to his Chicago home, and then everything would be on an even kilter again. She supposed ten days wasn't so bad. After all, what was ten days?

She remembered what Derrick said about liking to count things, and her mind took up the challenge. *Let's see, that was one week, three days. . .two hundred and forty hours. . .fourteen thousand and four hundred minutes. . .*

With Derrick joining in on all the family doings.

She punched her pillow, then turned off the light and threw herself down on her side. What kind of person liked to count things, anyway? It reminded her of that silly purple puppet on *Sesame Street*. And why was she dwelling on this? He was just another guest, after all. Most guests stayed two or three or even four days, so ten wasn't all that much more.

After long minutes of staring into darkness, Taylor realized she'd forgotten to brush her teeth. Grumbling, she flicked on the light again and headed for her private bathroom.

Eight hundred and sixty-four thousand seconds.

Ten days was really an eternity.

Chapter 2

With a satisfied smile, Derrick strode toward the stables after a filling breakfast. He'd never had hot salsa on scrambled eggs before—and over steak, yet—but the combination wasn't half bad. And he'd never considered pinto beans to be a breakfast dish, but the helping he'd eaten was actually tasty. A frosty chill lingered in the air though the sun was out, and he could see his breath form a white fog, even smell the trace of jalapeño peppers as he exhaled. The spicy meal had warmed his blood and set his motor running. He was ready for anything—be it a fidgety horse or a prickly female.

The female stepped outside the dim stables, leading a dark gray horse. With the reins in one hand, she settled her fists on her jean-clad hips. "You're late."

Derrick held up his hands in mock defense. "Not my fault. Chad wanted to talk to me about something. I promise to be on time tomorrow."

"Humph." Taylor's gaze slid down his form, and she arched a brow. "Let me guess. You bought that outfit just for this week."

"Is there something wrong with it?" Derrick looked down at

his black designer jeans and cream-colored Western shirt with the red braid. They matched the red cowboy boots he'd found on clearance, and the black felt hat went nicely with the outfit.

Her mouth flickered at the corners. "As long as the jeans are tough and the boots are durable, it'll work, I guess." She dipped her head and pulled down the brim of her tan cowboy hat as she turned toward the horse, as though to hide the amusement he detected in her eyes. He noticed that beneath her brown suede jacket her plaid shirt and jeans weren't flashy, but looked worn and comfortable. As did her brown leather boots.

"Today we'll just go over the basics," Taylor said. "Mounting, dismounting, learning the commands, getting a feel for the saddle and how to use the reins. I've already saddled Thunder, so I'll show you how to do that tomorrow."

"Thunder?" Derrick darted an uncertain look toward the gray beast.

Taylor smiled. "Not to worry. Thunder really should have been called *Breeze*. He's a good old boy, aren't you?" She affectionately stroked the white blaze along the horse's forehead.

He tossed his head as if nodding, and she smiled. Derrick liked her smile when it was real. Not fake or mocking or tight. Just nice and easy, a sweet spread of her lips that put a sparkle in her eyes. Last night when he'd met her, she'd been wearing light makeup on her eyelids, cheeks, and lips, and her hair was done up in curls pinned on top of her head. Today her face was scrubbed fresh, and he spotted a sprinkling of freckles on her nose and cheeks. Her thick hair was pulled back in one long ponytail that brushed her shoulder blades. He preferred this look to the glamorous one of yesterday. It fit her better.

She glanced in his direction and frowned. "What are you smiling at?"

"Nothing." He sensed it was smarter to keep his thoughts to himself.

Her narrowed eyes continued to survey him. "All right, then. Let's get started. First, put your left boot in the stirrup and your left hand on the saddle. Then hoist yourself up and throw your right leg over the horse. I'll hold the reins and keep the horse steady."

"Yes, ma'am," he said in his best Texas drawl as he tipped his hat. "Anything to please."

He settled his heel against the stirrup and followed the rest of her directions, but his right leg wouldn't cooperate. The new jeans were stiff and tight and he couldn't swing his leg all the way over. If he tried, he might rip the seam.

"Is there a problem?" she asked when he tried a second time and remained precariously perched, one boot in the stirrup, both arms clutched across the smooth cowhide saddle, and his right leg raised like a dog at a hydrant. The horse nickered and moved its head as though trying to look back to see what kind of idiot he was paired with.

"Uh, no," Derrick grunted. "Almost have it now." Instead of trying to move his leg higher, he shifted his upper body by giving a little jump to hoist himself over. The slick sole of his boot slipped off the metal stirrup, his chin hit the saddle, and he landed in the dust at Taylor's feet.

He looked up. Her head was lowered as she rubbed the middle of her forehead with three fingers. He brushed his hand along the underside of his chin to check for blood. Seeing none, he shrugged.

"Maybe I can get a refund on the outfit."

At this, she let out a laughing snort, as if she couldn't hold back any longer. He liked the sound of it and grinned. She lifted her head and met his gaze, her smile as wide as his, then she shook her head as though exasperated.

"Are you all right?"

"Sure. I'm tough."

"Okay, then. Go ask my mother to loan you a pair of Will's jeans. You look like you wear the same size. I'll wait for you here."

Derrick picked up his hat from the ground where it had fallen and managed to climb to his feet, though awkwardly, as the stiff denim pressed hard into his skin. Maybe he shouldn't have washed the jeans before wearing them or dried them on high heat. He'd worn jeans before, of course, but yesterday morning he'd done a rush packing job and had put all the new clothes on a fast dry cycle. Obviously a big mistake. At least the shirt had survived.

He headed toward the main house, embarrassed, but glad he'd been the one to make Taylor laugh. According to Chad, she didn't do much of that anymore.

❦

Sunlight poured over the tall man in the saddle as Taylor watched him guide Thunder in a circle around the stable yard. The Yank caught on quick, she'd give him that. Once he returned wearing a pair of smooth, faded blue jeans—ones that didn't look as if they would cut off his circulation if he sneezed—he'd succeeded in mounting the horse. A bit awkwardly, but he'd gotten up there.

"Chad-tells-me-this-is-a-working-ranch," Derrick said, his words bouncing up and down with his body as the horse started at a trot.

Taylor grinned at how funny he sounded, even if she was

exasperated that his questions seemed to increase with the horse's speed. She'd never known a man who liked to talk much, but this one did. "The cowhands work on another part of the ranch, away from the B and B. The only time you'll see any of them up close and personal is when one of them, probably Buddy, will show you how to rope a cow."

"You-won't-be-doing-that?"

"Nope. That goes beyond my level of expertise." Unease pricked her. Hopefully he would be satisfied with her answer and not pry.

"How-big-is-this-ranch?"

"Over two thousand acres. My great-grandfather trained mustangs here, but now we raise beef cattle." She stood in the middle of the corral, turning in slow circles as she watched his progress. "Since you're so interested in the life of a cowboy, I guess you should've come to the B and B earlier. We had a five-day cattle drive several weeks ago. Two of our guests went with Chad, my father, and the cowhands to experience a real Wild West adventure."

"Sorry-to-have-missed-it," Derrick said in staccato bursts. "But-Chad-told-me-about-the-Saturday-night-campout. He-said-you're-in-charge-of-that."

Taylor stiffened in irritated surprise. So she'd been volunteered to host another function without her knowledge? Did her brothers think she had nothing else to do?

Derrick glanced her way. "I'm-looking-forward-to-it."

Peeved, for a wild moment Taylor thought about slapping Thunder's rump and sending the horse into a fast gallop that would take its talkative rider far from her. Maybe then Derrick would lose interest in future lessons. Of course she wouldn't endanger any guest's life by doing something as crazy as that, but the delectable thought still made her grin.

Derrick rode the horse in another full circle. A dog's rapid barking suddenly yipped through the air, seizing Taylor's attention. A brown flash of fur zipped past Thunder, followed by a black one. The horse spooked, whinnying in fright, then took off like a shot out of the stable yard. Taylor groaned when she saw that someone had left the gate open.

"Hold on!" she called to Derrick.

His face tensed as he clutched the reins and pommel in a white-knuckled grip, doing his best to stay astride the horse as it cleared the gate. Taylor mounted her mustang saddled nearby. She prodded the white-spotted gelding into a hard run, soon catching up to Thunder, who was over a mile away from the stable. Thankfully, the city boy hadn't fallen. He was draped over the horse, his thighs squeezing the saddle.

"Pull on the reins to stop him," she called. "Don't squeeze your legs tight. That only makes him run faster."

"What?"

"Don't squeeze your legs!"

"How am I supposed to stay on?" he shouted incredulously.

"Unwrap your arms from around his neck, and pull on the reins."

Tight-lipped, Derrick straightened from his hunched-over position and followed her orders.

"Easy, Thunder," she commanded, reaching for the horse's reins and pulling on them harder. "Whoa, boy."

The horse slowed to a walk, then came to a standstill. Taylor reined in Stardust and looked over at Derrick. His hat was missing, and his face was stretched in an expression of pain. In fact, he looked a little green around the gills.

"Are you okay?" she asked.

"What happened?" Derrick's words sounded vague.

"Some dog was chasing a squirrel. I've never seen it around here before."

"The dog or the squirrel?" He groaned, pushing a hand to his stomach. "Never mind. That was some ride."

Her remorse deepened. "Sorry."

"It wasn't your fault."

Maybe not, but she still felt guilty. Hadn't she pictured the scenario of Thunder galloping off with Derrick only moments before it actually happened?

"Are you going to throw up?" she asked.

"I don't think so, but my stomach feels like it's still on a wild ride. Must be something I ate."

"I never thought jalapeños made great breakfast material, but my brother likes things hot and spicy. We do serve normal breakfasts here, too. Before our lesson tomorrow, I'll make you a ham and cheese omelet with hash browns and pumpkin-nut muffins—to make up for what happened just now," she added hastily when she saw his face relax and his eyes brighten. No use giving him the wrong idea.

"It sounds like something to look forward to. When I can think about food again."

"Good." She shifted in the saddle. "We should be getting back now. I'll show you how to unsaddle Thunder. Then your lesson will be over for today and you can go lie down if you want. Do you remember how to give the command for Thunder to walk?"

"Sure." He lifted the reins, leaned forward, and clicked his tongue against the roof of his mouth. Thunder began to move slowly forward in a straight line, in the opposite direction of the stables. "Uh, how do I get him to turn?" Derrick called over his shoulder when the horse carried him closer to a fringe of bare cottonwoods.

"Use the reins. Gently pull one rein to the side in the direction you want Thunder to go."

She watched as Derrick got the horse under control and swung him around, then prodded Stardust to walk beside Thunder. She was uncomfortably aware of the casual glances Derrick cast her way, but she didn't look at him. She might feel guilty about the riding lesson and want to make up for it, but that was as far as her feelings went. He was Chad's friend and a temporary guest. Nothing more.

At the gate, a blond-haired woman and child waited. A black puppy fidgeted in the boy's arms. "I'm sorry," the woman said. "We couldn't find anyone to sit with Pepper, and he doesn't like kennels. The lady who owns the place said it would be okay if we brought him. As soon as we got out of the car, he jumped out and ran this way. I'm Rhea Graystone, and this is my son, Brandon."

"Pleased to meet you. I'm Taylor Summerall, and this is one of our guests, Derrick Freeborn," she said with a smile and a polite tip of her hat. "In the future, please keep your dog away from the stables. There's a fenced-in backyard where he can run. The horses don't know him and can get easily spooked, like what happened with Derrick just now."

Rhea's gaze went to Derrick, and she frowned. "Are you all right?"

"No real harm done," he said. "The ride was an adventure, but I think I'd better get back to my room. If you don't mind, I'd rather learn how to unsaddle another day."

Concern pricked Taylor again. "We'll have a better lesson tomorrow." She gave him directions on how to dismount, slipping off her own horse first as an example. As she led both Stardust and Thunder to the stable, she watched Derrick limp to the main house. The Yank had gumption, a friendly personality—and he wasn't hard to look at, either.

Frowning, Taylor turned away and busied herself with unsaddling both horses.

⁂

"Is there something about me your sister doesn't like?" Derrick asked Chad as he helped himself to a thick slice of pumpkin pie and cup of eggnog after the roast beef and potato dinner. The dessert table was set out in buffet, all-you-can-eat style, and Derrick was taking advantage of it. In the background of the cozy family room the stereo speakers played a silly Christmas country ditty, a song Derrick didn't recognize. Something about the singer's grandma getting run over by a reindeer.

"Interesting song," Derrick commented.

Chad chuckled. "Yeah, Dad likes to listen to the radio in the evenings for the local news. About Taylor. . ." He looked toward his sister, who stood across the room, her body language rigid as she stared into the tranquil fire. "She's like that with all the guys," Chad said. "She takes off running like a frightened calf being chased by a coyote if anyone gets too close."

Derrick mulled over the information while he let the rich, creamy eggnog slide over his tongue. "Why? Did she get hurt? She doesn't seem like the shy type."

Chad let out a loud guffaw. "Taylor—shy? Not my sister," he added more quietly when she turned and looked their way, her gaze sharp. A repentant look crossed his face. "Go easy on her, Derrick. She lost a fiancé two years ago and hasn't gotten over it yet."

"Two years is a long time to grieve over a broken relationship."

"Yeah, that's what we all think," Chad relented. "But it wasn't that kind of breakup. Kevin was killed in a freak accident, and Taylor was there when it happened."

Before Derrick could inquire further, Taylor began walking across the maroon-colored pile carpet toward them. "And what are you two old buddies chatting about?" she asked sweetly, the look in her eyes suspicious.

"Oh, just what two old friends usually wind up talking about," Chad shot back. "The past."

"Yeah, but whose?"

A hint of red seeped beneath Chad's skin. "I just remembered. Mom wants me to help move some furniture in the banquet room. I'll be back in a few." He weaseled away through the exit into the lobby.

"Chicken," Taylor muttered under her breath. She pinpointed Derrick with her pale blue eyes. The gemstone-blue sweater she wore brought out the narrow rim of darker blue around her stunning irises. "What about you? Are you brave enough to tell the truth?"

"We were talking about you," Derrick admitted, feeling a little sheepish.

"I gathered that when I heard Chad blurt my name. So what did he tell you?"

"Among other things, he told me you lost your fiancé in an accident."

Surprise jolted her expression, and a flash of pain tinged her eyes. "He shouldn't have done that."

"Maybe not. Anyway, I'm sorry."

Taylor shrugged and looked beyond him. She lifted her crystal cup and took a sip of eggnog.

"I lost someone close, too, once. My kid sister. I know it's not the same thing, but I just wanted you to know I understand."

She was quiet a moment before she sought his gaze. "How'd it happen?"

"She was in a carpool with a bunch of kids in a station wagon. Another car ran a red light and broadsided them. Jenny was sitting by the door and was the only one killed. She was eight at the time."

Her brows pulled down in a sympathetic frown. "That must have been hard."

"It was. I had a lot of guilt to deal with."

"Guilt?"

"I was sixteen and had just gotten my license. I was the one who was supposed to pick her up from school. But I ran into some friends and forgot." He cleared his throat. The words were still difficult to speak, though time had eased the pain and he'd already dealt with the guilt years ago through counseling.

Her expression softened. She laid her hand on the sleeve of the green turtleneck he'd thrown on before dinner. "I'm sorry," she said. "Believe me, I know how difficult that must have been."

Somehow the tables had turned. His initial reason for bringing up the subject was to get her to talk about losing Kevin; but now she was the one doling out sympathy. He wasn't even sure why he spoke about the experience with Jenny, unless it was to reassure Taylor that others dealt with similar tragedies and survived. He'd only known the woman twenty-four hours, but already he felt connected to her in some odd way.

Whether or not she would have spoken about what happened two years ago, Derrick would never know. At that moment, Taylor's mom glided up to them. "I'm so glad y'all could come and be with us this Christmas, Derrick," she enthused in a Southern drawl that would've sounded more at home in Georgia than Texas. Dressed in a shimmering white pantsuit flared at the legs and sleeves, the woman with the reddish-brown hair and pale blue eyes, much like Taylor's, was the picture of a charming hostess. "It's so nice to get to know one of Chad's friends."

"It's a pleasure to be here, Mrs. Summerall. Thanks for having me."

"Anytime. And please, call me Charla. Now where was it that Chad said your mother and her new husband went off to on their honeymoon?"

"They took a Caribbean cruise."

"Oh, yes, how lovely! It must be wonderful to get away from all that cold weather y'all have up North. Brrrr," she said with a little mock-rubbing of her arms. "Which reminds me, Taylor. I heard on the weather radio this morning that it may drop to the twenties Saturday night. Be sure to wear your thermals, and take the insulated sleeping bags."

Taylor's cheeks went pink. "Actually, maybe we should call off the campout if there's bad weather forecasted."

"Oh, no, the skies are supposed to be clear that night. And the Graystones—not the couple getting married, but their grandson and his wife—have expressed an interest in participating. They used to live in Michigan, so I'm sure they wouldn't mind the chilly temperature. And I'll bet Derrick, here, has seen his share of cold weather, too."

Derrick nodded, though he wasn't sure he wanted to sleep on the frozen ground if it was going to be all that cold.

As if reading his mind, Charla chuckled. "We have the latest in winter-weather camping gear, so don't you worry. We won't let you turn into an icicle."

Derrick let out a sound resembling a short laugh, though he still wasn't too sure. "You mentioned a wedding here this weekend?"

"The Graystones are celebrating their golden wedding anniversary," Taylor answered. "They'll be renewing their wedding vows."

"Which reminds me," Charla said. "I need to call Mabel and make sure she can play the piano for the reception. You're welcome to come, if you'd like, Derrick. The Graystones are a very sweet and outgoing couple. They've spent every anniversary with us since we opened four years ago. And Taylor is going to sing. Now you be sure to help yourself to those pumpkin cookies." She smiled at Derrick, then disappeared as quickly as she'd come.

"You're going to sing?"

Taylor went a shade redder. "I'm not that great or anything. I'm just free." She grinned self-consciously. "Don't feel obligated to come. The Graystones are the type who don't want anyone to feel left out, and they asked Mom to give a blanket invitation to any guests staying here. But you're the only one staying, besides the Graystones' family, of course."

"Actually, I'd like to come." When Charla first spoke of it, the thought of attending hadn't crossed Derrick's mind. Hearing that Taylor would sing raised his interest level by ten points. Saturday couldn't get here fast enough. Though if he were going to ride a horse to the campsite, as Chad had said he would have to do, he would need a lot more improvement. Tomorrow's riding lesson just had to go better. And hopefully his relationship with the teacher would improve, too.

Chapter 3

"Mom, I can't find the gold and crimson poinsettias." Taylor stood on a ladder and searched the high shelves of the storage closet, sorting through the stacks of thick plastic zippered cases that had once contained sheet sets or comforters. Now they were containers for silk flowers, arranged by theme and color for every occasion.

"Taylor, if it was a rattlesnake it would've bitten you," her mom said, exasperation starting to show through her usual poise. It was always like that the day before a big event took place. Mom often got high-strung, worried that this or that might go wrong. "Near your left elbow, under the blue orchids and white daisies."

"Oh." Taylor nabbed the light but bulky pillow-sized case from the stack, let it fall the several feet to the carpet, then stepped down from the ladder to reclaim it.

"White tablecloths with the gold lacy edging, or gold tablecloths with embroidered roses?"

Taylor worked to free the zipper on the case. It stuck, and she tugged harder. As she worked to loosen the metal teeth, she thought about her morning ride.

"Taylor! Did you hear me?"

Taylor looked up. "What? Oh, sorry, Mom. I was off in another world."

"One with Derrick in it?"

Taylor frowned. "Why would you say that?"

"Because since he arrived four days ago, you've acted differently."

"Differently?" Taylor shook her head. "No, I'm the same. I sure hope, though, that Mabel will be feeling well enough to play tomorrow. But if I have to sing a cappella, I guess I can manage." She steered the conversation to the wedding, sure that this was the appropriate path on which to sidetrack her mother. "Hopefully, I won't prove to be too much of a disappointment."

"You'll do fine, dear. You have a lovely voice. Now, which tablecloths do you think will work best?"

"The lacy ones." Taylor held the flower case to her chest. "I'll just go put these in some vases."

"Use the glass ones with the gold flecks. I think that would be a nice touch."

Taylor moved away before her mother could reintroduce their prior conversation. It annoyed her that the entire family seemed bent on hitching her with Derrick. Robert and Will, with their pathetically obvious efforts to make sure Taylor sat beside Derrick at dinner every night. Dad, with his never-ending questions regarding Derrick's job—at one point, Taylor wouldn't have been surprised if her father had asked to see Derrick's annual tax returns for the last two years. And good old Chad, who'd lassoed her into giving Derrick riding lessons and taking him on the campout tomorrow night. At least her older brother had taken over the calf-roping lesson, since Buddy wasn't available. Taylor wasn't sure she could've handled that.

Regardless, this morning, curiosity had compelled her to

peek inside the building that housed the life-sized mechanical horse and calf. Derrick had sat atop the horse, his profile to her. Some wisenheimer had fastened a red velvet Santa hat to the fiberglass calf, which whizzed away from the stationary horse on a fifteen-foot track, making it harder for the rider to lasso it. Taylor wondered why Chad had turned the ride to expert level, then realized Derrick probably wouldn't have been happy with trying to rope a stationary calf. His first awkward attempts brought loud guffaws from both men, and Taylor grinned. That's one thing that amazed Taylor about Derrick. He had the ability to laugh at himself and get others laughing with him, not at him. Also, he was persistent. After four days of riding lessons, he was getting better. He'd taken a hard fall or two to reach that mark, though she'd tried to show him the proper way to relax and take a fall. He might have had the trim, muscular build of a cowboy, but he was as clumsy as a gangly junior high kid.

As Taylor stood in the banquet room and arranged metallic gold roses and poinsettias with the deep crimson ones, adding silk greenery as needed, Derrick's disappointed words from that morning came back to haunt her. "But don't I get to rope a real calf?" he'd asked Chad when the lesson was over.

Then as now, Taylor felt an awkward lump clog her throat, bringing with it the sting of tears. At the barn, she'd lifted her hand to swipe them away, painfully knocking her elbow against the door, alerting both men to her presence. Chad's expression turned sympathetic as realization hit, and he opened his mouth to speak. But she shook her head and backed up, then turned and hurried home, her fast walk soon speeding into a run as memories took hold and tears dribbled down her cheeks.

The bitter image of two years ago soured the sweet silliness of Derrick's morning lesson, and she swallowed the emotion down hard. She would not cry again. Viciously, she jammed a piece of greenery deep into a vase.

"Ouch!" an amused male voice said from behind her. "I hope that wasn't aimed at me for being such a lousy student this week."

Startled, she spun around. The smile on Derrick's face faded to worry. "Hey, are you crying?" He spanned the ten-foot distance between them.

"I'm fine." Briskly she wiped under her eyes with the back of her free hand and lifted her chin, hoping to give the impression of being in control. "You shouldn't sneak up on people like that."

"Sorry. Carpet muffles sound." He looked around the formal banquet room in the throes of being decorated. "Anything I can do to help?"

"You're a guest."

"Yeah, but you guys have made me feel like part of your family. I'd like to contribute something."

Taylor shrugged. "You can set up the folding tables and chairs. They're in the closet, outside the door. We'll need six tables. The guests will sit in the center of the room, and the guests of honor will sit at the dining room table that Chad moved against the wall over there."

Derrick went to retrieve the items. Taylor tried to concentrate on the flower arrangements, but the constant clanging as Derrick set up the metal furniture, and dropped a chair in the process, drew her attention his way. She watched the muscles in his back and shoulders bunch and ripple under the thin maroon pullover as he went about his task. The ends of dark hair brushing the lower edge of his collar curled like shining, mocha gift ribbons. They were clumped together and damp, as if he'd just gotten out of a shower.

"Must you make so much noise?" she bit out.

Still in his hunched-over position, he looked over his shoulder in surprise. "Sorry. The table leg was stuck, and I was trying to bang it into place."

Instant remorse hit. "No, I'm sorry. I shouldn't have snapped." She massaged her right temple with the fingertips of one hand. "You were nice to offer to help, and I'm acting like a shrew."

"Headache?"

She nodded. "I'm pretty well finished with these. Could you tell Mom I went to lie down for a while?"

"Sure." He straightened and faced her. "I hope you feel better soon."

"Thanks." Taylor left the room and went upstairs. Why did the guy have to be so nice? It would be easier to be indifferent toward him if he weren't so helpful and kind. And the way her stomach quivered when he looked at her with those velvety brown eyes didn't help matters, either. What was happening to her?

Awed, Derrick watched Taylor the following morning. She stood at the front of the gaily decorated banquet room, clothed in a mellow white floor-length gown rimmed in lace. Something shiny sparkled all over her hair, like silvery moondust. Her hair was anchored on top of her head in a waterfall of curls, as it had been the first time he'd met her.

She was beautiful.

Derrick found it hard to catch his breath as he listened to

her sing with the voice of an angel, which she resembled. No background music marred the pure, sweet notes as she sang to the golden wedding couple a song Taylor had told him was played on their original wedding day, "Oh, Promise Me."

Tears glistened in both Mr. Graystone's and his wife's eyes as Taylor finished the last hauntingly sweet verse. Afterward, the white-haired gentleman turned to the smiling woman he had lived beside for half of a century and tenderly kissed her. Once they broke apart, the guests clapped and cheered, and corks of champagne were popped.

"To another fifty years, as great as the first," Mr. Graystone's son called out, lifting his glass.

"Hear, hear!" The elderly gentleman laughed, giving his plump wife a squeeze.

Derrick watched Taylor, who mixed with the guests, accepting their praise and serving white-frosted lemon cake to whoever wanted it. Though she was outgoing, Derrick could see how stiffly she carried herself. It was some time before he could get her alone.

"You sing beautifully," he said.

"Thank you." Her face and smile looked as rigid as porcelain, and just as ready to crack. "I wish we would've had piano music to go with it, though."

She started to move away, and Derrick grappled for words to keep her with him. "Are we still on for tonight?"

"The weather situation hasn't changed, if that's what you mean."

"I can handle the cold."

"Then I guess we're on. I'll see you at the stable at five."

"Taylor?"

She turned, her brows lifted.

"Is anything wrong? You don't act as if you're feeling well. Is the headache back?"

The stiffly polite look diminished, and a trace of genuine warmth touched her pale blue eyes. "I'm okay. Thanks for asking. Weddings are just sometimes difficult for me."

"Because of Kevin?" he asked softly.

"Partly."

She attempted a smile, one that trembled at the corners. Derrick suddenly had a strong urge to kiss that smile into full bloom but took a swig of his sherbet-covered punch instead.

"I'd better go prepare for tonight," she said. "The campout is only a few hours away."

For Derrick, those hours crawled by. He'd already packed his gear that morning, so he spent the time at his windows, watching Taylor and her brothers entering and exiting one of the ranch buildings as they geared up for the night ahead. He would have gone down to help, but he sensed that Taylor needed some distance, to sort things out. That he was getting to her was obvious, and he wasn't sure how that made him feel. Could she ever think about him the way he was starting to think about her?

At five before five, Derrick hoisted his backpack from the wide brown leather saddle used to decorate the dark-paneled corner of the room. He plucked his hat from the two-foot-high bronze cowboy statue on the oak dresser, slapped it on his head, and headed for the stable.

The horses for the young Graystones and their two small sons were already saddled, and Taylor was making adjustments to one of the horse's stirrups. She looked up as he approached. "Ready?"

"I sure am." Under her supervision, he saddled Thunder.

When she didn't have to correct him once, as had been the case before, he grinned. "Did I pass, teacher?"

She smiled. "With flying colors. But now comes the real test."

Derrick curbed his anxiety. He'd never been on an hour-long trail ride. Or an overnight campout. Would he prove to be too much of a city boy to handle it? During his last visit, the doctor had told him he needed to take it easy, that his life was too stressful, especially with the new job, and at the rate he kept it up, he'd have a heart attack before hitting thirty. Derrick wouldn't call the past four days of learning to ride, being captive on a runaway horse, and learning how to rope a calf easy, but he'd had fun. And he'd never felt better a day in his life. Thinking about work, Derrick frowned. Chicago, with its steel and glass skyscrapers and congested traffic, seemed a world away.

Riding Thunder, who plodded behind Stardust along a grassy hill, Derrick inhaled a deep breath of chilly air. Sunset painted the far-reaching sky with splashes of red, purple, and gold. Acres of wheat-colored grass shifted slightly in the breeze, and short, squat trees lined the snakelike stream to his right. A herd of white-faced brown cattle grazed nearby. A cowboy rode between them, probably counting them, as Chad had said they needed to do each day. For grins, Derrick took up the challenge from his place on the hill.

Taylor reined in her horse, waiting for Derrick to catch up. "Doing all right?" she asked.

He smiled. "Just counting the cows."

She grinned, then laughed. "I had to ask! Anyway, I wanted to let you know that we should reach camp before dark. Will and Robert went there earlier to set up for us."

"I was wondering where the tents were."

"Since we were getting such a late start because of the golden wedding, I asked my brothers to set them up in advance."

"It was a nice ceremony. I don't usually go to that sort of thing, but I was glad to be there."

"Yeah, it was nice." Taylor's gaze grew introspective. "It's nice to know that two people who've lived together so long can still love one another so much."

"It takes a lot of love to make a marriage work," Derrick agreed. "And commitment. You have to want the same things."

Taylor threw him a sharp glance, then looked away. "Yeah. I need to check on the others." Her expression now grim, she headed a few yards back down the trail to where the Graystone bunch rode.

Derrick wondered what he'd said to reap her curt words.

⁂

Taylor stared into the sizzling, crackling campfire. Wrapped in several layers of clothes and sitting close to the moderate blaze, she felt toasty warm on the outside. But inside, her heart was a lump of ice.

She watched Derrick joke with the two Graystone boys as he squished a fat marshmallow on a pointed stick and held it in the middle of the flames. It caught fire, and he quickly withdrew it and blew the flame out. "That's okay," he said with a smile. "I like mine cinder-black."

Taylor blew out a breath in amused exasperation. "Don't you know how to do anything, city boy?" She impaled a marshmallow on a stick and held it over the tip of the flames, rotating it until the white, puffy square turned a delicious golden-brown. Taking it from the fire, she trapped it between two graham crackers and a section of a semisweet chocolate bar then offered it his way. "Here."

Instead of taking the s'mores, which she held near his face, Derrick opened his mouth for the treat. She hesitated, heart beating fast, then crammed the thing halfway into his mouth, withdrawing her hand as quickly as she could.

"Thanks," he said, mouth full. He brushed away the downpour of crumbs that had fallen to his jacket as a result of her hasty gesture. His eyes were laughing at her, and she quickly looked away to make her own snack.

"Let's sing Christmas carols!" eleven-year-old Brandon Graystone suggested. "I brought my harmonica."

Taylor grinned. "I'll get my guitar."

"You play guitar, too?" Derrick asked.

"Yep, though I'd reserve any praise until you hear me. I'm not that good."

"That's what you led me to believe about your singing."

Taylor pretended not to hear Derrick's words. She walked past the blanketed horses tied near the fire and toward her tent to claim the guitar case her brothers had brought earlier in the pickup, along with the rest of the bulky gear. A camp stove nearby held a hot pot of coffee, and she refilled her tin mug before going back to the circle. The stove was used to heat the dinner stew, the coffee, and the hot water for cocoa for the kids— but it couldn't toast marshmallows. For that, a campfire was needed. Besides, singing around a stove didn't produce half the fun singing around a campfire did. And the guests expected it.

After Taylor reclaimed her spot next to Derrick and tuned her guitar, she strummed out a Texas-style version of "Deck the Halls." Brandon joined in with his harmonica, if not expertly, then exuberantly. But his playing didn't sound any worse than Taylor's. She ignored the chords struck wrong and belted out a round of carols, giving them a Western twang, with everybody merrily joining in and having a rollicking good time.

After awhile, the songs grew more mellow, more worshipful, and the others stopped singing, instead listening to Taylor. Her eyes half closed, a smile on her face, she strummed her guitar and sang her two favorites: "The Holly and the Ivy" and "What Child Is This?" Then she ended with the slow and peaceful "Silent Night." With the stars twinkling above, and not even a breeze to stir the few leaves left on the nearby cottonwoods, the song seemed fitting.

"That was beautiful," Rhea Graystone said softly. "I can't remember having such a good time."

"Me, either!" Brandon said. "Can we do it again tomorrow?"

They all laughed, and Derrick mussed the boy's hair. Brandon giggled. Derrick then jabbed the boy's side in a tickle, and Brandon squealed, laughing louder. His eight-year-old brother, Joshua, obviously not wanting to be left out, jumped up behind Derrick and, growling like a bear, pretended to put him in a choke hold. Derrick reached behind with both hands and tickled him.

"Not so close to the fire, guys," Taylor warned softly.

Derrick was so good with kids. He would make a great father someday. Kevin never wanted them, though he'd told Taylor that after they were married five years and settled into their life together, maybe he'd give in to her desire for children and think about having one then. Again Taylor thought about Derrick's words on the ride out here, of how a good marriage was based on commitment and wanting the same things.

"It's your bedtime," Mr. Graystone said. "Say good night to everyone."

"Aw, do we have to, Dad?" Joshua asked.

"I'm fixing to hit my bedroll, too," Derrick said.

"Fixing?" Brandon giggled. "You're beginning to sound like a Texan!"

"That wouldn't be so bad, would it?" Derrick shot back, his tone light. His gaze caught Taylor's for a few body-tingling seconds, and she hurriedly stood. "It's time for everyone to hit their bedrolls. I need to shut down and get camp ready for the night."

"I'll help." Derrick rose to join her.

"No, that's okay—"

"I insist."

Taylor didn't bother to argue. It had been a long, emotional day. The sooner they were cleaned up, the sooner she could zip herself into her own tent and insulated sleeping bag. The Graystones said their good nights and departed to their tent, and Taylor and Derrick made the camp ready for the evening. The mournful cry of a coyote sailed miles beyond the trees.

Derrick looked her way. "He sure sounds lonesome."

"Wait." Taylor turned from the low fire and held up her hand to listen, satisfied when another howl came from a different direction.

Derrick grinned. "His girlfriend calling him to come see her?"

"Nope. His wife chastising him for staying out too late."

Derrick laughed softly, the sound burying itself deep inside Taylor's heart. He moved closer, until the orange glow from the flames bathed his face. "I really enjoyed today, Taylor. And tonight. With you."

She sought for a witty comment but couldn't find one. Nor could she break away from the tenderness in his eyes.

"Taylor?" he asked quietly. His hand moved to brush the side of her head and the curls now hanging loose. He fingered them as though they were threads of the most delicate gold, fit only for royalty. He stared a moment longer, his eyes as dark as obsidian shimmering in the night. Then he slowly lowered his mouth to hers.

Warm, velvet, intoxicating... The words to describe his kiss shot through Taylor's mind. He wrapped his arms around her, and rational thought fled as she melted into his embrace.

A coyote's howl coming from closer than before broke them apart. They stared at one another a moment before Taylor stepped away from his arms and moved to put out the fire.

"Are we safe here?" Derrick asked.

Safe? That depended on what he was referring to. Right now, coyotes were the least of her worries. "Sure. The tents have zippers, and the food is securely stashed away." Once she finished with the fire, only scant moonlight touched them. She shoved her bare hands into fur-lined pockets. "I guess it's time to turn in. I'll see you in the morning."

"Good night, Taylor," he said as she walked off. "Sleep well."

Safely inside her tent, Taylor stripped down to a comfortable two layers and snuggled deep inside her thick sleeping bag. She reached for a thermos of hot chocolate she'd brought with her, but took only a few sips for warmth before she screwed the cap back on and lay down.

Why had she let Derrick kiss her? And why had she kissed him back? Had she lost all the good sense God gave her? That was easy to do when Derrick was near, when the warmth of his touch and his mouth played a melody on her heart. But it wasn't wise. He would be leaving in less than a week. And Taylor was no longer counting the hours until he would go.

Chapter 4

"Hey, Taylor—wake up!"

At the sound of an excited child's voice, Taylor groggily came to. Feeling the chill bite her face, she burrowed deeper into her warm sleeping bag and tried to go back to sleep.

"Taylor, come out and see!"

The summons came again, followed by a raspy knock on the stiff tent cloth, and she held back a groan, remembering where she was. "Okay, okay, I'm coming." She made quick work of putting on her other layers of clothing, jumping up and down a little in the freezing-cold air, pulled on her boots over her thick socks, and followed it with her jacket and hat. Unzipping the tent, she stepped outside. Her eyes widened, and she lifted her gaze to the pearl gray sky, gasping in delight.

Numerous white flakes drifted gently down to touch the brown earth. A few caught Taylor on the cheeks and nose, and she giggled at their icy kiss.

"Another thing I didn't expect to see in this part of Texas," Derrick said from nearby. "Snow."

She grinned at him. "Oh, we get our share, sometimes. Several inches anyway. But I can't remember ever getting any this close to Christmas." She pocketed her hands and closed her eyes in enjoyment, her face still positioned toward the sky. "It feels like a real white Christmas now, though it'll probably melt by tomorrow. If it sticks at all."

"It's starting to stick in some places," Joshua pointed out excitedly.

"Try shoveling feet of the stuff off your sidewalk every winter," Derrick cut in. "You'd get tired of it soon enough. When I get home, I imagine I'll have a few feet to plow through just to reach the steps of my apartment building. My landlord is a couch potato and doesn't always take care of things like that."

Taylor eyed him. His words were spoken in jest, but it further reminded her that they lived in two different worlds. And Derrick was going home to his in three days.

She moved toward the camp stove. "I'll get the coffee on and heat the rest of the stew. Then we'll break camp."

Once they'd eaten a hot breakfast and cleaned up, they left the campsite. The tents remained, since her brothers had told Taylor they'd see to taking them down. With the unexpected weather situation, Taylor felt relieved about that. She wanted to get everyone back to the ranch house as soon as possible. Blizzard-type conditions hit once in a rare moon, but it could get messy and turn to sleet.

Ten minutes into the ride, Brandon called out to Taylor, "What's that green stuff in those branches up there?"

She turned her head to look at where he pointed. "Mistletoe," she yelled back.

"You mean the Christmas-kissy stuff?" Joshua piped up. Taylor chuckled. "Yeah."

"Let's get some," Brandon called out.

"Why would you want some old kissy-stuff?" his brother asked, clearly disgusted.

"For Granny and Gramps's anniversary," Brandon shot back. "They said they met at a Christmas dance and kissed under the mistletoe for the first time. So can we get some?"

Taylor studied the nearest tree and the moss-colored, white-berried clump hanging from its second branch. "It's not all that high, but I'm not doing any climbing. Sorry. And I didn't bring a rifle to shoot it down, either."

"You mean you can shoot, too?" Derrick asked in wonder.

She grinned at him. "I was raised on a cattle ranch, remember?"

"Will you get it down for me, Dad?" Brandon begged.

"Do we really need it?" Mr. Graystone asked, doubt etched in his voice as he looked the fifteen or so feet up the tree.

"It's Christmas! And we didn't get to have any fun and cut down a pine this year since we had to come to Texas instead. I want to give Granny and Gramps a present, too, like everyone else did!"

"I'll get it for you," Derrick offered. Taylor swung her gaze his way, watching as he dismounted. Not gracefully, but at least he didn't fall.

Was he out of his mind? Judging from this last week, outdoor, sportsman-type activities weren't in his field. The poor guy could trip on strands of hay a few inches deep.

"I don't think you should try it," Taylor said.

"I'll be all right. Not far from where I live there's a place that offers rock climbing. It has an indoor rock wall over three stories high. I go there sometimes to unwind."

Well, that explained where his muscles and fine physique came from. Though Taylor wondered how he could keep from plummeting from such a height when on his first day at the ranch he'd fallen off a horse—and that was before he was even in the saddle!

"I want to do this for the Graystones," he added. "They were nice enough to invite me to their golden wedding anniversary. I'd like to repay the gesture and do something nice for them." He tugged his suede gloves more tightly onto his fingers then grabbed the lowest branch, swinging himself up into the tree. Taylor tensed, watching as he moved higher. Visions of his broken body and her needing to gallop away on Stardust to call an ambulance came to mind. How fast could she reach the ranch for help?

"Derrick," she called out in warning. "The branches might be slick or something. Come on down."

"No, they're fine," he grunted. "Almost there."

Heart in her mouth, Taylor watched as he reached the clump of green. At least he was wearing rubber-soled hiking shoes this time, and not those slick-soled red cowboy boots. With his arm anchored around a thick limb, he tore off the plant where it had attached itself to the tree. The greenery fell, rustling through the branches, until it hit the snow-speckled earth. Brandon let out a whoop of jubilation and jumped down from his saddle. Taylor didn't breathe until Derrick reached safety. At the last limb, he lost his grip and fell. His feet went out from under him as his shoes hit the ground.

Taylor quickly dismounted and ran his way, dropping to her hands and knees beside him. "Are you all right?" she demanded.

"Sure. I'm tough, remember? Just got the wind knocked out of me is all."

"That was a really stupid thing to do," Taylor couldn't resist saying. Nor could she resist the smile that crept to her face in answer to his boyish grin.

"I sure hope you took out an extra large insurance policy." She shook her head and straightened to her knees, settling her palms on her thighs. "You are the most accident-prone person I've ever met."

He chuckled and held out his hand. "Help me up?"

Taylor nodded and grabbed both his hands. Once he was almost on his feet, however, his heavier weight unbalanced her slighter one, and she found herself falling against his chest. His arms flew around her back. In surprise, she looked up, and their gazes locked.

"Thanks," he said.

"Sure," she whispered. Flustered, realizing the Graystones must be watching, she pushed away from him. She offered the best smile she could, though it felt feeble. "Let's get on back now. I want to get these horses some water and into a warm barn."

Taylor mounted Stardust and waited for Derrick to do the same with Thunder. Talk about falling. . . . She was doing exactly that—for Derrick. Would the impact when she hit bottom once he left the ranch shatter her heart? She was from the country; he was from the city. Both were happy with life as it was and didn't want to change. Besides, there was Kevin. A full two days had passed without her once thinking of her former fiancé. Was that wrong? After all, if it hadn't been for Taylor, Kevin would still be alive today.

⚜

That evening, before the scheduled hayride, Derrick looked for Taylor in all the public rooms of the ranch house but couldn't find her.

226

"I saw her go to the stable earlier, while it was still light outside," Brandon offered.

Derrick thanked the boy and walked toward the wooden building. He fingered the sprig of mistletoe he'd torn from Brandon's anniversary gift to his grandparents before letting the large bough fall from the tree. Did he dare use it? The sweet kiss Derrick shared with Taylor by the campfire last night had warmed his soul and made him hungry for more. But was he pushing things too fast?

The cool wind chapped his ears. He'd left his cowboy hat in his room, but he kept walking instead of turning around to get it. He was accustomed to cold much worse than this, but he could do without the white stuff that went along with it. This morning's unexpected snowfall amounted to an accumulation of not quite three inches, and Derrick crunched through it, eyeing the pasty gray clouds that forecasted more to come in the next few hours. At least the weather prediction according to the guy on the radio was that it would warm up day after tomorrow.

Once he entered the barn, Taylor straightened from her bent position and glanced his way. Her set jaw clearly told him he was intruding. "What do you want?" she asked.

The snow outside might be melting soon, but inside things appeared as if they would remain buried in invisible frost. "The hayride is starting in a few minutes. I was hoping you might join us."

"Sorry. Can't." He could now see the wetness shimmering in her eyes. "Buttercup's sick, and I'm waiting for the vet in town to get home so he can get the message I left on his answering machine. Our regular vet is off visiting family in Missouri. I can't leave her when she's this sick."

Derrick gazed into the stall where Taylor worked. A horse

Derrick remembered seeing before restlessly moved within the confined area. She let out a frantic whinny, as if in pain. Rivulets of sweat ran down the tan-colored coat as if she'd been ridden hard.

"What's wrong with her?" Derrick asked, moving closer.

"I don't know, but I suspect colic." Worried lines creased Taylor's forehead. "She's been eating her bedding, and with all the other symptoms I've seen, that's a sure sign."

"Colic—isn't that what babies get when they have too much gas?"

The look she sent his way was sober. "Yes, but in a horse it can be deadly if it's not treated soon. It can be a symptom of a bigger problem. I just wish I knew where the vet was. Robert drove into town to try to find him." She again bent down to the trough, and now Derrick could see she was removing the horse's feed.

"Anything I can do?" he asked quietly.

"I wouldn't want you to miss your hayride."

"I'd rather stay here with you and help however I can."

"Thank you." Her voice and the look she gave him this time were soft. "I have to remove all her food as long as she's like this. She needs plenty of water, though, if she'll even drink it. Take that pail and fill this other trough with it. The pump's over there."

Derrick set to work on the assigned task. Halfway through, he heard a loud crackling sound and turned to see that the horse had lowered herself to the ground and now lay on the hay. Taylor went to the mare and knelt down, stroking her long neck.

"It's okay, girl," she whispered. "We'll get you help soon. I've done all I know to do."

Sensing that Taylor was about ready to cry, Derrick finished pouring the rest of the water from the bucket into the trough then sat beside her. He took hold of her other hand, the one not stroking the horse's neck, and hoped he wasn't bungling forth where he wasn't wanted.

"Father," he said, "we turn this matter over to You. Not even a sparrow escapes Your notice, and You know how special this horse is to Taylor. We ask that You send a vet soon to save this animal, that You relieve any pain or pressure she's feeling, and give Taylor peace, in Jesus' name."

"Amen." Taylor ended the prayer. She looked at him. "Thank you. Buttercup *is* special. She's Stardust's mother, and we've had her since I was a kid. I know she's old for a horse, but I'm not ready to lose her yet."

The sorrow in her eyes suggested a deeper pain, one not yet healed. But she needed to heal. The grieving had gone on too long.

"Tell me about Kevin," Derrick said quietly.

She stiffened and pulled her hand from beneath his. Her mouth tightened and an angry spark jumped into her eyes. Maybe he was being nosy, but at least he'd gotten her mind off the present circumstances.

"Two years is a long time to hold something in, Taylor. There's a season for everything—even sorrow—but yours has gone on too long. Maybe you think I don't have any business talking about it, and I probably don't, but you need to let go of the grief. Holding on to it is a lot like not taking care of an infection. It eats away at the skin, and the wound can't heal. You have to treat the infection and get rid of it before healing can begin. Believe me, I know what I'm talking about. That's the way the counselor put it to me after my sister died. Until I talked about it and dealt with the way I felt, I didn't have much interest in continuing on with life. I wasn't suicidal or anything. I just didn't care what happened."

Her expression softened as she lifted her gaze to Derrick's. Under Taylor's gentle hand, the horse had ceased her constant fidgeting, though she jerked her body or legs from time to time. The animal seemed to rest easier now than she had when Derrick first entered the stable.

"We met at a rodeo," Taylor said at last. "Kevin was one of the spectators there, like me. We sat beside each other, started talking, and realized we had a lot of similar interests. One date led to another, and soon we were a steady item. We got engaged three months later."

Her hand stopped stroking Buttercup's neck and just lay there. She lowered her gaze to look at it. "He led me to believe he was more experienced with ranch work than he really was. When he lost his job at a pet store, I spoke up for him and got him a job here. Only he wasn't much of a cowboy, more of a show-off, really. Not in an arrogant way. More like a big kid trying to impress."

"What happened to him?" Derrick gently prodded when she went silent.

Her face clouded. "He was working the cattle with my father and Chad. I was there, too. He hadn't had a lot of experience with roping yet, but he managed to rope a calf. He grinned up at me, proud of what he'd done. Even said, 'See, Taylor. I told you I could do it. And you didn't think I could.' That's when it happened."

She shut her eyes tight. "While he was removing the rope, his horse spooked and ran, like what happened with you the other day. His hand was still caught in the rope. He was dragged for almost a mile. When we got to him, he was almost dead." A tear slipped out from between her closed lashes. "I held him in my arms while my brother rode to get help, but he died before Chad could get back."

Derrick moved his hand to cover hers. "Taylor, I'm so sorry—"

"No!" She snatched her hand back, and her eyes popped open. "Don't you dare tell me how it was just a freak accident that could've happened to anyone. I'm the one who begged Dad to give Kevin the job! Even after I saw what a mistake that was, I'm the one who encouraged Dad to keep Kevin on."

Derrick noted the flash of fire in her pale blue eyes, the remorse buried there, and understood. She blamed herself for Kevin's death. Remembering how guilt-ridden he felt after his sister was killed, Derrick held back the automatic reaction to want to respond as passionately as she did and try to convince her she wasn't to blame. Through his own experience he knew that could only make things worse. Instead he directed his gaze to the ground and the hay strewn there. He picked up a piece and began threading the yellow strand through his fingers.

"Okay, I won't tell you any of those things." He sensed her surprise in the way her body gave a little jump. "But I sure thought you had more sense than to get engaged to a guy who couldn't make a decision for himself."

Taylor bristled, like Derrick thought she would. "Kevin was very much his own man," she said, tight-lipped. "He made plenty of decisions."

"Maybe. But from what you told me, he needed you to lead him around like a horse. Even find another job for him."

"That's not true! When an opening came up at the ranch, Kevin asked me to speak to Dad about hiring him. So I did. But I thought he knew more about ranch life, as much as he talked about horses and cows."

"Hmm. So what you're saying is that it was his decision to keep that information to himself, so he could land a job here. Right?"

"Yes." The word came out uncertain. She drew her brows together as if he'd presented her with an unexpected set of equations and she didn't know the answer. "But when I found out he was inexperienced, I should have told Dad to let him go."

"That would have been hard on a relationship," Derrick mused. "I can see why you didn't. Also, it seems to me that your dad is one smart guy. Smart enough to have seen Kevin's inexperience and judge whether to let him go. Without your say in the matter."

She rubbed the space between her brows with three fingers. "I don't know. Maybe."

"Just how does one get experience at ranch life? Don't they have to live it firsthand?"

"You're confusing me, Derrick."

"Sorry. I'm just trying to get you to think about something you've obviously never considered."

"And what's that?"

"Kevin was an adult, capable of making his own choices. If he wanted something badly enough, he sounded like the type to go after it. You couldn't have stopped him."

She fidgeted, moving her upper body in a slight turn, as though to crack her back. She looked uncomfortable, both physically and emotionally. It was time to drop the subject. He'd given her enough to consider.

"You look tired," he said. "I may not be as soft as a pillow, but I'm here if you'd like to lean against me while we wait."

Taylor hesitated at least half a minute, then nodded and

rested her back against his shoulder. She smelled like a mixture of hay and fresh flowers. Bracing one hand on the floor, Derrick slung his other arm around her, to help keep her in place. He dipped his head to inhale the clean scent of her hair, deciding it smelled like the lilac candles his mother favored. Soft strands of her curls brushed against his cheek. For a wild moment, Derrick thought about unearthing the mistletoe sprig from his pocket, but now wasn't a good time. He didn't want to take advantage of her with a surprise kiss when she was so vulnerable.

The horse gave another painful whinny and moved her head as though to rise, but quickly laid it back down. Derrick felt Taylor tense.

"Favorite Christmas carol," he said, hoping to get her mind off the situation and lighten the mood.

"What?" She turned her head sideways to look at him.

"What's your favorite Christmas carol? And why?"

"Oh. 'The Holly and the Ivy,' I guess, because when I hear the song on the radio or CD, a bunch of angelic-sounding kids are usually singing it. Children's voices are so sweet, and the carol has such an old-world English sound. Have you ever heard it?"

"Only last night at the campfire when you sang it." He wouldn't mind owning a compilation of Taylor singing carols and strumming her guitar. "Favorite Christmas movie?"

"Is this a game?"

"You could say that. When I was a boy, Mom and I used to play this and other games like it when we were driving long distances to visit relatives over the holidays. It helped to pass the time."

"As long as you don't count any wrong answers."

He chuckled. "No counting in this game. Or wrong answers. It's a way to get to know you and what you like."

"Okay, then. *Miracle in the Wilderness.* Because it was set in the 1800s with pioneers and Native Americans. And the Christmas story of Christ's birth was told and later expressed in a way they could understand. I especially liked that."

"Favorite Christmas book?"

"Except for my Bible, I don't get a lot of reading in. Mom belongs to an inspirational romance club that sent her some Christmas-themed books that look pretty interesting. I might try to read one or two of those in the coming weeks."

"What about your favorite Christmas kids' show?"

"That's easy. The Charlie Brown one."

"Why?"

"I loved it when Linus recited the passage of Jesus' birth from the Bible, then later the kids all helped Charlie Brown feel better about his sad choice of a tree."

"Christmas song from a movie?"

" 'I'll Be Home for Christmas'—because I like Judy Garland and her movies." She paused. "I don't hear you telling me any of yours."

He chuckled. "Okay. 'Jingle Bells' for a favorite carol— because I always got to ring the handbells when we went caroling. Mom headed the group. She was the church choir director, and I was the youngest kid there. She couldn't afford a sitter in those days, so I always got dragged around with her." He grinned at the memory. He loved his mom and all she'd sacrificed for him. He hoped her new marriage made her happy.

"What else?" Taylor prodded.

"For a Christmas movie—*It's a Wonderful Life*, because I

rooted for the guy all the way through and was glad when he asked God to get him back home. Christmas book—I've only read *A Christmas Carol*, and that was long ago. It was required reading for school, but it held my interest, and I liked the way it ended. Kids' show—*The Grinch*, 'cause he was such a crusty old guy but had a good heart underneath it all. He saved his dog."

She looked sideways at him again, and he gave her a big smile.

"You're a pretty nice guy yourself," she admitted.

"Thanks." He lifted his eyebrows in amused surprise at the compliment. "But I hope that doesn't mean you think me crusty or old."

Pink stained her cheeks, and she turned her head back around. "What have you learned about me? Or dare I even ask?"

"Sure. You're a sweet, down-home girl who enjoys the simple pleasures of life. You have a strong faith in God and a sensitive heart. And I'll bet you even cried when Charlie Brown saw the decked-out tree and all those kids yelled, 'Merry Christmas, Charlie Brown!'"

"Did not." The grin lifting her lips said otherwise. "Well, maybe a little."

He chuckled and hugged her closer to him for a moment. If not for the horse's condition, this would be perfect. The soft yellow glow of the inside lights, the warmth of her pressed against him. . . Cozy. Something he could definitely get used to.

"Now it's your turn to be rated," she said, interrupting his train of thought. "Judging from what you said, I think you're a guy who wants everyone everywhere to overcome their problems, especially those people whom others give up on. You see the good in everyone, so you want all to succeed, and you do what you can to help, even if it means just rooting for people."

"Not a bad analysis," he mused. "But I'm not sure I'm as golden-hearted as that. With all the trouble at my new job, I'm about ready to quit from the stress."

"Trouble?"

"Someone's been mismanaging the accounts at the firm I work for. Probably the former accountant, though I'm just assuming. An investigation is under way now. I'm exempt from being suspect, because I was hired a little over a month ago. But soon I'll have to go back into the ugly corporate jungle."

Taylor stiffened against him. "In three days."

"Yeah." Derrick grew somber. He didn't want to leave but had no choice. If the situation went to trial, he might have to testify. He wished he could take Taylor with him to Chicago.

The sudden thought surprised him.

Even if their relationship did progress to something bigger, he could never ask her to leave the ranch she loved. She belonged here, and instinctively Derrick knew she would wither up in a huge congested city, with no horse to ride over the vast, empty land, or campouts in the middle of the peaceful woods. She was every inch a country girl. He couldn't change that—nor did he want to.

A movement at the stable door alerted them both to company. Robert strode in, followed by a squat, middle-aged man wearing gray slacks and a white dress shirt under his long, unbuttoned trench coat. A black satchel was in his hand.

Robert lifted his brow upon nearing the stall and seeing Taylor snug against Derrick. She quickly leaned forward and scrambled to her feet. "You're the vet?" she asked, walking toward the newcomer.

"Yes, ma'am. Howard Feldman's the name. It's a good thing your brother found me when he did. Me and my wife were just fixing to head on over to her parents' place in the next county. Now, what have we here?" He approached Buttercup, and Derrick rose from his sitting position.

"I'll go back to the house now and get out of your way," he said.

Taylor offered him a faint smile. "Thanks for keeping me company."

As Derrick retraced the shallow impressions his footsteps had made in the snow, he wondered about the cheerless look in her eyes. Was it only concern for her horse? Or had something else been said to make her look like her world was nearing the brink of collapse?

Chapter 5

After an enormous Christmas dinner featuring barbecued roast beef, buttery mashed potatoes, onion-flavored green beans, corn on the cob, and much more, Derrick joined the Summeralls in the family room. Taylor passed out the gifts that had mysteriously accumulated under the tree this past week, and Derrick was surprised when she handed him a thin, square-shaped one. His brows lifted.

"You shouldn't have, Taylor."

"Oh, it's not from me," she hastened to say. "It's from the family, though Chad picked it out."

Derrick nodded his friend's way and opened the shiny blue wrap. Pleasure shot through him when he saw a CD of gospel hymns with Taylor's smiling face on the cover.

Taylor pierced her brother with a glare. "He's right, Chad. You really shouldn't have."

"Oh, lighten up, Taylor," Robert said with a grin.

Derrick looked from Chad to Taylor then back again. "But how. . . ?"

"Yesterday you told me how much you enjoyed Taylor's singing," Chad explained. "And I remembered that she'd done that years ago. A friend of Dad's is a local radio DJ—he's the one we listen to every night—and in exchange for him staying here with his family one weekend, he got permission to let us borrow the studio to make that. It was during her senior year in high school, if I remember right."

Derrick looked at the picture on the cover again. Taylor's eyes sparkled with a childlike innocence and glow, as if nothing in her world had ever gone wrong. Obviously the photo was taken before Kevin's accident. "This is great! Thanks. I can't wait to pop it into my player at home."

"And thank you," Charla Summerall said from across the room, an unwrapped box in her lap. "We always do love these sausage and cheese sets. I can't wait to try them all."

Derrick smiled then noticed that Taylor had picked up his present to her, shaped exactly as his gift had been. From her place on the sofa, she shot him an uncertain look.

"It won't bite," he said with a grin.

Pink flushed her cheeks, but she slid her short nail under the flap and opened it. "Oh, Derrick. . ." She smiled up at him. "The best of Judy Garland. Thank you."

Derrick was glad he'd agreed to go Christmas shopping with Chad yesterday and had found that CD. Yet before he could answer her, Lou Summerall stood and faced his wife. A commanding figure who towered well over six feet, with graying hair and swarthy skin, Lou was the type of man to capture the attention of a roomful of people.

"And now for your gift, Charla darlin'."

"Oh, but. . ." She touched the diamond drop necklace around her neck. "Isn't this it?"

Lou chuckled. "That's just from me. But this next gift is from your sons, too. Now, close your eyes."

"This is all so mysterious," she drawled.

Derrick heard Taylor gasp and turned to look. Chad and Will carried what appeared to be a big, varnished oak cabinet and set it in front of their mother.

"You can open your eyes now," Lou prodded.

She did so and squealed. "Oh—how beautiful! Will, you must've been the one to burn those scrolls into the wood. They look just like something you did when you were a boy in wood shop. But. . .where will I put it? It doesn't have any legs."

At this, all three of her sons laughed. Lou bent down and said quietly, "It's not supposed to have any legs. It's for the kitchen we're going to remodel for you, the one you've been begging me to do for years. This is just one of the cabinets. There are five more like it out in the shed. And new drawers, too."

"Oh, Lou!" She threw her arms around her husband, almost pulling him down to her lap with the exuberance of her hug, then just as suddenly she released him and jumped up. "And I know just where they'll go, too. Come along with me, all of you. This is so wonderful—you're all so wonderful—I can't wait!" She hurried from the room.

Shaking their heads and smiling, the Summerall men followed. Before Taylor could rise to join them, Derrick spoke. "You have one more present."

She wrinkled her brow and looked in the immediate area around her. "Are you sure?"

"Yes." He rose from his chair and walked across the room to take a seat beside her on the sofa. "I'm glad to hear Buttercup's doing better."

Taylor searched the discarded gift wrap around her feet. "She's able to eat again. I'm so thankful she got through this crisis and we were able to find a skilled vet."

She located the rectangular-shaped box in the same style

of glossy green paper that Derrick had used to wrap the CD. This time when she opened her gift, she laughed. "*A Charlie Brown Christmas*! Oh, how perfect, Derrick. Thank you."

"We can cuddle up on the couch and watch it tonight, after the others go to bed."

At his low words, she seemed suddenly hesitant. "Are you trying to tell me that you're interested in me?"

"Would you mind very much if I was?"

"No, I don't think so. But what would be the point? You're leaving for Chicago tomorrow—"

He shook his head slightly, lifting his fingers to barely touch her lips when she opened her mouth to say more. "Let's take this one step at a time," he suggested, pulling his other hand from his pants pocket.

"What's that you have there?"

He held up the tiny sprig of mistletoe for her inspection. This time her whole face turned pink, but she didn't pull away. That fact encouraged him.

"In keeping with the Christmas tradition," he murmured, raising it above her head. He slowly drew closer, watching her beautiful blue eyes dilate. . .and close. Then he shut his own eyes and tenderly kissed her.

<hr />

Later, in her room, Taylor stood at her window with its view of the side lawn and stared at the red luminaries glowing in the dark. She couldn't believe she'd let Derrick kiss her a second time. Worse, she'd kissed him back. . .and liked it. Then an hour ago they'd sat side by side on the couch, eating soft pralines and watching the Peanuts gang learn the true meaning of Christmas. She couldn't remember a more enjoyable time, unless she counted the other night, by the campfire. . .

The muted ring of her bedside phone caught her attention, and she moved to grab it on the third ring, taking note of the steady yellow glow of one of the buttons. An inside call. No doubt Chad was calling to apologize for something.

"Hello?"

"I hope I didn't wake you."

Her heart began a funny cadence as warmth rushed to her face. "Derrick. No—I. . ." She fought for control. He probably needed towels or something. She couldn't remember if she'd stocked his room with enough of them. "I hope there's not a problem."

"No. I just wanted to hear your voice."

The tingling warmth shot down through her fingers and toes, but she couldn't think of anything to say.

"I've enjoyed my stay here with your family. And tonight, with you," his low voice caressed her ear several seconds later.

"I'm glad. You're welcome to come visit us again anytime." She winced when she realized how professional she sounded.

"Is that a personal invitation?"

How to answer that? "Um. . .sure."

A longer pause ensued. "By the way, those pralines were delicious. Chad told me you made them."

"Yes. I'll have Mom box some up for you for your plane trip, if you'd like." There. She'd said it. He was going. The reminder put the starch back into her bones. How could he play with her emotions like this, when he knew how it might hurt her?

"I'll miss you, Taylor."

Her eyes slid shut, and she swallowed hard. "Yeah," she whispered.

"Are you all right? You sound upset."

"I'm just tired. I'll see you in the morning at breakfast."

"Okay." He sounded disappointed. "Good night."

Frowning, Taylor hung up the phone and went to the bathroom sink. Bending over, she rinsed the sting from her eyes with cold water. The phone rang again.

She was there on the second ring.

"Hi," she said breathlessly into the receiver. "I'm sorry I was so hard to talk to a minute ago—"

"Taylor?" Chad asked. "What are you talking about?"

Her heart did a little nosedive. "Oh, hi, Chad. Nothing. That was a wonderful present you guys gave Mom. I haven't seen her face light up like that in a long time."

"Then I'm forgiven?"

Taylor couldn't help the small grin that lifted her lips. She blotted her damp face with the hand towel she'd grabbed before sprinting from the bathroom. "For what this time?"

"For pairing you off with Derrick and asking you to keep him company these past ten days."

Her amusement evaporated, and she focused on the lavender lamp shade.

"I noticed that you seemed to be getting along pretty well with each other today. So maybe it wasn't all a complete waste of your time?"

"No, it was fine." She tossed the towel onto the bed and bent over to pull the blankets down.

"Did you know that Dad offered Derrick a job managing the books?"

She froze in shock, then snapped to a stand. "No, I didn't. What did he say?"

"He thanked Dad but said he had to get back to Chicago."

Of course. He must miss the big city life.

"Are you there?"

"Yeah. Listen, I'm pretty tired. I think I'll turn in now."

"Okay. I just wanted to call and assure you that I had your best interests in mind from the start. Maybe I came off like an uncaring jerk at the beginning, but I really do care about you, Taylor."

"I know." She smiled, and another set of tears pricked her eyes. It was a rarity for Chad to talk about his emotions, so this was a milestone. "I love you, too, big brother. Good night."

Once Taylor hung up the phone, she finished getting ready for bed then slid between the cold sheets. She curled her body around a pillow she held in an effort to warm up. Tomorrow Derrick would be gone, and life would go on as it had before he came. Any far-reaching, misty dream she'd entertained of him staying had evaporated in the harsh light of reality. Her dad offered him the chance, and he'd turned it down. Flat. Derrick belonged in the city. Yet, at this moment, Taylor felt he would take her heart with him when he went.

Chapter 6

Derrick stood at the window of his fifth-floor apartment and studied the bustling city below. Lights from building windows and cars pierced the darkness of the evening sky. Now and then a horn would honk from the direction of a street still under repairs, shattering the relative stillness. A fresh snow was falling, but it would soon turn the sooty gray of what was already on the ground. That's one thing he liked about Texas. The snow stayed white, probably because it melted within a matter of days, and there hadn't been such a heavy accumulation that shoveling was necessary. In fact, the white stuff hadn't been much of a bother at all.

In the background, Taylor's clear, sweet voice sang to him from his stereo speakers. He had played the CD almost non-stop since his return home. It was almost as good as having her there with him. He'd never missed a person so much, and only three days had passed since he left the ranch. How could a girl he'd known for such a short time affect him so strongly?

Because you're in love with her, his mind whispered back.

Derrick pulled away from the window and surveyed the empty, stark room decorated in brass, black, and dim white. It was true. He loved the short, sassy cowgirl, and Chad probably knew it, too. Why else, at the airport, would he have kept introducing the subject of Taylor? Chad's questions about their time together had been offhand, but frequent enough for him to realize that his buddy suspected Derrick's feelings ran deep.

He missed Taylor horribly.

A burning smell invaded his nostrils and made Derrick grimace. *Oh, no. I must've forgotten to set the timer.*

He rushed into his compact kitchen, pulled on the checkered mitts, and withdrew his charred pre-made lasagna dinner from the oven. Smoke swept upward, setting off the smoke alarm. A shrill blare penetrated the area, and he felt as if his eardrums might burst. Leaving the cardboard tray of burnt food on the rack, he shed his mitts and disengaged the alarm.

The sudden quiet brought welcome relief, though it seemed invasive, too. After such a din, the silence gave the impression of being underlined, and Derrick felt even more alone, especially since the last track on the CD had ended.

He took a fork and removed the top layer of burnt cheese from his dinner, glad to see that the noodles, meat, and red sauce underneath looked okay to eat. Still, even unburned, this meal couldn't compare to the homemade meals that Taylor's mom served at the ranch.

The phone rang, and Derrick grabbed it, thankful to whoever was on the other end. He needed someone to talk to right now to save him from his blue-without-you thoughts. "Hello?"

"Derrick," his boss said. "Sorry to call so late, but this is important."

"Not a problem." Derrick leaned against the counter. "I'm listening."

Five minutes later he hung up the receiver, feeling stunned. Was this God's hand at work?

Taylor reclined on the couch, with her head against a round pillow cushion, and took advantage of the downtime to read the last chapter of her mother's Christmas-themed suspense book. Who would have thought a Christian romance could have such an impact on her life? All of the many different methods God used to encourage His people amazed her.

Like the heroine in the book who was upset about a brother on trial for murder, Taylor blamed herself for a loved one's choices. She'd felt responsible for Kevin's death because she'd gotten him the job at the ranch. Yet, Derrick was right. Kevin had made his own choices, and regardless of what Taylor might have said or done otherwise, he would have acted as he wanted. God didn't hold her responsible for what had happened to Kevin. Taylor had been the one to slap on her own self-made handcuffs and fasten them tightly around her wrists.

While reading the novel these past few days, she'd been led to put down the book at times and search out scriptures mentioned in the story. Portions that enlightened the heroine to the truth, as well as other verses. God's promises from the verses of Jeremiah especially helped Taylor:

" 'For I know the plans I have for you,' declares the Lord, 'plans to prosper you and not to harm you, plans to give you hope and a future. Then you will call upon me and come and pray to me, and I will listen to you. You will seek me and find me when you seek me with all your heart.' "

Taylor had been doing exactly that, especially over her feelings concerning Derrick. She'd thought about him for almost a week, ever since the day he left, and she'd come to the knowledge that it was all right for her to love again—that God desired to give her a future, one filled with hope. Was that future with Derrick?

Chad had Derrick's phone number. Maybe in the new year she would break down and give him a call. If things between them were meant to progress, they would. Long distance and differing lifestyles didn't matter if she and Derrick were supposed to be together. She'd been pouring her heart out to God for almost a week now, and she was convinced that He'd heard her. Whatever happened, His plans for her were best.

Taylor finished the story, which ended in a cozy-warm way to make her feel good inside. She put the book down and stretched, then sank back against the cushion. The heroine had ended up making the decision to move to the hero's state to share his life, and Taylor's mind wandered back to Derrick. What if they did start seeing each other and their relationship matured to such a point that God told her to move to Chicago? Could she do that?

She thought about the fresh country air, riding Stardust, and the acres and acres of empty, wild, beautiful land on which she lived. It would be difficult to leave the home she loved behind, but there was such a thing as visits. And the twenty-first century did make it easy to cover a thousand miles or more. Her time with the Lord this past week had helped Taylor understand that if God were behind a possible move on her part, she wouldn't be happy doing otherwise. Yet He'd have to make the directive very clear to her for her to do such a thing as leave Texas.

Taylor's face warmed. Here she was planning out their married life together, when she and Derrick had never even been out on an official date!

"Hey, there you are."

Chad's loud voice interrupted her thoughts, and she shot to a sitting position. She felt embarrassed that she'd been dreaming like a silly schoolgirl who'd linked her and her boyfriend's names in a hand-drawn heart. Good thing no one could read her thoughts!

"Don't tell me you haven't got any plans for New Year's Eve?" Chad asked, his gaze taking in her rumpled sweatshirt and jeans. He was spruced up in a nice pair of black slacks and a patterned sweater.

"I thought I'd just stay home and watch the ball in New York come down on TV. Besides, if the Masons want anything, with Dad and Mom gone to the dance, and you and Robert and Will all on dates, someone has to stay behind and keep things running."

"The Masons are on their honeymoon," Chad argued with a grin. "I doubt you'll be getting any phone calls from their room."

"Maybe not, but I'd rather stay home tonight. I might even start another one of these novels. Mom has a shelf full of them, and they're really good. Much better than I expected."

Chad feigned an expression of horror. "Oh no! Not another romance junkie in the house! Life was bad enough when it was just Mom, but now you've been bit by the bug, too?"

Taylor chuckled. "Yeah, I guess I have."

"Well, I'll quit trying to push you out of the house then. From what I've seen, there's no known cure for the romance junkie. I'll talk to you later."

"Are you bringing Karen to dinner tomorrow?"

Chad's face actually turned a shade of salmon. "I plan to. You'll like her, I think. She was raised on a ranch, too, and she's different from those 'empty-headed females' I brought home in the past. I believe that's what you called them." His tone lightened to teasing.

"I look forward to meeting her then. It's time you found a nice girl to settle down with."

"Don't rush me." He seemed nervous. "Listen, as long as you're not going anywhere, can I borrow your car? My truck's been stalling on me lately, and I wouldn't want the old girl to go temperamental while I'm with Karen."

"Sure. The keys are in my bedroom on the bureau."

"Thanks."

Taylor chuckled and watched Chad hurry from the room. Obviously a romance bug of a different sort had bitten her brother.

With hours to while away until midnight and no guests who needed her, Taylor enjoyed a leisurely shower, dried her hair with a blow dryer, zipped herself into a pair of faded blue jeans, and pulled on one of her softest, fluffiest sweaters. Taking her desire to pamper herself to another level, she grabbed a pint of peppermint ice cream from the freezer and a spoon from the drawer. Sock-footed, she padded back to the couch. She made herself comfortable and spooned what was left of the decadently sweet stuff into her mouth, her gaze going out the window over the decorated lawn. She crunched down on the candy pieces, thinking.

Not quite the way she'd thought she would spend New Year's Eve, but this wasn't so bad. It was better than going to the community dance alone.

Ice cream finished, a glance at the wall clock told her she still had a little more than an hour to kill before midnight. She remembered that Mom had asked her to make another batch of soft pralines for New Year's Day. Might as well take care of that now.

To keep her company, she switched on the tabletop radio in the kitchen. It was set at her dad's station, and she left the dial there, enjoying the oldies music. She had just set the cooked candy mixture aside to cool when a soft drink commercial ended and the station jingle played. The DJ's deep, fluid voice captured her attention:

"This might seem a week late to some of you folks out there, but since the caller assures me that there really are twelve days of Christmas—and don't we have the song to prove it?—I thought I'd go ahead and play the requested tune one last time. This goes out to Taylor from Derrick."

Taylor froze, spoon in midair, her eyes going wide. Her gaze whipped to the black box on her mother's kitchen counter. From its small speaker, strains of "I'll Be Home for Christmas" floated through the kitchen. The singer wasn't Judy Garland, but even if it had been the Abominable Snowman, Taylor probably wouldn't have known the difference. She stood, disbelieving, her mouth open.

Surely the DJ meant another Taylor and Derrick. It had to be one of those strange-but-true coincidences. Their names weren't all that common, but this sort of thing happened occasionally, didn't it? What other explanation could there be? Derrick wouldn't be calling from Chicago to request a song.

Her heart calmed to a steadier beat. She retrieved the pecan halves from the cabinet and had just sprinkled a few into a measuring cup when the DJ came on the air again.

"Well, there you have it. Since I know this little lady personally, I agreed to deliver a message along with the song. Taylor, if you're out there and are listening—you get yourself off that ranch and on down to the bus station on McGregor Street as quick as you can. Derrick will be outside waiting for you."

Taylor dropped the one-pound bag, and pecans scattered all over the tiles.

❧

Derrick cast a nervous smile toward the crowd who'd gathered, then glanced at his wristwatch again. What if she didn't show? Maybe it had been a mistake to call the DJ and have the man relay his message to Taylor. Ever since the song aired, curious people had trickled into the bus depot like those in New York Times Square who'd eagerly waited for the ball to drop an hour ago. Cars drove up and parked, some keeping watch inside, while others joined Derrick and took a spot on the sidewalk that stretched in front of the cement building. Derrick quit counting the onlookers when he reached fifty-five. Honestly! Didn't these people have anything better to do on New Year's Eve than to stand outside a bus depot?

Derrick didn't want to think about the possibility of Taylor not making an appearance, but the thought had darted through his mind these past thirty minutes like a persistent gnat. She might not have been listening to the radio tonight. She might have gone to a party or a dance. Why had he assumed that she'd be sitting at home anyway? Or that she'd be interested in furthering their relationship? He should have thought this through. If he had ordered a taxi and quietly arrived at The Silver Spur, at least he would have been saved the humiliation and disappointment if she didn't show.

An elderly woman walked up to him, pulling her down coat closer around her neck. "What time do you have?" she asked, her breath misting in the air.

Derrick looked at his watch. "Fifteen 'til."

She smiled. "Chin up, young man. She'll show."

Derrick's face warmed. He wished he could be so sure.

The minutes crawled by on inchworm feet. More cars pulled up. More people got out. He wished the radio station that the Summeralls listened to wasn't as popular as it obviously was. The town was small, but apparently everyone in the vicinity who'd been listening had turned out to watch.

Suddenly, Derrick heard what sounded like horse hooves clattering over blacktop. He turned to look, as did the rest of the crowd. Taylor came riding around the corner on Stardust, her hair catching the glow of outside lights and bouncing around her shoulders.

"There she is!" an excited little girl cried out.

The crowd cheered. As Taylor drew close, Derrick saw the disbelief that made her eyes go round when she noticed the two long lines of smiling faces and those who craned their heads from the windows of their cars. Her face was flushed, whether from the ride or from embarrassment, Derrick didn't know. If she felt like he did, it was probably a little of both.

He moved forward, almost stumbling over his own feet in his eagerness to be with her. She spotted him, and her expression relaxed as she gave him one of the biggest smiles he'd ever seen. In a matter of seconds, they reached each other. Taylor dismounted, a bystander took the reins, and she moved into Derrick's arms. Another cheer went up.

"It's so good to hold you again," Derrick murmured in her ear, lifting her off the ground. He laid his cheek against her soft, sweet-smelling hair. After a few seconds passed, he reluctantly loosed his tight hold and set her back on her feet. Near to bursting with his news and unable to contain it any longer, he blurted, "I'm out of a job!"

She drew her brows together in confusion. "You sound happy about it."

"I am. The firm's gone bankrupt, though I'm sorry for those involved. I don't have to testify in court, either. They caught the embezzler, and word has it that he'll plea-bargain to get a lighter sentence."

Her brow creased as if she were desperately trying to figure out his words.

He laughed. "Taylor, I have nothing to keep me in Chicago anymore! If your dad still has that position for a personal accountant open, I'd like to take it. I've found I really like Texas. Especially the people here." His hands moved to cradle her chilled face. "And I love you."

"Really, Derrick?" Her eyes shone.

"Yes. I couldn't stop thinking about you all this past week. I want to spend as much time as I can getting to know you, getting to know everything about you."

"I'd like that," she said shyly. "Because I think I love you, too."

Though it was thirty-two degrees, the admission warmed him clear through. He studied every inch of her face, every curve, every freckle. His gaze lifted to her shimmering blue one and locked.

"What are you thinking?" she whispered.

"I'm just counting the stars in your eyes."

She grinned and wrapped her arms around him. "Be quiet and kiss me, city boy."

"With pleasure." He dipped his head and touched his lips to her soft ones. They were icy-cold and he quickly warmed them, enjoying the desirable task.

Car horns began to honk. Party whistles and blowers blew. Stardust whinnied.

"Happy New Year!" someone shouted from nearby.

Derrick broke the kiss, his face only inches from Taylor's.

"Happy New Year," she whispered.

He smiled. "Happy New Year." Bending down, he reclaimed her lips until Stardust's loud whinny broke them apart a second time.

"We'd better get out of here," Taylor said, giggling, "before we have to chase another runaway horse. Stardust is more stable than the others, but I don't want to take any chances. I'll give you a ride back to the ranch. One of the boys can come and pick up your luggage later. I assume you left it inside?"

Derrick nodded, and she mounted and reclaimed the reins while he awkwardly swung up behind her. He wrapped his arms around her waist. "This'll be a great year, Taylor, for both of us. It's a brand-new start, the best year yet."

Taylor smiled and settled back against his chest for the ride home.

Epilogue

One year later

They're coming!"

The excited squeal from outside met Taylor's ears, and automatically she covered her styled-for-the-occasion hair with her free hand. She walked quickly past numerous pots of red and white poinsettias placed on the edge of the stairs, and rows of sweet-smelling pine garland that draped the walls. Her other hand she kept firmly wrapped around Derrick's.

Before they could make it to the sunny outdoors, he stopped her at the door.

"What?" she asked, wondering if they'd forgotten something. Their luggage was at the bus station being guarded by Robert and Will.

Derrick pointedly looked at the mistletoe hanging above their heads, and Taylor grinned. He bent his head toward her. His kiss took her breath away, even if it was brief.

"You ready for this?" he asked, eyes twinkling.

She matched his smile. "Ready when you are."

He opened the door, and together they raced outside, trying

in vain to cover their heads while showers of heart-shaped rice rained down on them from the guests lined up along the steps and sidewalk of the ranch house. They both laughed as they ran toward Stardust, saddled and waiting for the short ride that would take Taylor and her new husband to the depot, where they would catch a bus for the airport, then be on their way to a honeymoon cruise in the Caribbean. Chad held Stardust's reins to keep him steady, and Karen looped her arm through his, her new engagement ring catching flashes of light.

Taylor took a moment to hug the woman who'd become such a good friend. "I'm so glad you're going to be my sister." She looked toward her brother. "Thanks, Chad. For everything. And yes, you're definitely forgiven."

She chuckled at the confusion that crossed his face, and gave him a quick hug, too. Then she hugged her parents. Her mom whispered in her ear, "What was that all about?"

"Chad forced me to give lessons to Derrick when he first came here a year ago," Taylor explained before she moved away.

"Ah," her mom said, a twinkle in her eye. "Then, I'm glad he did. I've never seen you so happy."

"Welcome to the family, Taylor," Derrick's mom said, wrapping Taylor and Derrick in a close hug. "You both have a wonderful life together. And believe me, you'll love the cruise."

A group of Taylor's small cousins moved in and began throwing handfuls of rice at close range.

"We'd better get out of here." Taylor laughed. "I'll call you when we reach the hotel, Mom. See y'all in two weeks."

Derrick mounted the gelding with expertise. His past year on the ranch had served him well, riding with Taylor almost every day. Her city boy was now a fine horseman. He held out one hand to her and helped to pull her up on the saddle. She was glad she'd worn her gray wool slacks, fuzzy white top, and gray snakeskin boots. Her mother's suggestion of a blouse with a full skirt for a going-away outfit would never have worked in this chilly December weather. Even with her thermals and new down jacket she felt cold, and she wrapped her arms tightly around Derrick's middle.

"Mm," he said with a backward smile her way. "That's nice. You can do that anytime you'd like, Mrs. Freeborn."

Smiling, she snuggled closer. *Mrs. Freeborn.* She could hear that name from sunup to sundown and never get tired of it.

"Are you ready to ride off into the sunset together?" he asked.

She raised her brows at the corny line. "Only if you don't stop to count the cows."

He laughed, a pleasant, rich sound that shook the air. Taylor knew she'd never grow tired of that laugh, either. Nor of his infectious smile.

They waved their good-byes to family and friends who'd come to share in the joy of their Christmas wedding. Then Derrick prodded Stardust into a gallop, and they rode across the wide land together. Ahead of them, the magnificent red ball of the sun dipped beyond the horizon and tinted the clouds with mellow rose and violet. The guests' parting calls of good wishes became a pleasant background murmur in Taylor's ears. Smiling, she laid her cheek against the suede material covering Derrick's broad back. She had hope again, and the assurance of a bright future with this wonderful man who possessed a heart as big as Texas.

God's promises really did come true.

TAYLOR'S SOFT PRALINES
(Ultra-rich, ultra sweet, ultra creamy)

¾ c. milk
2 c. sugar + 1 c. sugar
1¾ c. pecan halves or peanuts
1 t. vanilla

Over low heat, cook milk and 2 cups sugar in 4-quart saucepan, stirring frequently. Meanwhile, caramelize 1 cup sugar in skillet over low heat, achieving a syrupy, golden brown appearance, and stirring as needed so sugar doesn't burn. Add to milk mixture. Cook to soft ball stage, stirring all the while. Cool until lukewarm. Add vanilla and nuts. Beat until creamy and spread thickly on waxed paper. Break apart into pieces when dry.

Enjoy!

PAMELA GRIFFIN

Pamela lives in North Central Texas and divides her time among God, family, and writing. Her main goal in writing Christian fiction is to encourage others and plant seeds of faith through entertaining stories that minister to the wounded spirit. Christmas is her favorite time of year, and she enjoys writing stories centered on the season. She has contracted over twenty novels and novellas and loves hearing from her readers. You can visit her at: http://users.waymark.net/words_of_honey/.

Christmas in the City

by Debby Mayne

Dedication
I'd like to dedicate this story to Lori Welch,
a faithful follower of Christ,
who offers comfort and kindness to her friends.

Acknowledgments
Thanks to Rev. Fred Bouton for sharing
the details about prison ministries in New York.
Thanks to Rev. Scott Welch for offering
such great sermons and inspirational wisdom.

*Blessed be God, even the Father of our Lord Jesus Christ,
the Father of mercies, and the God of all comfort;
who comforteth us in all our tribulation, that we may
be able to comfort them which are in any trouble, by the comfort
wherewith we ourselves are comforted of God.*
2 CORINTHIANS 1:3–4

Chapter 1

No other student in the Northeast Culinary Institute could create a raspberry soufflé that came close to Kathryn Anderson's. In fact, her entire final exam—spinach crepes with crab dressing, chicken asparagus soup, fresh-baked multigrain bread, ginger shrimp, and raspberry soufflé—won top honors across the board. Kathryn was on her way to realizing her dream of becoming a world-class chef.

"Hey, Kathryn," Peter Townsley whispered from behind, "wanna go out with the rest of us tonight? We figured we might as well celebrate before anyone has to leave."

"Sorry, Peter, but I can't. I promised my aunt I'd come to her place after the exam."

Peter nodded his understanding and smiled. "Tell Miss Celia I said hi. She makes the best homemade biscuits I've ever tasted."

"Will do." After Kathryn finished cleaning her section of the training kitchen, she joined the other students and waited for the verdict.

Three hours later, Kathryn walked past Rockefeller Center Plaza, her coveted certificate secured in the briefcase she clutched at her side. She'd won the dessert competition as well as best overall. Aunt Celia would be so proud.

Who would've imagined that Kathryn Anderson, daughter of Bette Anderson, queen of dinner theater in Boise, Idaho, would have so much as even thought of being a chef? Her mother was the least domestic person she knew, but summers spent at Aunt Celia's boardinghouse in Soho had given Kathryn a hint of what she wanted to do with her life.

Workers scurried around the plaza steps, getting the gargantuan Christmas tree ready for the lighting ceremony that would take place in a few nights. She inhaled deeply, taking in the scent of impending snow. Just maybe this would be a white Christmas—most likely Kathryn's last, since she'd agreed to an apprenticeship in the kitchen of the Don Cesar in St. Petersburg, Florida. Although she looked forward to the sun and sandy beaches, she'd miss the change of seasons.

The subway was crowded with holiday shoppers, most of them toting bags with store logos emblazoned on the sides. She hadn't even begun her shopping yet, but she would soon—before she left New York.

Once aboard the train, Kathryn found herself daydreaming about having her own kitchen, creating delectable delights for the most discriminating diners. As the subway train slid to a stop at the Houston station, Kathryn edged toward the door. She stepped off and took a quick glance around, enjoying all the sights and sounds of the city. This had been her home for three years, and she'd loved every minute of it.

Since Aunt Celia's place was only four blocks from the station, Kathryn walked the distance, looking right and left, nodding to shopkeepers who stood in their doorways, glancing up at the sky. Kathryn inhaled deeply and allowed the cold, crisp air to fill her lungs as she rounded the last corner, heading toward her aunt's. She was still amazed that Aunt Celia had continued to hold out on selling the last of the boardinghouses in trendy Soho, since real estate had shot sky-high. The three-story stone house with the wraparound porch immediately came into full view.

She blinked. Reverend Stan Jarrett, one of Aunt Celia's regulars, stood on the front porch, wearing an expression of anticipation and looking more handsome than ever.

"Hello, Kathryn," the man said as she drew closer. "I've been watching for you."

"Why?" she asked. "Where's Aunt Celia?"

He nodded toward the front door. "Let's go inside. We need to talk."

A quick knot formed in her stomach.

Once inside, the entire downstairs of the house seemed eerily quiet, opposite of how it had been the last time she'd been there.

"Have a seat," he said as he rubbed his chin.

"What's going on, Reverend Jarrett?" she asked.

"Please call me Stan." The hint of smile quickly faded. "I have some disconcerting news."

"Bad news?" Kathryn's insides tightened.

He glanced over his shoulder, and Kathryn followed his line of vision to see Mona and Bonnie, two of Aunt Celia's valued and trusted workers, standing in the doorway, their eyes round, and their bodies tense with anticipation. Stan turned back to her.

"Your aunt had to be taken to the hospital this morning," he blurted.

"Hospital?" she shrieked. "What happened? What's wrong?"

"She broke her hip, twisted her ankle, and dislocated her arm," Stan replied.

Kathryn sank back in her seat. "How did that happen?"

"According to her, she slipped on the ice on the bottom step when she was taking out the garbage," Stan replied. "No one saw it happen. She said she lost her breath, but you wouldn't have known it, hearing her scream."

"She screamed?"

"Oh, yes," Mona replied as she stepped closer, filling the room with her expansive presence. "Miss Celia has a strong set of lungs. The fall didn't change that one bit."

Kathryn quickly stood. "I need to go see her."

"I'll go with you," Stan said. "But first, we need to discuss this place."

"This place?" Kathryn repeated, gesturing around the room. Then she realized that without her aunt here, there was no one to run the boardinghouse. Both Mona and Bonnie had families, so they went home after all the dishes were washed and put away.

"I realize it might put a crimp in your plans, but I was hoping you'd stick around for a while, at least until your aunt gets back on her feet."

Images of sun and sandy beaches flitted through Kathryn's mind as she wrestled with her decision. She knew what she wanted, but she also knew what would be the right thing to do. Aunt Celia had led her to the Lord at a very young age. No way would Kathryn let Aunt Celia down.

"Of course, I'll hang around here until she's better," Kathryn said emphatically.

Stan grinned. "That's what I thought you'd say. Ready to pay her a visit?"

Kathryn offered a stiff nod as she stood on shaky legs.

"Let me peek into the kitchen," she said. "We might need to pick up a few things on the way back from the hospital."

"Take your time," he told her. "Miss Celia's not going anywhere."

Stan fully understood what Kathryn must be feeling at this moment. He'd experienced enough disappointment of his own. He could see the frustration on her face, and he felt protective of the diminutive strawberry blond. He'd forced himself not to act on his attraction to Miss Celia's niece in the past.

"We're running low on sugar and eggs," Kathryn said as she exited the kitchen. "I don't know why Aunt Celia doesn't have more delivered."

"She's been doing this a long time," Stan reminded her. "I think she probably knows how to run this place with her eyes closed."

Kathryn now sported a frown but didn't say a word. He knew she needed time to mentally adjust to this change of plans.

They walked all the way to the hospital in the blustery winds that whipped around the cold, gray buildings. Awnings, which had protected shoppers in the hot summer, now flapped and made slapping sounds. Kathryn didn't seem to be aware of the world around her as she leaned into the wind and forged ahead.

Finally, she slowed her pace. "Which do you think would be better for dinner tomorrow night—marinated lamb served with a mint and basil sauce or shrimp served on a bed of fresh arugula?"

"What's wrong with fried chicken or pork chops?"

"You're kidding, right?"

"No, I'm not kidding. People come to Miss Celia's for home cooking, not gourmet fare. They can get the fancy stuff anywhere else."

"Well, I think they'd appreciate something a little different. We can stop off at a butcher on the way back."

Stan decided not to argue. "Fine with me. I'll eat anything you put in front of me."

She tossed him a look he couldn't interpret, so he didn't worry about it. If she was mad, she'd get over it. If she wanted answers, she needed to ask the questions.

Miss Celia was propped up in bed when they walked into her room. "Hey, you two. I hear the weather's awful."

"You should know, Miss Celia," Stan said. "Gotta stay off those icy steps."

She grimaced. "Don't I know it." Then she turned to Kathryn. "I sure hope this isn't too much of an inconvenience for you to help out for a few weeks—at least until I can come home."

Stan quickly glanced at Kathryn to see her response. To his surprise, she didn't give away any of the frustration he'd seen earlier. She shook her head and genuinely smiled at her aunt. "No, of course not, silly. I'm more than happy to help out."

"Are you sure, Kathryn?" Miss Celia asked.

"You know I don't lie. Relax. Everything's under control."

A smile widened Miss Celia's face. "You're such a good girl." She glanced at Stan. "Take care of her, okay?"

He started to promise to do just that, but he noticed how Kathryn's entire body tensed. Kathryn spoke up.

"I'm perfectly capable of taking care of myself and your boardinghouse, Aunt Celia. Now get some rest so you can heal. Let me know if there's anything I can do."

Miss Celia chuckled. "Bossy little thing, isn't she?"

He didn't comment. He knew better.

On the way back to Miss Celia's City House, they found a

butcher who stayed open late. Stan watched in amazement as Kathryn expertly placed her order and put it on a tab.

He waited until they left before he asked, "Wasn't that sort of expensive?"

"Maybe a little, but it's not like I'll have to do that every day. Starting tomorrow, I'll be doing all the ordering from the wholesale warehouse."

They arrived back at the house to find everything clean and put away. A note from Mona said there were two plates of leftovers in the refrigerator.

"You'll be working hard tomorrow," Stan said. "Sit down and let me serve you."

She paused then nodded. He was by her side five minutes later with two steaming plates of food and mugs of tea.

"How long will you be here this time, Stan?" Kathryn asked, between bites of food.

"I'm not sure. I'm still on loan from Nashville, but the prison ministry here needs people."

She suddenly started choking and coughing. "Prison ministry? What is that?"

Chapter 2

"Y ou didn't know that's what I did?"

"I knew you were a pastor, but I've never heard of a prison ministry. What, exactly, do you do?"

He paused to consider whether to give her the long or the short version and decided on the latter. "I visit inmates in prison to let them know that they still have hope through Christ."

"Why would you do that?"

Her words gave away her lack of understanding, so he knew he needed to tread lightly on the subject. "Everyone needs to know about Christ."

She held her mug a few inches from her lips. "I know that's what the Bible says, but I can't imagine criminals actually paying attention to the Bible."

She obviously didn't know about his past.

Kathryn's eyes had begun to droop. He stood and nodded to the door.

"Why don't you go on to your room and get some rest while I clean up?" he told her. "We can talk after breakfast in the morning."

"Are you sure you don't mind?" she asked.

"Positive. I want to do it."

Without an argument, she nodded. "I am pretty sleepy. It's been a long day."

Stan wasn't sleepy, so he headed back to the hospital for a quick visit with Miss Celia. The wind had died down, and it didn't feel nearly as cold.

"I knew you'd be back," Miss Celia said with a twinkle in her eye when he walked into her room.

"You're a smart woman."

"Think you can work on my niece while you're around, Stan?"

"Work on her? What do you mean?"

Celia cleared her throat as she gathered her thoughts. When she spoke, the words were deliberate and strong.

"My niece is very sweet, but she's rather misguided. Unfortunately, my brother was a lousy father to her. She has trust issues because he was never completely honest with her. When she found out some of his long absences were spent in jail, she was very hurt."

Stan should have figured as much.

"Was he a guilty man?" he asked.

"Unlike you, yes."

"That's awful."

"I know. I'm also concerned about her walk with the Lord. She goes to church with me as often as she can, but I'm not sure how deep her faith is."

"I'll see what I can do."

"She believes in God, so it shouldn't be too hard."

"That's a good start, I agree," he said with a nod. "But what does she understand about the gospel message?"

"Not much, I'm afraid. Whenever I try to bring it up, she

has to run off somewhere. I'm sure her reasons are legitimate. Still, it's hard to witness to someone who has one foot out the door."

"Yes, I know," he agreed. "It took a prison term for me to stay still long enough to listen."

Miss Celia looked him in the eye. "That should have never happened to such a nice young man as you."

"I agree. And that leads to another subject. What, exactly, does Kathryn know about my past? She seemed shocked when I said I had a prison ministry."

Miss Celia tightened her lips and folded her hands. "Not much. Just that you're in the ministry, and you travel quite a bit."

"I guess I need to tell her about my prison term and a few of the details if I'm going to stay in the house with her in charge."

"It'll come as a shock to her."

"You're right. I'll be very careful how I tell her. Hopefully, I won't scare her too much. In the meantime, you need to concentrate on healing."

Her eyes quickly misted. "I feel awful that I won't be able to make it to her graduation ceremony."

He patted her hand. "I'm sure she understands, Miss Celia." He straightened and moved toward the door.

"Come back and see me soon, okay, Stan?"

"Yes, of course," he said as he left the room. As he stepped outside, he wrapped his jacket tightly around his chest and shoved his hands in his pockets.

Miss Celia's City House was dark when he returned. He used one of the keys Miss Celia handed out to her boarders and let himself in; then he took two steps at a time going up the stairs. After making the long walk to and from the hospital twice in the same evening, he was ready for bed.

The next morning, he came down for breakfast just as Mona and Bonnie were clearing the tables.

"Where's Kathryn?" he asked, grabbing a biscuit out of the basket before Mona could whisk it off the table.

"She left for school already. She said she'd be back around three."

"I'll be back around five. Tell her to let me know if she needs any help." Stan stuffed a bite of the freshly buttered biscuit into his mouth.

Mona grinned. "Okay."

He saw the gleam in her eye, but he chose to ignore the unspoken thoughts.

❦

Stan was late getting away from the prison, so when he arrived at Miss Celia's, dinner was in full swing. And so was the commotion in the dining room.

"Yuck!" one of the businesswomen said. "I don't like all this rich food."

"Me, neither," the man across from her replied. "What's wrong with normal food?"

Kathryn appeared at the door leading to the kitchen, a helpless, frantic expression on her face. His protective urge kicked into high gear. Stan crossed the dining room in three long strides, nudging her back into the kitchen.

"What's happening out there?" he asked softly as he stood at the kitchen door.

She looked up at him with fear. "Mutiny."

"I was afraid that might happen."

Kathryn planted her floured fist on her hip and glared at

him. "I just wanted to do something really special for them."

That simple statement reminded him of all Jesus had done for humanity and how little His efforts were appreciated. But this was not the time to tell her that. Instead, he ushered her deeper into the kitchen to make sure no one else could hear.

"I have a simple suggestion," he said. "If you want to offer gourmet food, why don't you give them a choice?"

"That's sort of hard," she said. "And expensive."

"Maybe, but you won't have so many angry people, and you can get a feel for what they want."

"Yeah, but—"

She was interrupted by Mona, who pushed through the kitchen, a huge tray filled with uneaten portions of lamb. "They're mad," Mona said. "That one lady—the one with the big mouth—says she's not staying here next time she comes to New York."

Stan turned to Kathryn whose bottom lip was between her teeth. She needed to make a decision—quick.

"Just a minute," she said before running toward the dining room. She returned a minute later, looking dejected. "I promised them meatloaf tomorrow night. Aunt Celia's recipe."

"I'm sorry, Kathryn," Stan said.

"Yeah, me, too." Kathryn turned her back on him, grabbed a plate from the returned tray, and began scraping the contents into the garbage.

"Whoa, wait a minute," Stan said. "I know some people who would love that food."

"Your prisoners?" she asked sarcastically.

He nodded. "I'll have to bring a little extra for the guards, too."

Kathryn paused then nodded. "Yeah, I guess it's not a good

idea to waste food when there are people who'll eat it, even if they are convicts."

Stan felt a thud in his chest.

⚜

The snowstorm had returned by the next morning, only now there were no signs of it letting up. Stan carried sacks of food to the prison, garnering curious glances from people as he boarded the train. He smiled and nodded but didn't say a word. He was relieved that his favorite guard was on duty so he wouldn't get hassled about bringing in the food.

"Wow!" one of the men in his Bible study said. "Someone can really cook."

As Stan left the prison, one of the guards told him the weather report was pretty harsh. "We're likely to get snowed in for a few days," he said.

The next morning, Stan glanced outside and saw a blanket of white snow hiding the sidewalks and a layer of ice with thick mounds of snow covering the street. He wasn't going anywhere.

"Good thing we ordered extra food," Kathryn said as he arrived at the breakfast table. "All roads in the city are impassable, so Mona and Bonnie can't come to work." She sniffled. "And my graduation ceremony has been put off until everything clears up."

"Have you called your aunt?" he asked.

Kathryn nodded. "She said she took physical therapy twice today, and it wore her out. I feel awful that I can't go see her."

"I'm sure she understands."

"She told me something else. Her physical therapist said she might need to go to a rehab facility for a few months, maybe even up to a year. She's not coming straight home from the hospital."

Stan thought he saw Kathryn's chin quiver. "Will you be able to stick around?"

"Of course. I wouldn't think of doing anything else. Aunt Celia has made so many sacrifices for me, it would be wrong of me to leave."

"Sacrifices," Stan repeated.

"What?" Kathryn stopped and stared at him.

"Life is full of sacrifices."

"What are you talking about, Stan?"

Stan shrugged. "I was just thinking about how Mary and Joseph had to make so many sacrifices when God told them they'd be parents to the Christ child."

"Sounds more like an honor than a sacrifice to me."

"Yes, it was, and fortunately, they saw it that way. But think about it. They had to sacrifice their reputations when Mary became pregnant and they weren't yet married. Then they sacrificed their comfort to travel the distance. Another thing they sacrificed was dignity, parading in front of all those people who knew Mary was about to bear a child. Giving birth in a stable was another sacrifice." After a brief pause, he added, "And you know all the sacrifices Jesus made to witness to His followers."

Kathryn frowned and gulped. "Makes me feel petty."

"I wouldn't say that," Stan argued.

"Then what are you saying?" Kathryn asked.

"Just that the Lord understands and appreciates what it means for you to make sacrifices for the sake of others."

***

The remainder of the week, Kathryn stuck close to the menu her aunt had posted on the kitchen bulletin board. Although she'd accepted the boarders' simple tastes, Stan saw that her shoulders were sagging and her step had lost its bounce. The more he got to know her, the more he cared about her feelings.

"What's wrong, Kathryn?" he asked.

"Nothing."

"Come on. I can tell something's bugging you."

Her jaw tightened; then she spun around. "I called the head chef at the Don Cesar and told him it would be awhile before I could come down there."

"Was he okay with that?" Stan asked.

She rubbed her nose with the back of her hand. "He told me he couldn't wait very long."

"Sounds like he still wants you."

"That would be wishful thinking on my part. I told him to go ahead and bring in another apprentice. I have to stick around here until Aunt Celia returns."

"Trust that the Lord will provide what you're supposed to have." He knew this would be the perfect time for him to tell her about his past, but the words wouldn't come. His fear of her turning away from him overshadowed what he felt he needed to do.

"I'm working on it," she said as she turned back to her work.

❦

Kathryn wasn't sure what had just happened, but she did know that whenever Stan was around, she felt a sense of peace, like everything would be okay, as he'd promised. His faith in God was strong and very evident. He made her want to learn more about God and why He allowed such things to happen. She'd always believed in God, and she knew about Jesus, but she never fully understood the depth of His love for humanity until Stan came along and made it seem so simple.

"You'll be okay, Kathryn," he said. "In fact, you're a very strong woman, just like your aunt."

She smiled. "Thanks."

Later that day, the streets were clear enough for Stan to go to work. "As soon as flights resume, I need to take a trip to Nashville," he told her.

A familiar dread washed over her as she remembered how her father had flitted in and out of her life.

Everything seemed to overshadow her graduation the next day. Wasn't she supposed to be happy? When they were able to come back to work, Mona and Bonnie told her to enjoy her big day.

How could she enjoy it under the circumstances?

When Kathryn arrived at the institute, all the students and teaching chefs were chattering about how their families had struggled to change their plans. They made her painfully aware that she was the only one in the graduating class without someone there to witness the ceremony. She steeled herself against the pain.

At precisely five minutes before seven o'clock, the students lined up in alphabetical order, with Kathryn Anderson at the front of the line. She stood at the edge of the curtain, scanning the crowd, trying to imagine where Aunt Celia would have sat had she been there.

What? She blinked and leaned forward to get a better look. *What is* he *doing here?*

Stan Jarrett sat in the third row, dressed in a suit, and looking up at the stage expectantly. He looked more handsome than ever. If she didn't watch out, she could definitely fall in love with him.

Chapter 3

A momentary joy spread over Katherine as she studied the man who'd brought her comfort over the past several weeks. She wanted to talk to him, but there wasn't time.

After the final name was called, the administrator of the school invited all of the friends and family of the graduates to come up and sample some of the culinary delights. Kathryn hung out on the edge of the stage, watching as Stan made his way up.

Her heart raced as he came up to her. "Congratulations, Kathryn. Your aunt is very proud of you."

"I know she is. Did she put you up to coming?"

"No," he said firmly. "I came on my own. I've never been to a culinary school graduation before."

"And you've always wondered what it was like, right?"

He smiled back. "Something like that." He nodded toward the buffet. "And I'm dying to try that big brown, white, and beige thing in the center of the table."

"That big brown, white, and beige thing is a meringue. C'mon, let's go see what we can grab before the rest of the vultures polish it off."

She led him by the hand to the table. Several of her classmates looked at Stan and offered questioning glances, but no one said anything.

"Did you make any of this stuff?"

Kathryn nodded. "I helped with most of it, but I made the cheesecake by myself."

"Wow!" he said, after sampling the food on his plate. "This is incredible—especially the cheesecake. Can you cook all this?"

She nodded. "I hesitate to admit it, but yes."

"Why do you put it like that?"

"Aunt Celia's boarders, remember?"

"Oh yeah, the boarders. Well, you might want to fix them what they want, but if you ever get the urge to do something fancy, I'm all taste buds."

"That's nice to know. Thanks for the offer."

Being with Stan felt so natural—comfortable even. Stan was really a great guy, and she couldn't deny the tingle she felt when he looked at her with that twinkle in his eye and the mischievous grin.

"Hey, Kathryn," Chef Latour said as he gently placed his arm around her shoulder. "When do you leave for Florida?"

"I'm not going anytime soon."

"What?" Chef Latour said with obvious dismay. "Don't tell me they changed their minds. Let me go call my friend and straighten this out. You will be the best chef in the East, and they should feel privileged you'd consider them."

"Oh, no, that's not it."

Chef Latour glanced at Stan with an accusing glare. "Do you have something to do with this?"

"No, I—"

"It's my aunt," Kathryn blurted. "She fell and has to stay in the hospital."

A look of remorse crossed Chef Latour's face. "Oh my, I'm so sorry. If there's anything I can do, please let me know."

After he left, Stan leaned over and whispered, "Wanna go home?"

Kathryn inhaled, allowing her senses to experience his close proximity and clean scent. She nodded.

"Why don't we walk to the next station?" she said. "I need to get rid of some of this energy."

"If you can handle the cold, then I certainly can." He gently placed his arm around her shoulder, and she allowed herself to snuggle into his warmth.

Conversation between them felt natural. He asked questions about her plans for the future, and she admitted she wasn't sure now. Then she turned the questions back to him.

"Why are you involved in the prison ministry?" she asked.

She felt him tense, but after a few seconds, he relaxed a little. "This is something I feel called to do."

"Wouldn't you reach more people if you became a pulpit preacher?"

"I'm not sure. I talk to a lot of people in jail. If I can bring comfort to hurting people and let them know where they can spend eternity, I feel like I need to continue doing that."

"Those people have done crimes, though. Shouldn't they suffer for the pain they've caused others?"

"Oh, trust me, Kathryn, they're suffering plenty."

"You sound like you feel sorry for them."

"Some of them might even be innocent."

"Come on, Stan. You can't be that naive. People don't get thrown in jail if they've never committed a crime."

"Some do," he argued.

"I don't believe that for a minute."

They walked in silence the rest of the way to Miss Celia's City House. Kathryn knew something had changed between them during the conversation, but she couldn't put her finger on exactly what.

⁂

As they arrived at the boardinghouse, Stan couldn't think of a reason to keep her from going up to her room, although he wanted to be with her just a little longer.

She took one step up, turned, and smiled. "Thanks for coming to the ceremony, Stan. That was very sweet of you."

"I wouldn't have missed it for anything."

Their gazes locked for several seconds before Kathryn turned and ran up the stairs. He felt an odd sensation burning in his gut as she disappeared behind the upstairs wall.

The next morning, Stan stopped off to see Miss Celia on his way to work. She'd just finished breakfast and was wrestling with a newspaper.

"This thing's so big, I almost can't read it anymore," she grumbled.

"Well, good morning to you, too, Miss Celia."

"Sorry." She folded the paper and put it down on the bed beside her. "It's just so frustrating to be in this bed while the whole world is out there moving around."

"I can imagine."

She snorted. "I s'pose it's sort of like how your prisoners feel most days."

"Yes, except they can walk and move around."

"This is worse, huh?" she said. "I just might have to break out of this prison if the doctor doesn't release me soon."

"You can't do that, Miss Celia. I was just kidding."

"I know you were. So how's it going with my niece?"

"She seems to be okay," he said.

"Uh-huh. Tell me another good one. C'mon, Stan. I've known you for a while. I see that hangdog expression you've had since you first walked in here. You can tell me what's on your mind."

He shrugged. "I don't know for sure myself, so how can I tell you? Besides, it's almost time for your therapy, and I have a bunch of inmates waiting to hear the rest of Matthew. I'm reading the New Testament to my small group."

"The whole New Testament?"

"Yes. I just hope I don't get transferred before I'm finished."

"That'll take you forever, but that's okay with me. I like having you here."

"And I like being here."

Stan had gotten almost to the door when she called out his name. He quickly turned and faced her.

"You might want to start thinking of a way to let Kathryn know about your incarceration. I'd love to see the two of you get to know each other better, and she needs honesty."

Miss Celia could see right through him. But after all she'd been through, how could he tell Kathryn he'd spent nearly three months as an inmate?

"I'll look for an opening in conversation," he said.

"Just don't wait too long," Miss Celia advised.

He pursed his lips, offered a crisp nod, then left.

Stan knew he would have been bitter had the Lord not come into his life when he hit rock bottom. He would still be in jail had the robber for whom Stan was mistaken not held up another convenience store. Although he wouldn't wish his experience on anyone, Stan knew the Lord had used it for overall good.

He reflected on how he'd begun his relationship with the Lord. When the group of men from the prison ministry had left Bibles, he'd picked one up and carried it back to his cell because there wasn't anything better to do. As he read and reread the promises of the Lord, Stan's view of life had gradually changed. By the time he was released, he possessed a whole different attitude and purpose for living, and he was eager to serve the Lord. His prayers had been answered, and he'd been given the opportunity through Prison Fellowship.

The train ride to the prison was long, so he had time to think about how to tell Kathryn about his past. But no matter what he said, he knew it would hit her with a jolt and she would put up the shield he'd seen so many times.

After arriving at the prison, he stepped into the first room, took off his belt and shoelaces, and waited for his locker assignment for his personal belongings. He knew the drill. Nothing was allowed on the other side that would enable a prisoner to escape, hurt someone, or commit suicide.

The group waited for him in the visitation area. One of the prisoners had been coming for weeks, while the others were newer and more skeptical. He kept his personal greetings low-key. In prison, trust was one gift that had to be earned—and that often took much longer than in the outside world.

He finished reading the book of Matthew and asked the men if they had any questions. For a while, it appeared no one would say a word, but then one of the newcomers lifted his hand.

"Yes, Rodney?" Stan said. "You have a question?"

"Why didn't Jesus just wipe out all those people who were mocking him? Maybe people would have listened. He didn't have to die like that."

Stan smiled. He'd heard that question before. "One thing I've learned is that God doesn't always take the easy way out. In fact, what he did for mankind by allowing Jesus to be crucified was probably more difficult than anything any of us will have to face."

Another of the prisoners snorted, stuck out his legs in front of him, and slouched down in his seat as he folded his arms, virtually shutting out the world around him. "I don't know about that, man. This place can be pretty rough."

"Yes, I know," Stan agreed. "But imagine how much worse it would be if you had guards taunting you with sticks and then having to walk to your death, carrying a heavy cross, knowing you were about to be nailed to it and left there to die."

"Yeah, that's extreme," the inmate said. "But I'm like Rodney. I don't see why Jesus didn't just perform a miracle and get down from that cross."

"I think the answers to your questions will become clearer as we go deeper into the New Testament."

Later that night, Stan shared the questions with Kathryn. She nodded.

"I've often wondered the same thing," she said. "But then I've also wondered why Adam and Eve could have been so foolish to blatantly disobey God, when they had everything handed to them that they could possibly want."

Stan grinned. "I guess they were acting like spoiled children in the Garden of Eden."

"Sure appears that way," Kathryn said. "And now we all have to suffer."

She'd just given him another opportunity to tell her about his past. He cleared his throat, opened his mouth, and then watched her eyes light up.

"Oh, I forgot to tell you," she said with excitement. "I had some Key limes shipped up from Florida, and I made you a pie this afternoon."

He felt as if someone had knocked the wind out of him. "You're very sweet, Kathryn."

He watched her blush, which left his pulse racing. "I like doing things for you, Stan," she said softly.

Each day, he vowed to discuss his past with Kathryn, but something always came up. Miss Celia became more and more stern with him, showing her disapproval over his silence. He wanted to do the right thing—and he fully intended to. Someday.

"Christmas is coming soon, Miss Celia," he reminded her during one of his daily visits.

"Yeah, and all I want from you is for you to tell my niece about what you went through."

Now he had no choice. "Okay. I'll do it."

"Good boy."

Later that night, after Mona and Bonnie left, Stan joined Kathryn in the kitchen. "Would you like to talk for a little while before bedtime?" he asked.

She nodded, her eyes wide, her smile wider. Stan took a step closer to her. She was particularly beautiful when she smiled, and her kindness touched his heart in a way nothing else could. Suddenly, he felt an overwhelming urge to kiss her.

⁂❦⁃

Kathryn followed him to the sitting room then stopped when he turned toward her. He slowly reached out, took her hand, and kissed the back of her fingers, leaving her senses heightened at the point of contact. There was no doubt she was falling in love with him, and there was nothing she could do to stop it.

"Kathryn," he whispered softly, as he pulled her into his arms. She tilted her face up to his and slowly melted into his embrace, knowing she was about to be kissed.

Chapter 4

As Stan's lips found hers, Kathryn let out a sigh. His kiss was tender—just like the man.

He quickly pulled away from the kiss, which had rendered her incapable of speaking. He led her to the loveseat by the window.

Stan sat in silence for a few moments before he shook his head. "I'm sorry if I upset you, Kathryn."

A chuckle escaped her throat, and she found her voice. "You didn't upset me. I liked it."

"So did I. Very much." He glanced away then turned back to her. "What are you thinking?"

"Nothing."

"Just empty thoughts?"

Kathryn started to nod, but instead, she turned and looked him in the eye. "No. It's just that. . ."

How could she tell him he'd turned her entire world upside down? He totally confused her and made her wish she'd never met him, yet she wanted to be near him all the time.

"Just that *what?*" he asked slowly.

"Nothing," she replied.

As quickly as his smile appeared, it left, and he removed his hands from hers. "We need to move slowly."

Her heart fell. "You're right."

He sat and stared at his steepled hands as if he'd never seen them before. Kathryn's stomach let out a loud rumble.

"Still hungry?" he asked, his voice sounding hoarse.

"No. Just a little nervous. Are you okay?"

Kathryn held her breath as he gazed deeply into her eyes once again. The tugging sensation at her heart was more noticeable than before the kiss. In a way, she regretted it, but the feeling was so nice, she wouldn't have traded it for anything. Conflicting emotions swelled inside her.

"You look like the nervous one," he replied. "Why don't we call it a night? We both have some thinking to do."

The warmth of his lips on hers lingered as she left Stan alone. She knew he didn't want to part ways any more than she did, but it was for their own good. He'd brought her to her senses and let her know without words that his mission was stronger than anything between them.

As she undressed and got ready for bed, all Kathryn could think about was how wonderful and natural it felt to kiss and be kissed by Stan. Kathryn slipped beneath the covers and hunkered down with her head on the soft, down pillow. She shut her eyes and asked God to give her wisdom and the ability to understand what was going on in her life. More things than she could count had cropped up, confusing her and making her wonder if she'd ever accomplish her goal.

She must have fallen asleep soon after she ended her prayer, because when she opened her eyes and blinked, it was light outside. One quick glance at her alarm clock let her know she'd overslept.

Swinging her legs over the side of the bed, Kathryn rubbed

her eyes. She quickly got up, washed her face, brushed her teeth, dressed, and flew down to the kitchen, where Bonnie was scurrying back and forth between the dining room and kitchen. Glancing around the crowded dining room, she noticed one person who wasn't there.

"Where's Stan?"

"He had to go back to Nashville," Bonnie said over her shoulder before disappearing behind the swinging kitchen door.

Kathryn was right on her heels. "What?"

"His supervisor with the ministry called and said he needed to come back. They were shorthanded, and they needed him."

Kathryn felt a quick thud in her chest as that old resentment crept up and caught her off guard. "Well, good," she said sarcastically. "Now maybe we can get some work done."

Bonnie opened her mouth, but then quickly closed it and shook her head. Good thing, too. Kathryn didn't feel like listening to excuses or sympathetic apologies.

"I need to get moving," Kathryn said as she scurried around the kitchen.

Bonnie followed close behind.

When the delivery people came half an hour later, Kathryn had to check the order. Bonnie busied herself by getting lunch ready for the boarders and local businesspeople who came during the week.

After lunch cleanup, Kathryn shoved her arms in her coat. "I need to go see Aunt Celia for a little while. I'll be back in an hour or two."

"Take your time," Bonnie said, then winked and offered an understanding smile.

Kathryn forced herself to smile back, even though she felt

overwhelmed at the moment. She was being thrown so many curveballs lately, and she wasn't sure what to do with them all.

Aunt Celia didn't act the least bit surprised when she told her about Stan leaving. "That's something you'll have to accept about him."

"I know, but. . ."

Kathryn wasn't sure how to say what she felt about Stan. But when she glanced up at her aunt, she had a feeling she didn't have to say anything. Aunt Celia was a smart woman.

Finally, after a moment of silence, Aunt Celia sighed. "All this therapy's wearing me out. I barely have time to read my Bible."

"I wish there was something I could do," Kathryn said.

"I know, sweetheart. But this is only temporary."

"Is there any way you'll be able to come home for Christmas?" Kathryn asked.

Aunt Celia cleared her throat. "I'm working on it. It's still a couple weeks away."

"Want me to talk to the doctors?"

"It's my physical therapist who's holding things up. He's afraid I'll do something stupid and fall again."

"What if I promise to keep an eye on you and not let you do anything risky?"

"That might work," she said with a chuckle. "Someone needs to keep an eye on me, I s'pose."

"I need to get back. Call me later, okay?"

Kathryn had made it to the door when her aunt's voice made her pause. "I'm sorry about Stan."

"Hey, Stan has a job to do. It's no big deal."

"When change comes in life, it only means that the Lord has something else in store for us. You might not see it right away, but it's generally better than anything we could have planned."

As Kathryn left the hospital, she thought about that last comment. She wished she had that kind of faith.

※◎※

Two weeks later, Miss Celia was waiting at her hospital room door, ready to go home. "I thought you'd never get here," she told Kathryn. "Let's go!"

Chapter 5

I'm sure he'd be here if he could," Aunt Celia said as Kathryn wheeled her up the ramp Stan had made and to the front door. Kathryn had talked the physical therapist into releasing her aunt for a few days. It was Christmas Eve, and most of the boarders had gone home to be with their own families. Only a few lonely people stayed behind. "Hold on for a minute, dear. Let me catch my breath before we go inside. It's been a long time."

"I understand," Kathryn said. "This must be hard for you."

"Not hard, exactly. Just overwhelming. I miss being here more than you can ever imagine."

Once they were inside the house, the boarders who were still there greeted them and then went to their own rooms. Aunt Celia let out a long sigh.

"I love this place, but I know I can't hold on to it forever."

"What are you talking about?" Kathryn said, suddenly feeling a tightening in her abdomen. She couldn't fathom Aunt Celia not having her boardinghouse. "You'll be up and around in no time. Your physical therapist even told me you were doing great and should expect a full recovery."

With sadness in her eyes, Aunt Celia studied Kathryn. "I've

worked hard all my life. I've had quite a bit of time to think lately, and I might be ready for something different."

Kathryn felt the urge to change the subject. "Let's go into the kitchen and see if Mona and Bonnie left you a plate."

After they sat down to reheated leftovers, Aunt Celia said the blessing then turned to Kathryn. "I sure do wish Stan could be here."

"Me, too," Kathryn murmured so softly she wasn't sure her aunt could hear.

After they ate dinner, mostly in silence, Kathryn wheeled her aunt to the bedroom she'd prepared downstairs. "If you need me, just ring this," she said, pointing to the bell on the nightstand.

Aunt Celia chuckled. "You're a dear, but you're also a glutton for punishment."

The next morning was Christmas, so Kathryn quickly gathered all the gifts she'd stored in her closet. They were all small things that her aunt could use in the rehab center, like a coin purse to keep her change for the vending machines, a lap robe, a lightweight sweater that she could easily pull on and off, and some paperback novels Kathryn knew she enjoyed.

"You shouldn't have," Aunt Celia said as she opened the last of her gifts. "You did way too much for me. It's enough that you're running this place while I'm laid up."

"I really wanted to do it," Kathryn replied, thrilled her aunt liked everything.

"I have something for you, too," Aunt Celia said. She pulled out the Bible that once belonged to her mother, Kathryn's grandmother. "She'd want you to have this, I'm sure."

Kathryn opened the Bible and lingered on the page with

the family tree. She felt her throat constrict as tears welled in her eyes.

"Dad's name is in here," she said, her voice shaking.

"Yes, so it is," Aunt Celia said softly. "I'm just sorry he never stuck around long enough to listen to our mother share her faith."

"I've always wondered about that. How did Dad miss the wonderful message of God's love?"

Aunt Celia took Kathryn's hand and held it. "This is probably a good time to share some things with you."

Kathryn sat and listened to the story of her wanderlust father, who left home when he was still in his teens. He always thought there was something better out there, and he didn't want to miss out on anything—especially a chance to grab his fortune. She hadn't seen him in years.

"Too bad he was such a liar," Kathryn said.

Aunt Celia sighed and shook her head. "I don't think he started out that way. He just got caught up in the excitement of latching onto a better life, and he had a lapse in judgment."

"A lapse that destroyed his family," Kathryn reminded her.

Aunt Celia leveled her with a serious look. "No, Kathryn. It did injure the family, but it didn't destroy us. You and I still have each other, and we have the love of Christ. I pray every day for your mother, but that's all we can do. Your father may change one of these days, but you have to move forward, even if he doesn't."

Kathryn slowly nodded. "Yes, you're right, Aunt Celia. And I'm thankful to have you."

"Not any more thankful than I am to have you. Being here right now is the best Christmas present I could possibly have."

"Time to get breakfast ready for the lonely boarders,"

Kathryn said. "I picked up a few gifts for them."

"We're doing everything we can," Reverend Martin said when Stan expressed his desire to return to New York right after Christmas. "It's just that we're so shorthanded with the flu going around and everyone wanting time with their families."

"I understand," Stan replied. And he did.

It was mid-January before he managed to go back to New York. He was thankful for the flexibility in his ministry, but it was time to settle down.

Stan's pulse quickened at the sight of Kathryn as she entered the front door and breezed past him, heading for the kitchen. She was a woman on a mission. He liked that about her. Nothing about Kathryn was halfway.

"How's your aunt?" he asked. "Did she have a nice Christmas?"

Kathryn nodded. "It was pleasant. I just wish she could have stayed longer."

Kathryn stood several feet from him, appearing to be intentionally keeping her distance. "I wish I could've been here," he said, feeling awkward.

"Aunt Celia would have like that."

"How about you?" he asked.

Her lower lip trembled as she stared at her hands and then looked up at him. "To be honest, I'm not sure."

Her comment hit him like a ton of bricks. He gulped. "Thanks for being honest, Kathryn."

Her opinion mattered more than he wanted it to. He was falling in love with her, a disaster in the making.

"I have to start dinner, Stan," she said as she backed away

from him and slid out of the room, leaving him alone. He felt like the floor beneath him might open up and swallow him alive.

He finally went up to his room to prepare the lesson for the next day. But, no matter how hard he tried to focus on his work, his conversation with Kathryn kept creeping into his head, forcing him to give up and rely solely on prayer.

Squeezing his eyes shut, he begged for some direction that would knock him upside the head. "Otherwise, Lord, I might miss what you want for me. Amen."

The aroma of spices and seasonings wafted up to him, drawing him back down a couple of hours later.

Stan entered the dining room in time to hear more grumbling among the boarders. He instantly felt the urge to protect her. Although he managed to quiet them for now, he suspected they'd pick up where they left off after he was gone.

He bowed his head and said a prayer of thanksgiving for any food he was fortunate to have.

Kathryn suddenly appeared at the door, holding a platter of some fancy stuffed bird. Stan held his breath, waiting for someone to make a wisecrack, but then Mona was right behind her with a very large meatloaf, sliced and doused with ketchup, just like the other boarders liked it.

"We're giving you a choice," Kathryn announced. "You can have the traditional boardinghouse food, or you can have something different." She looked around the room then added, "Something special."

Stan raised his hand, which Kathryn immediately acknowledged. "May I have some of both?"

Taking his lead, the other boarders requested both. Stan's earlier indignation faded, and he was grateful for the softening of the boarders.

People literally ate double their usual amount. Kathryn stood around and observed in amazement while Stan watched her. He loved seeing her happy, knowing she'd brought something good into the lives of these people. Her earlier dour expression had softened, which lifted his heart.

After the rest of the boarders had gone to their rooms, Stan stood. He picked up his own plate and stacked it with the others at his table. When he appeared at the kitchen door, Kathryn met him and tried to take the stack from him.

"No," he said as he turned away, preventing her from grabbing the plates. "I'm helping clean up."

"You don't need to do that," she said, avoiding his gaze.

"I've already told you before, I like doing this."

Kathryn paused then said, "Okay, suit yourself. Just put 'em in the sink." She left him and went out to the dining room to gather up some more of the dirty dinnerware.

Stan had already begun loading the dishwasher when she came back. "The sink was full," he explained.

Without saying a word, she put her stack on the counter and went back for more. Mona had gone home for the day, so that left Bonnie as the only hired help there. Stan knew if he didn't help, Kathryn would still be cleaning long after Bonnie went home. He might be a slow, but at least they could make progress a little faster.

When they finished, Kathryn wiped her hands on a towel. "Thanks again, Stan. I wish you didn't feel like you had to do that, but I really appreciate it."

"I don't feel like I have to," he replied. "I truly like doing it."

"What's your game, Stan?"

"Game?"

Her forehead crinkled. "You waltz in and out of here like

298

nothing else matters but your prisoners. I don't get it."

"Please, Kathryn, let me explain, okay?"

"Not tonight, Stan. I have a lot on my mind."

He knew now wasn't the right time to press. "Okay, fine, Kathryn, but we do need to talk."

He turned to go up to his room and hesitated as he reached the door.

"Stan?"

Spinning on his heel, he looked at her.

"Do you really think they liked dinner? The boarders, I mean."

"They cleaned their plates, didn't they?"

She offered a hint of a smile, which gave him a tiny speck of hope. "G'night, Stan."

"Good night, Kathryn. Get some rest."

As he watched Kathryn ascend the stairs, Stan knew he'd have no peace until he told her everything. First thing tomorrow.

<hr/>

After breakfast the next morning, Kathryn cast curious glances his way. Finally, she said, "Aren't you supposed to be working?"

"We need to talk."

"Okay," she said, her voice cracking. "Let me finish here."

Once the breakfast dishes had been washed and put away, she turned to him. "You wanted to talk, so talk."

He joined her at the kitchen table. They sat in silence until Stan knew he had to speak. "Okay, this is hard, but I guess I'd better speak my mind. I really like you, Kathryn. I've never felt this way about a woman before."

She managed a shaky grin as she looked him in the eye, her guard not quite as high. "I have a confession to make."

"A confession?"

Kathryn opened her mouth then shook her head. "Nothing. It doesn't matter. Go on. So you were saying you never felt this way before?"

"Yes. But. . ."

"Here it comes," she said, the shield returning. "There's always a *but*."

"Unfortunately, my ministry is based in Nashville. I'm part of a loan program of prison ministers. Until recently, I've been more than happy to travel. But things have changed. I've applied for a job working directly for the prison here in New York, but there's no guarantee it'll come through."

"It probably won't come through," she said sarcastically.

The defeat he heard in her voice broke his heart. "Kathryn," he began as he reached for her hand.

"Don't," she said. "I don't want to hear any more."

"Things would have been much simpler if we'd met under different circumstances. My life is such a mess."

She looked at him straight on, defiance evident in her eyes. "I'm the one who's a mess. Your life is the one with meaning. I bet you've always known exactly where you were going in your life, haven't you?"

Chapter 6

The sudden look of anguish in his eyes tore at her heart. Had she been too hard on him?

"No, not really," he said. "There's something you should know about me."

"And that is?"

"It's something I did. . .or, rather, didn't do in my past."

"I'm not in the mood to play games, Stan. Just spit it out."

She watched him swallow hard before leveling her with a gaze that was downright scary. He looked like a completely different person.

"I spent three months in prison," he blurted as he looked away, "for a crime I didn't commit."

"You what?" she asked. She felt her body stiffen. Surely she'd heard wrong.

"A few years ago, I was working a job I didn't care for, repairing computers in an electronics store. I'd been trying to find something else to do with my life, and I confided in one of the other techs about it. He said he thought I was nuts because we made decent money and quite a few people had been getting laid off. Our jobs were secure, but that didn't affect how I felt about my job."

"How did that get you thrown in jail?" Kathryn asked as she edged away from him.

"I thought he'd forgotten about our talk, but obviously he hadn't. The local convenience store was robbed several weeks later, and when they put the guy's image from the store security videotape on TV, the tech at work thought the robber looked like me. He called the hotline and told them I wasn't happy with my job and that he thought I was the guy who robbed the convenience store."

"How did that get you sent to jail? Job dissatisfaction isn't a crime." She studied him before adding, "And from what I've seen, those videotapes aren't the best in the world. Lots of people have similar features to yours." *But none that came together so well*, she thought.

"No, but when the police came to interview me at work, I wasn't exactly polite about it."

"Did you resist arrest?"

"No," he said with a sardonic chuckle. "In fact, they didn't even arrest me right away. I told them they were barking up the wrong tree, but they insisted I answer their questions. I told them to get out. They told me I had no choice but to cooperate, and eventually, the argument escalated until my boss told me to go home and not to come back."

"That's awful," Kathryn said. "But I don't understand why you didn't cooperate from the beginning. That doesn't sound like you."

"Maybe not now, but back then I had a chip on my shoulder. Until I had a personal relationship with the Lord, I wasn't the most agreeable guy around."

This was news Kathryn needed to pay attention to. From her personal experience, people didn't change. They only hid the truth. At such deception, her father had been the best she'd ever seen—that is, until now.

"They made me go to a lineup," he continued, "and the manager of the convenience store picked me, of all people. Then they hauled me off to jail."

"You said you were only there for three months. That doesn't seem long for armed robbery." Kathryn continued to edge farther away from him.

"The guy who'd actually robbed the store did it again. This time, he was sloppy and got caught. When it came out that he'd robbed the one I'd been accused of, all charges were dropped."

"Did you try to get your old job back?"

"No," he said. "While I was in prison, I developed an interest in the ministry. This might sound strange to you, but I saw that time in prison as a message to change my life. I noticed firsthand that when people have committed a crime and they're caught, they tend to be more open to hearing the gospel."

"That does seem strange. I would have thought the opposite." Kathryn now felt numb. She wasn't sure if she should believe him, but she did know she needed to stay as far away from him as she could get.

"In some people, you'll see extreme bitterness. But in others, once they have nothing to do but think about how they've hurt other people and messed up their own lives, they want to do something to change things. Their vulnerabilities have been exposed, so they tend to go one way or another."

"So that's how you got into the prison ministry, huh?"

"Yep. That's it in a nutshell."

Kathryn hated secrets. And now that she'd learned Stan's secret, she felt betrayed not only by him but by herself. She'd allowed herself to feel something for this man—this ex-con.

Silence fell between them as she mentally processed what he'd told her. Finally, he stood and nodded. "Guess I'd better get on to my room. I have to prepare for tomorrow."

She watched him leave the room, his head hanging. Her limbs felt numb, so she waited several minutes before trying to stand.

⁂

Stan figured it was a mistake to blurt it all out so fast, but once he'd gotten started, he couldn't seem to stop. Okay, so now the ball was in Kathryn's court. He'd have to give her time to sort through all he'd told her. Kathryn obviously didn't understand what he'd gone through, and he had to admit, neither did he. He'd forgiven the man who'd been responsible for his being in jail, but the memories hadn't been as easily erased from his mind.

Flashbacks kept him from sleeping as they haunted him all night. He went down to breakfast feeling like a beaten man. Kathryn did a double take when she saw him, but she didn't give him even a hint of a smile.

On the way to the prison, he stopped off and saw Miss Celia. "Hey, Stan, you look rough." She narrowed her focus then slowly shook her head. "You told Kathryn, didn't you?"

"Afraid so," he replied. "And now I know it was a mistake. I should have waited."

"Did you tell her all the details?"

"As much as I could."

"Then don't worry about it."

He huffed. "That's easy for you to say, Miss Celia. She loves you no matter what."

"Well, that might be so, but it has nothing to do with the two of you."

"I know." He leaned over and gave her a quick peck on the cheek. "Gotta run. The men are waiting to hear more about Jesus."

"How's the New Testament coming along?" she asked.

"Good. They've asked some thought-provoking questions."

"Yeah," she said. "And I bet some of them are designed to trip you up."

"I'm sure."

"Hold on a minute, Stan. I want you to tell me something."

Thinking Miss Celia had a question about his ministry, he stepped back into the room. "Okay, whatever you want to know."

"Do you love my niece?"

He froze in place. That simple question—those five words—had stunned him.

"Uh. . ." He glanced down at his feet. "Yes, I do, Miss Celia."

"Well, you better figure out how to let her know that, too. I can only stall her so long."

"Stall her? I don't want you to do that."

Miss Celia offered one of her I-know-what-I'm-doing lopsided grins. "Looks to me like you might need some help."

"I appreciate the offer, but I think we should let the Lord work through this without any interference."

A contrite expression instantly formed on her face. She nodded. "Yes, you're absolutely right. I'll behave."

He offered a grin and a wave. "Thanks for the offer, though. It's very sweet of you."

"Sweet?" she said with a cackle. "That's a new one." She paused for a second before looking coyly up at him. "You think I'm sweet?"

"Yes," he replied. "You're one of the sweetest people I've ever met."

Her eyes misted over. "You're a good boy, Stan. Most people would have come out of your situation with hardened hearts. But you've taken lemons and made lemonade. I wish more people were like you."

"Don't go getting all mushy on me, Miss Celia. You know that makes me uncomfortable."

She giggled. "It's fun making a man squirm."

"You're too much," he said as he left the room.

About halfway through the Bible study with the inmates, he was interrupted by one of the men who'd attended since the beginning but hadn't opened his mouth until now.

"Hey, Rev, I got a question for you," the man said, as he folded his arms over his chest and narrowed his eyes.

"What's that, George?"

"You got something else on your mind?" He shook his head and smirked. "Looks like you might be thinkin' about some woman or somethin'."

Might as well be honest. These guys would see right through him.

"Yeah, afraid so."

All the men hooted and made cat sounds. "We knew it. You can't hide nothin' from the boys."

"Okay, so now that you're on to me, would you mind praying for me?" he asked.

They all exchanged glances then nodded. George spoke up. "Ya gotta tell us exactly what to pray for, man, or we won't know what to say to God."

Chapter 7

Stan told them just enough to get them all smiling then said he really needed to go. "Hey, man, you need to let the lady know how you feel," George said. "Women like stuff like that."

"Thanks, George. I'll do my best."

His cell phone rang the second he got it back from the prison guards. "We need you back in Nashville, Stan."

A knot formed in his chest. "What happened?"

"Some of the prisoners got a little rowdy, and now Joe's in the hospital."

"I'll be there as soon as I can."

Stan had always known he was in a high-risk profession, but this was the first time he'd personally known someone who'd gotten hurt. He said a prayer for his friend Joe and then went inside to let Kathryn know he was leaving again.

"Just let us know when we need to get your room ready again," she said without any sign of emotion.

<hr/>

Kathryn's conviction had now officially been reinforced. She never should have let her guard down—not even a smidgen.

Stan wasn't any better than her father; in fact, he may have been worse. Her father had never claimed to be a godly man.

Why Aunt Celia had insisted on her keeping a room for Stan, Kathryn couldn't imagine. They had a waiting list of boarders. But she'd learned early on that arguing with Aunt Celia wouldn't do her a bit of good.

Each time Stan showed up over the next several months, Kathryn forced herself to keep her distance. Finally, autumn came and went, and Aunt Celia was making sounds about coming home before Christmas—permanently. The physical therapist at the rehab center was aggressively pushing her to work hard.

A whole year had passed since Aunt Celia's fall. Stan continued to travel back and forth between New York and Nashville.

"We have some things to discuss," Aunt Celia said a week before she was due to go home.

"I need to get a downstairs room ready for you."

"That's great, but my room is the least of my concerns. I've been doing quite a bit of thinking." She glanced down then added, "About the City House."

"Not about *giving up* the City House, I hope," Kathryn replied.

"Yes, dear, that's exactly what I want to discuss. I've had some offers, and I don't want to let an opportunity get away."

Kathryn felt that sick feeling as she let herself imagine her aunt retiring. She couldn't look her in the eye.

"Have you been reading your Bible, Kathryn?"

"Not only have I been reading my Bible, you'll be pleased to know I've been going to your church. Everyone wants to stop by when you get home."

"All my friends at church are such dears," Aunt Celia said. "They've been visiting and bringing me presents."

Kathryn chuckled. "Don't expect to keep getting all those presents after you get home."

"I hope they don't bring me anything because, to be honest with you, it's embarrassing. I never know what to say."

◈

Stan was waiting for Kathryn when she returned to the boardinghouse. "Your room's ready," she said flatly.

"Can we talk?"

She shrugged. "About what?"

He looked at her then sighed. "Never mind. You don't look like you're in the mood for a chat—at least not with me."

Kathryn wished she didn't feel that familiar tug at her heart when he looked at her like that. Finally, she conceded. "Maybe later, okay?"

A flicker of hope appeared in his eyes. "Great. Tonight?"

"Fine. Tonight after dinner."

They had the routine down from before. Eat dinner, gather and wash dishes, and head to the sitting room. Kathryn was there first, and she started the conversation.

"Aunt Celia is coming home soon, and she's talking about selling this place."

◈

"When?" Stan said.

"Day after tomorrow," Kathryn replied.

"And she wants to sell this place?"

Miss Celia had discussed several options she'd been considering since her accident, and although he'd miss having this wonderful place to stay, he thought she might be right—maybe it was time to move on to the next phase of her life. She needed a change.

Kathryn looked at him and nodded. Her expression was rigid. Determined. Rehearsed.

"Tell you what, Kathryn," he said. "I'll tell the guys at the prison you need me here, and I'll stick around to make sure everything's okay when she returns."

He knew he'd said the wrong thing the second he saw her jaw tighten even more. "I don't need you to do that. I'm perfectly capable—"

"I know you're capable, but I want to be here. Miss Celia has done so much for me, I can't imagine not helping at least a little."

He watched as she thought it over, now realizing he hadn't given her much choice. "Okay, I guess that would be all right. She'll probably like it."

"Do we need to get a downstairs room ready?" he asked. "She's always had the room on the second floor, but that won't work. At least not yet. It might be a while before she can navigate the stairs."

Kathryn groaned. "I'll have to do some shuffling of guests. There's nothing available on the main floor."

"I thought Gus was leaving."

"Not for another week," Kathryn said. "But his room would be perfect. I'll talk to him in the morning after breakfast."

"You'd better get some rest," Stan advised. "You'll need it. I have a feeling you'll be very busy while she's here."

She sighed. "No doubt."

As Kathryn ascended the stairs, he saw her shoulders sag, the weight of the world dragging her down. He wished he could say or do something to make her feel better, but he knew from experience there were just some things that she had to handle on her own.

Kathryn shut her bedroom door behind her before slumping into the chair by the door. She'd had her whole life planned, but nothing was turning out right. To top it off, she felt guilty for dreading the time Aunt Celia would be home.

The more she thought about everything, the more confused she got. Her head ached, and she felt the weight on her shoulders as burdens kept piling on, brick by brick.

With a heavy sigh, Kathryn stood and got ready for bed. After crawling beneath the covers, she rummaged around and found her Bible, then settled back on her propped up pillows.

Aunt Celia had called and mentioned something about the book of Luke, chapter twenty-three, verses forty through forty-one. Kathryn found the verses. After reading the scripture ahead of it, she understood that this was where Jesus was talking to the criminals when he'd been nailed to the cross. After one of them had hurled insults, the other said, " 'Don't you fear God,' he said, 'since you are under the same sentence? . . . For we are getting what our deeds deserve. But this man has done nothing wrong.' "

Kathryn turned the Bible upside down on her comforter, shut her eyes, and thought about how this verse applied to her life. She knew Jesus was the perfect example of how people should be; her aunt had taught her that early in life. Aunt Celia was the wisest woman she knew, and she was also loving in a totally unconditional way. She never expected anything in return from anyone, including her own brother.

After being disappointed time after time by her parents, Kathryn had a difficult time trusting anyone—except Aunt Celia, who'd never let her down. Her father had lied his way through everything with her and her mother, and her mother had gotten into community theater as a hobby. When she'd been discovered by the man who opened the tiny dinner theater on the edge of town, she jumped at the chance to get paid and call herself a professional actress. From then on, she left Kathryn home alone most nights.

The summers she spent with Aunt Celia were the only times Kathryn felt as though someone cared enough about her to give her the attention she needed. Her aunt always sent her home with recipes, which Kathryn then embellished. The first positive words out of her mother's mouth were, "Wow, girl, you cook like the chefs in the fine restaurants of New York."

That set Kathryn to thinking about a future in the restaurant business. If she could do this on her own without any training, she wondered what she could do if she had the best teachers in the world.

After high school, she remained at home while she went to the community college and got a liberal arts degree, worked retail, and saved her money for her goal.

Aunt Celia had been delighted and encouraged her to follow her dream. Even her mother thought it sounded exciting.

So Kathryn embarked on a journey that she assumed would be filled with obstacles, but she'd determined to overcome them. And she had. Until now.

All the what-ifs fluttered through her mind. What if she never had an opportunity to work with a great chef, like the one at the Don Cesar? What if Aunt Celia needed more from her than she could give? What if Stan was right about God's plan?

Squeezing her eyes shut, she chewed on her bottom lip as she silently prayed.

Lord, thank You so much for the blessing of Aunt Celia. She has been my protector and anchor during troubled times. And thank You for the past three years and allowing me to complete the culinary program. That was truly a blessing. I'm coming to You with a heaviness on my heart and have no idea what to do with my life. Please give me some direction and guidance so I don't keep digging deeper into frustration. And Lord, while you're at it, I pray that You'll enlighten me and give me a peace about whatever relationship You want me to have with Stan. My attraction to him frightens me, and I know that's not what You want. I know You don't want me making deals with You, and that's not what this is, but I do intend to listen more closely in church and read my Bible more often. Your word is so rich and filled with answers I haven't exactly paid attention to in the past. I want to live a life that is pleasing to You, Lord. Amen.

Kathryn knew her prayer was awkward, but she also knew the Lord understood. She was taking baby steps in her walk with the Lord, and there were times she staggered.

The next day was filled with meal preparation, washing sheets, vacuuming the foyer, dusting, and getting the downstairs room ready for Aunt Celia. One of the boarders was happy to move upstairs, since he'd been a regular customer at the City House for years. He even helped them move the furniture around to make it easier to maneuver the wheelchair.

Finally, the day was over, the last dish from dinner put away, and all the boarders in their rooms—except Stan. He remained behind, obviously waiting for Kathryn.

"I have to go back to Nashville before Christmas," he said without pause.

Okay, so what else is new? She just stared at him.

"I did promise to be here to help with your aunt."

"Yes, I know, but I can deal with it." Just like she'd had to deal with her father's empty promises throughout her childhood.

He glanced down and stared at his shoes as silence fell between them. Kathryn figured there was nothing left to say, so she turned to go to her room.

"No, wait," he said quickly.

She spun around. "What?"

"Kathryn, I'm really sorry. I'll be here for a little while, though, so I can make sure all the heavy lifting is done before I go."

"You don't have to," she said.

"You're right, I don't. But I want to."

She sighed. "Okay, whatever."

This time, he let her go. She walked slowly up the stairs, but he didn't try to stop her. She'd been at Miss Celia's for a year, yet she still couldn't figure out what was going on with Stan.

As hard as it was to walk away, it was even harder to kneel beside her bed. She lowered her face into her hands and let the frustrations take over. One thing Kathryn didn't do, though, was cry. She'd learned long ago that crying didn't do her any good. Besides, if someone saw her red-eyed and tear-streaked, they would feel sorry for her, and she hated pity.

Finally, she stammered over another prayer, this one expressing her disappointment but willingness to continue to try to walk in the path He had in mind for her—obviously without Stan.

"I've ordered a car to take her home," Stan said first thing the next morning.

"I was going to call a cab."

"Humor me. This is my way of paying her back for being so good to me."

"Okay," she said as numbness flooded her. "What time?"

He glanced at his watch. "I called when I got up this morning, and the nurse said the doctor would probably release her around ten."

"Fine."

Stan looked at her in silence for several seconds and then turned and walked away. She hated that tugging sensation at her chest as he disappeared from her life once again.

The excited murmurs from the guests showed how much Aunt Celia was loved. A couple of the men hung streamers, and one of the women had made a "WELCOME HOME, MISS CELIA" banner on her laptop computer and portable printer. Those who could arrange it took the day off from business meetings and school so they could greet Aunt Celia when she arrived. Kathryn pretended to be in a festive mood right along with the rest of them.

"Mind if I go to the rehab center with you?" Stan asked.

"Suit yourself." She didn't look him in the eye as they headed outside.

When they arrived at the rehab center, Aunt Celia was in her last therapy session. All the nursing assistants and technicians hugged her, saying to call and let them know how she was doing. True to form, Aunt Celia invited them to the City House for dinner one night soon, saying, "I'm sure my niece wouldn't mind making something fabulous. She's a trained chef, ya know."

The pride in her voice boosted Kathryn's mood. It was nice having someone recognize her talent rather than hearing the complaints about the "fancy cooking."

"Ready to hit the road?" Stan asked as he gripped the wheelchair handles and wheeled her out to the waiting car.

"You got that right. I'm ready to bust outta this joint."

The boardinghouse was suspiciously still as they pulled up in front. "It's good to be home," Aunt Celia said softly. "I hardly got any rest at the hospital."

Those words were barely out of her mouth when the door flung open and all twelve guests piled out onto the front porch. "Surprise!" they yelled. "Welcome home, Miss Celia!"

She covered her mouth with her hands as tears streamed down her cheeks. This was the first time Kathryn had ever seen her aunt cry, and if she hadn't looked away, she would be sobbing right along with her.

Chapter 8

S tan glanced at Kathryn and winked. She looked away and tried to blend in with the others.

Kathryn noticed Aunt Celia's smile beginning to fade after an hour of everyone talking at the same time. "Why don't we take you to your room for a while?" she whispered. "You look like you could use the rest."

Aunt Celia nodded gratefully. "You're right. I'm exhausted."

"Make way for Miss Celia," Gus said as he grabbed the wheelchair handles and pushed toward her room. He got to the door then nodded to Kathryn. "Why don't you take over from here? I don't want to force my way into a lady's room."

Aunt Celia appeared to bite back a smile, but she didn't say a word as Kathryn took over. Once the bedroom door was shut, with Kathryn and Aunt Celia inside, they looked at each other and laughed.

"This is all so sweet, but I was hoping to get a little shut-eye before having to face the crowd."

"I know," Kathryn said apologetically. "But you know how they are. They love you so much, they couldn't wait to see you."

"Wake me in time to help out with dinner," Aunt Celia said.

"You're kidding, right?"

"No, I'm not kidding. I'm back now, and I plan to do the work I've been doing practically all my life."

"If you insist," Kathryn said, knowing there was no point in arguing.

"What's going on between you and Stan?"

Kathryn did a double take. "What do you mean?"

"I've seen the way you two have been avoiding each other. Something's up."

"Nothing's up. He told me he was going back to Nashville in a few days. I think his time here has come to an end."

"Oh, I see."

Kathryn helped Aunt Celia to her bed; then she leaned over and planted a kiss on her cheek. "Get some rest. I'll be back in a few hours."

"Don't forget."

"Sleep tight." Kathryn shut the door behind her, looking down at the floor. She'd taken two steps without looking up when she was stopped by a shadow that suddenly appeared in the hallway. She blinked as she glanced toward the movement.

"Is she all squared away?" Stan asked. He took up half the hallway with his presence.

With a nod, Kathryn replied, "She wants me to wake her to help with dinner." She hoped he couldn't hear her heart pounding.

"That woman is a human dynamo. Nothing stops her, does it?"

"Never has," Kathryn said as she tried to edge around him. He paused then stepped to the side to let her pass.

As she brushed past him, she held her breath. His nearness unnerved her.

Once she was out of his sight, Kathryn leaned against the

wall. The instant she'd seen Stan standing in the hall looking at her, her knees had weakened, and she felt that odd sensation in the pit of her stomach. Now she barely had the strength to stand. Even imagining him in prison and remembering how he'd deserted her time after time didn't erase her desire to be with him. Avoiding him was the only way to get past that.

Dinner was a major production, since she wanted Aunt Celia to be proud of the fact that she could handle being in charge of the kitchen. An hour before dinner was to be served, Kathryn went to get her aunt.

"Hello, dear." Aunt Celia was sitting up in her bed and brushing her hair when Kathryn entered the room.

"You're awake."

"I got plenty of rest. I'm so happy to be here, I almost can't be still."

"I'm happy to have you back," Kathryn replied. "And so is everyone else."

They'd barely made it to the kitchen when Aunt Celia took control. "Put me to work."

Kathryn was amazed at how quickly her aunt had adjusted, and she said so. "I've been doing this practically all my life," Aunt Celia reminded her. "It's in my blood."

"You're amazing," Kathryn said.

Aunt Celia looked at her with a contemplative expression. "*God* is amazing. I'm letting Him do His work through me."

"Yes, God is amazing, isn't He?"

"So, how's your Bible reading coming along, Kathryn?"

"Just fine. I've been paying close attention whenever some-one mentions a verse," she said. "I'm using your mother's Bible."

"Good girl. That's what I was hoping you'd do." Aunt Celia

turned toward Bonnie and held out a bowl. "Here's the sauce. Let me take a look at the cake you're working on."

She quickly took the helm in the kitchen, which Kathryn was more than happy to let her have.

A party atmosphere hung over dinner, and Aunt Celia clearly enjoyed herself. But after the last of the boarders went to their rooms, she sighed.

"That was exhausting," she said. "I don't remember it being like this."

Stan was by her side in a flash. "That's because you were used to being in the thick of things."

"I suppose," she said. She sniffed and wheeled her chair to the kitchen door. "I'd like to help clean up, but I'm not sure I can do much."

"Not tonight," Mona said. "You're supposed to relax on your first night home. We'll clean up."

"Are you sure?"

Kathryn noticed her aunt didn't argue, which meant she had to be bone-tired.

"Positive," Mona replied. "Stan, you help Kathryn while I take Miss Celia back to her room."

Bonnie had to leave early, so Stan joined Kathryn in the kitchen. "Are you okay?" he asked.

"I'm fine."

"Okay, I won't push. I'm leaving in three days. I was sort of hoping. . ." He looked at her but didn't finish his sentence.

"Hoping what?"

Quickly turning his back to her, he said, "Nothing. Let's get this mess cleaned up, okay?"

By the time Mona returned from helping Aunt Celia, they'd washed all the dishes and most of the pots and pans.

Mona nudged Stan out of the way and told him that he could leave now.

After he was gone, she turned to Kathryn. "Everything will work out like it is supposed to."

"Yes, I know."

"God's plan is always greater than anything we can imagine."

Kathryn nodded as she lifted the scouring brush. They finished working side by side in silence.

For the next couple of days, Kathryn did her best to avoid Stan. But on the morning of his departure, he cornered her.

"I have something for you," he whispered.

"For me?"

"Yes," he said. He handed her a wrapped package. "Open it after I leave. I think it'll come in handy when you have questions."

Kathryn stood there and looked at the package she held in her hand. He reached out and gently touched her cheek. She quickly glanced up at him.

"Kathryn," he said softly, "you're a very good woman. I wish things could be different between us."

She couldn't speak. His touch was soft yet full of meaning— just like his words.

Chapter 9

For a moment, she thought he might try to kiss her. But he didn't. Instead, his lips twitched into a slight smile, and he tweaked her nose.

"I'll see you again soon, I hope," he told her. "I really care about you, Kathryn."

All she could do now was watch him as he walked away from her—out of her life—probably forever. All hope she had of things being different was gone.

Before going to her own room, she decided to check up on her aunt. "Come chat for a few minutes," Aunt Celia said, patting the bed beside her.

Kathryn did as she was told.

"What's that?" Aunt Celia asked, pointing to the package.

"A gift from Stan," Kathryn replied.

"About Stan," Aunt Celia began. Kathryn stiffened but remained seated. "What he said about his past is one hundred percent accurate. Before I allowed a former convict to stay in my boardinghouse, I had him checked out. He's a very good boy with a heart for Christ."

"You had him checked out?" Kathryn asked.

"Yes, of course I did. Running a boardinghouse is a huge

responsibility. I can't risk the safety of my boarders by letting just anyone stay here."

Kathryn instantly felt ashamed of herself for doubting Stan. "I should have known."

"Good night, sweetheart. I'll say a prayer for you, and you do the same for me."

Later that night, with nervous fingers, Kathryn tore into the gift Stan had left. It was a Bible concordance, with a bright blue cover and her name inscribed in gold lettering. He could not have given her a more thoughtful gift.

She lost track of time as she looked up all the questions she'd had about forgiveness, mercy, and grace. The verses she read made God's message very clear—that only through Him can we have a full life. And it involved total trust in the Lord and not in man.

It was past midnight when she finally snuggled under the covers and nestled her head on the pillow. Regrets filled her conscious thoughts. Maybe her relationship with Stan would have been different if she hadn't endured such a painful childhood. But then again, look at what he'd faced when being falsely accused. So what if her father hadn't been there when she'd needed him. It wasn't a good thing, but she'd survived. Now it was up to her to follow Christ and let go of her tortured past. She didn't have the right to transpose her hard feelings toward her father onto Stan, which was what she'd been doing since she'd learned about his past. She fell asleep wishing she'd allowed herself to follow God's lead with Stan.

The next several days were filled with a flurry of holiday arrangements. Most of the boarders planned to return to their homes.

Kathryn noticed her aunt's sincerity and warmth and how

well other people responded to her. Aunt Celia was a living, breathing example of what Christ wanted his followers to be like.

The days passed quickly, and one by one the people left Miss Celia's City House. The place grew very quiet. There wasn't much work for Mona and Bonnie, so Aunt Celia alternated their days off.

"Do you ever worry about anything, Aunt Celia?" Kathryn asked one evening as they sat in front of the fireplace in the sitting room.

"Sometimes," Aunt Celia admitted. "But I know I'm being watched after, so I pray about it, and let go."

"I'd like to be more like that," Kathryn said. "I worry way too much."

"You're right," Aunt Celia agreed. "You do worry too much. Just keep praying about it, and let Him work in your heart."

In spite of the fact that they only had a couple of boarders in the house, Aunt Celia insisted on decorating for Christmas. She did what she could by herself and told Kathryn where to put lights and holly.

"I think that wreath will look much better over there," she said, pointing to the door.

Suddenly, as if on command, the door opened. Aunt Celia turned to Kathryn with a curious glance then turned back to the door.

In walked Stan, grinning and bearing a stack of gifts that towered above his head. He peeked around his armload of packages. "Merry Christmas, Miss Celia. You didn't think I'd be able to stay away during this joyous time, did you?"

"Stan!" Aunt Celia squealed with delight. "Will you be here for Christmas?"

"No, I'm afraid not," he replied. "I'm leaving right after the Christmas Eve services. I'm scheduled to fly back to Nashville late Christmas Eve."

"This is wonderful, Stan," Aunt Celia said. "At least we have you for part of the holiday." She turned to Kathryn and winked. "Right, Kathryn?"

"Uh, right." Kathryn looked around, trying to find something to focus on besides Stan's penetrating gaze.

"Put those boxes down and come help us decorate the rest of this house."

Stan did as he was told. By dinnertime, the entire house was decorated in greenery, tiny white lights, and red velvet bows. Kathryn loved all the external trappings of Christmas. And now that she'd been studying her Bible, she understood the depth of what the celebration was truly about.

Stan could tell something was different about Kathryn, so he kept his distance until he had a better idea of what was going on with her. When he'd gotten the call about doing the sermon in New York, he'd jumped on it—mainly because it gave him another opportunity to see Kathryn.

"We're due for a terrible storm," Aunt Celia said during dinner. "I've heard we may get up to two feet of snow."

"That's pretty rough," Stan said. "But as long as public transportation continues to run, we should be okay."

"I don't think that'll be a problem," Aunt Celia said.

"I'm fine as long as I can get to the prison on Christmas Eve." He placed his fork on his plate and looked down. "I'll have to leave for the airport directly from the jail if I want to make my flight."

"Do you have to leave right away?" Miss Celia asked.

He sighed and nodded. "You know how it is."

Kathryn was very quiet through dinner. When the last person finished dessert, she jumped up and started gathering dishes.

"Need some help?" he asked.

"Not really," Kathryn said as she disappeared behind the swinging door.

"Don't ask, Stan," Miss Celia said. "Just do it."

"I think she's avoiding me."

"Of course she is. That girl's been through a lot. You'll have to prove yourself to her."

"I shouldn't have to prove myself to anyone," he argued.

Miss Celia's shook her head and gestured for him to follow her. "We need to talk," she told him.

Once they were sure no one was behind them, Miss Celia instructed him to close the door to the sitting room. "Apparently, there are some things you don't understand about my niece."

He shrugged. "Maybe you're right, but I do know she's determined to be a successful chef."

"My brother really did a number on her. He not only spent time in prison, he lied to her constantly."

"He lied? About what?"

"You name it, he lied about it. He kept promising to come back for her and her mother. He came back a couple of times, but he only stuck around until he had enough money to leave again."

"She told me about her father going to jail. That's hard on a kid. I see it all the time. At least she had her mother."

Miss Celia snickered. "What did she tell you about her mother?"

"Kathryn said she's an actress in local theater."

"Dinner theater in Boise, Idaho," Miss Celia said with disdain. "That's not exactly the most family-friendly profession a mother can have. She was gone all the time and often left Kathryn home alone until the wee hours of the night. When Kathryn got up, her mother was always sound asleep. They were like two ships passing in the night."

"That's even worse than I realized." No wonder she acted so distant each time he announced he was leaving.

Miss Celia sighed. "I tried to make things better for her when I had her here during the summers. I taught her how to cook because that mother of hers can't even boil an egg."

"She did mention something about having to cook her own meals, but she doesn't seem to have minded."

"You're right," Miss Celia agreed. "She's always been a natural in the kitchen. Unfortunately, she doesn't see the value in a simple, home-cooked meal. Her mother was pretentious, and she loved ordering gourmet foods, which was what Kathryn was brought up eating when she was at home. When she came here, she always doctored up everything I cooked for her."

"There's nothing wrong with being a gourmet chef," Stan said in Kathryn's defense.

"That's true. But there are times when I wish Kathryn would relax a little and not be so intense about her life. She wants to force things, when she needs to be quiet and pay attention to what the Lord wants for her."

"I think she's heading in that direction," Stan said.

"Well, she has been reading her Bible—and that concordance you gave her."

"I need to talk to her."

"You're a good boy, Stan," Miss Celia said. Was that a guilty glimmer in her eye?

"Thanks," he said. "I think."

She tilted her head back and let out a deep chuckle. "You think I'm up to something, don't you?"

"Miss Celia," he replied, "now that you bring it up, I *know* you're up to something."

"Smart boy."

Kathryn was wiping her hands on a towel right when Stan wheeled Miss Celia's chair into the kitchen. Miss Celia didn't give him a chance to say a word.

"Why don't the two of you go string some popcorn in the front room? I want to spend a little time alone in the kitchen."

Stan watched as Kathryn's eyes quickly developed a look of fear and helplessness. He wanted to give her an out, but he wasn't sure how to do it with Miss Celia sitting there glaring at them, almost as if daring either of them to argue.

Chapter 10

Kathryn finally nodded. "Okay, but I need to go to bed soon. I haven't finished my shopping, so I'm getting up early to get my work done."

"Don't worry about that, sweetie. There's not much to do around here when we only have a few guests."

Kathryn didn't utter another word as she quickly dropped the towel and headed toward the sitting room, where Miss Celia had instructed them to put the bowls of popcorn earlier. Stan was right behind her, unsure of what they'd talk about. He didn't want to tell her what he'd just discussed with her aunt, since he hadn't had time to digest all the information yet.

"Think we'll have a white Christmas?" Kathryn asked, breaking the silence between them.

"I hope so."

He studied her face as she picked up a kernel of corn and stabbed it with the needle. He wondered what she was thinking.

They strung popcorn in silence, with occasional comments about the weather for nearly an hour.

"I think this is enough," she finally said as she stood and carefully placed the strung popcorn in the bowl. "I'll ask Aunt Celia where she wants this hung, and then I think I'll go to bed."

Stan stood and followed her to her aunt's room, where she rapped on the door. Miss Celia had somehow managed to get herself into bed. She was propped up reading the Bible.

"Whatcha reading, Miss Celia?" Stan asked.

"Isaiah," she replied. "Chapter fifty-three is mighty powerful."

"That it is," Stan agreed.

"Aunt Celia, what would you like us to do with this?" Kathryn asked, holding up the bowl of strung popcorn.

"Just put that in some plastic bags in the kitchen," she instructed Kathryn. "We can hang that tomorrow."

⁂

Kathryn was too aware of Stan's presence as they headed upstairs to their rooms. When she got to the landing, she turned to face him.

"Thanks for all your help, Stan."

"My pleasure," he said, standing there looking down at her, his hands shoved into his pockets. He didn't look like he was eager to go anywhere.

Thoughts and emotions swirled inside her. Her resolve to accept Stan at face value hadn't been tested, and she wasn't sure what to do next.

"Do you have a big Christmas planned with your family?" Kathryn asked.

"No, not really. We generally just have a small get-together, and we exchange gifts. Most of the time, we go to Christmas Eve service together the night before, but things are a little different this year, with my ministry being what it is." His words were slow and slightly stilted, showing his discomfort.

"I bet it's hard on you."

"I'm fine with it. I don't get too hung up on expectations."

"Good night, Stan," Kathryn said, as she reluctantly turned her back and slipped into her room.

As the door closed behind her, she heard him say, "Good night, sweet Kathryn."

She crossed the room, sat on the edge of her bed, lifted her Bible, and turned to the same chapter her aunt had been reading. As she got ready for bed, she pondered the message and felt the impact from the words. With all of the Christmas decorations and festivities around her, Kathryn knew how easy it was to get lost in the worldly view of the season. She shut her eyes and began to pray.

> *Lord, You have revealed yourself to me in a way I never understood until now. All my life, I have tried to figure everything out on my own. But now, my eyes have been opened, thanks to Aunt Celia and. . .Stan. You have put me in the position of having to be still and listen, and for that, I thank You. Please continue to make my way clear and keep me close to You, Lord. Amen.*

When Kathryn awoke the next morning, she shivered. There was a slight break between the curtain panels, revealing the light dusting of snow that had accumulated on the pane and the pile of white fluff on the sill. Pulling her blanket to her chin, she sat up slightly to see if the snow was still falling.

"Whoa!" she said as she realized it was not only snowing, it was coming down fast.

She leaned over, grabbed her robe off the footboard, and then slipped her arms into it while remaining under the covers. A deep chill hung in the air, making her skin tingle as she quickly stuck out her feet and slid them into her big, fuzzy slippers. This was one of those mornings it was hard to get out of bed, but she had things to do.

Kathryn managed to shower and dress in record time, since she didn't want to be late getting a warm breakfast on the table. Aunt Celia was in the kitchen, waiting for her.

"G'morning, sweetie," Aunt Celia said. "The coffee will be ready in a few minutes."

The aroma of Aunt Celia's blueberry muffins—Kathryn's favorite—hung in the air. The coffeepot popped and sputtered as it brewed. Kathryn found comfort in the familiar morning sounds and smells.

"How did you manage to do all this?" Kathryn asked. "Did Mona come in?"

"No, dear, I did it by myself. But it wasn't too hard, since the girls put everything within my reach."

Kathryn remembered that Mona had suggested they do this, knowing Aunt Celia thrived on being independent. She said it would make Miss Celia crazy if she couldn't do a few things for herself.

"Have you looked outside?" Kathryn asked as she sat down across from her aunt to wait for the coffee.

"I sure have. It's lovely, isn't it?"

"Yes," Kathryn agreed. "And very cold. I wonder if Stan will be able to get around in all this."

"I was wondering the same thing." Aunt Celia frowned. "When I turned on the news this morning, the weather forecaster said there was some concern about having to shut down the airport. This is only the beginning of the storm."

Kathryn stiffened. "What'll he do?"

Aunt Celia shook her head. "Nothing he can do but stick

around here a few more days."

"Won't that mess up his plans?"

"Of course it will, but it's out of his hands. He'll be fine."

"Wow!" said a male voice from the kitchen door.

Both Kathryn and Aunt Celia turned around as Stan took a step toward them. Kathryn's pulse quickened.

"Have you looked outside?" he asked.

"Of course we have," Aunt Celia replied. "Help yourself to some coffee."

"Looks like we'll have our white Christmas after all," he said. "I need to leave for the jail early. It might take a little longer to get there."

Aunt Celia palmed the wheels of her chair, turning it around. "I need to go to my room for a little while. Kathryn, would you mind cooking some sausage links?"

"Sure, Aunt Celia. I'll be glad to fix some."

After she was gone, Stan put his coffee mug down on the table and leaned toward Kathryn. "You do realize you're the daughter your aunt never had, don't you?"

Kathryn nodded. "She's always been very good to me. We're closer than most mothers and daughters."

"You're very fortunate, you know."

"Yes."

"Your aunt's not the only one who loves being around you," he said before picking up his mug again and taking a sip. "I must admit, I hope the airport is closed. It'll give me an opportunity to spend one of the most revered days of the year with you and your aunt. Being with you makes me very happy, Kathryn."

Chapter 11

Kathryn's cheeks grew hot. "Uh. . ." She stood up and made her way over to the counter beside the stove. "I really need to start the sausage, Stan."

"Let me help," he said.

"You really don't have to."

"Would you like for me to leave you alone?" he asked softly.

Confusion flooded Kathryn. She wanted him there, next to her, and she wanted him to leave so she could think straight. And she needed to be alone to pray for guidance.

"It would probably be best if you did," she replied.

He didn't say a word, so all she heard was the swinging door as it flipped open and swished back and forth until it stilled. Now that she was alone in the kitchen, she could think logically, without the intrusion of his presence. When she exhaled, she felt as if the burdens of her past had lifted from her shoulders, allowing her to follow His lead as she prayed for direction.

Kathryn had the sausage ready in minutes. She carried a platter of sausage and a basket of Aunt Celia's muffins into the breakfast area right outside the kitchen. To her surprise, the only person there was Aunt Celia.

"Stan had to leave," Aunt Celia explained. "The weather

isn't going to improve, so I told him to go ahead to the prison."

Kathryn nodded as she poured two cups of coffee. "That's probably for the best." Disappointment muddied her thoughts.

Aunt Celia glared at her, lips pursed and jaws tight for several seconds before shaking her head. "I promised myself I'd stay out of this, but I'm afraid it's too much for me. Kathryn, why are you running away from Stan?"

"I'm not running."

"Maybe not physically, but you are emotionally. It's painful for me to watch you turn your back on something so special."

"You have to understand, Aunt Celia. It's been very hard for me to deal with my feelings about him."

Her voice trailed off as Aunt Celia nodded. "I understand, sweetheart, but Stan is nothing like your father."

Kathryn looked down at her feet and then back up at her aunt. "Yes, I know."

"Are you worried he's not telling the truth about his past?"

"At first I was, but not anymore," Kathryn admitted. "But there is one thing about him that baffles me."

"That he's not angry?" Aunt Celia said.

Kathryn nodded. "Most people would be fighting the system that unjustly accused them—but not Stan. He actually joined the ones who wrongly pointed their finger at him."

Aunt Celia smiled as she broke open a muffin and slathered it with softened butter. "His faith has provided him with the understanding that this is an unjust world we live in. Our rewards don't always come immediately. We seek eternal salvation through our faith in Christ, who never lets us down."

Kathryn hung her head as humility washed over her. "I'm so sorry, Aunt Celia," Kathryn said, her voice coming out in a squeak.

"Don't beat yourself up over this, dear. The Lord understands. After what you went through as a child, it would be difficult to trust anyone, especially a man."

"What can I do?" Kathryn asked.

"I know you care about Stan. I can see it in your eyes when you look at him."

"Am I that obvious?"

"Afraid so," Aunt Celia replied. "But if it's any consolation, he feels the same about you."

"You know it'll be difficult for me to have any kind of relationship with Stan, since he'll be in Tennessee and I'll be in Florida." She paused and then added, "After you fully recover, that is."

"Why don't you just relax and let the Lord take over?" Aunt Celia suggested. "In the meantime, enjoy your breakfast."

Just then, the phone rang, and Kathryn jumped. Fully expecting the call to be for Aunt Celia, she answered with a crisp, "Hello." It was the head chef at the Don Cesar.

"Kathryn, we have an unexpected opening in the kitchen. How soon can you be here?"

She glanced at Aunt Celia, who sat there picking at a muffin. Their conversation flashed through her mind, instantly letting her know what she had to do. "I'm sorry, but something has come up. I'm afraid you'll need to find someone else."

He gasped. "Are you certain of this? Working here is the opportunity of a lifetime."

"Yes, I know. But I can't." She felt no remorse whatsoever.

She hung up the phone as her chest constricted. In one quick moment, she'd erased the future she'd always thought she wanted. Aunt Celia looked at her but didn't say a word.

"That was the chef at the Don Cesar."

"I'm very sorry, Kathryn dear. There will be something else, although I'm sure you don't see it now."

"Don't you understand, Aunt Celia? I'm now free to follow the Lord's will."

⋘⊱⋙

Stan was so happy he could hardly contain himself. As soon as he'd walked in the front door of the prison, the head warden had cornered him.

"Congrats, Reverend. We had an unexpected job opening. You're now officially on staff. That is, if you still want the job."

"Are you kidding?" Stan asked.

"Nope, I'm serious as a judge. Your boys in the group you're preachin' to said they wanted you for the job, and the higher-ups actually listened." He chuckled and smacked his mouth. "Imagine that."

"Hey, thanks, pal. This is great news."

Miss Celia would be almost as happy as he was. She'd encouraged him to find a way to stay in New York since the need was so great. Telling her would be fun.

Then there was Kathryn. Stan blew out a long sigh as he thought about how much she'd come to mean to him. He didn't miss the irony of how he could now call New York his home while she'd be leaving for Florida when Miss Celia recovered.

Too bad, though. New York City agreed with her. He hadn't missed how she seemed to come alive as they went from the butcher to the green grocer. He wondered if she'd be happy in Florida.

Outside, Stan pulled his jacket tighter around him and leaned into the wind. The snow blew at a nearly forty-five-degree angle. The weather might be dreadful, but today it didn't bother him.

He stuck up his hand and captured the attention of one of the few cabs left on the street. Normally, he took the trains and walked, but these were extenuating circumstances, what with the weather and his eagerness to tell Miss Celia the good news.

The cab driver was chatty, talking about how he'd been hoping for a white Christmas. "I never expected this, though. I hope my kids aren't bouncing off the walls when I get home."

"Any idea how far behind schedule the flights are running at the airport?" Stan asked.

The cab driver lifted an eyebrow. "You're kidding, right? All flights today and tomorrow have been canceled."

An odd sort of peacefulness came over Stan as they inched toward Soho. He couldn't think of anything more enchanting than being snowbound with Kathryn and Miss Celia.

"Merry Christmas," Stan said, as the cab pulled to a stop in front of Miss Celia's City House.

After paying the driver, he carefully walked up the sidewalk to the steps. On the front door hung a green wreath with a large, red velvet bow. He had to use his shoulder to push the door open. He'd stayed here long enough to know it stuck with weather changes.

Miss Celia was sitting in the front room working on a jigsaw puzzle. "You alone?" he asked.

She glanced up, grinned, and nodded. "For now, anyway. Kathryn went up to nap. She's been working awfully hard lately, and I'm afraid she's not sleeping well at night. That girl has a lot on her mind."

"I'm sure she does."

Miss Celia looked up from her puzzle. "You look like you're ready to burst. What's going on?"

"You always could see right through me, Miss Celia." He paused a moment as she continued staring at him, waiting. "I've been offered a job on staff at the prison."

Miss Celia dropped the puzzle piece, and sincere joy lit up her face.

"I'm so happy for you, Stan."

"I hope you haven't already rented out my room."

Suddenly, her joyous expression turned cloudy. "I'm not sure yet."

"Hey, don't worry about it. I'm sure the Lord will provide something if you've got my room rented to someone else."

"It's not that," she said slowly. "It's just—"

Kathryn suddenly appeared. "Oh, hi, Stan," she said before turning to her aunt. "Do you think I should make cheesecake for dessert?"

"That would be wonderful," Miss Celia replied. "Won't it, Stan?"

"Absolutely, yes."

He saw the slight hint of a blush in her cheeks as she nodded. "Okay, then, we're having leg of lamb, asparagus tips, and cheesecake for dessert."

"I told her to pull out all the stops for dinner tonight," Miss Celia explained. "She must be getting tired of holding back."

"Actually, I've enjoyed cooking for your boarders, Aunt Celia," Kathryn said as she lingered in the doorway, "after I got used to it. I'd better get back to work."

Miss Celia cleared her throat. "Why don't you make yourself useful in the kitchen, Stan? I'm sure Kathryn could use a helping hand."

"Yes, of course." He pulled himself away from the table and left the room.

Kathryn was fully aware of what her aunt was up to, but now she didn't mind. Aunt Celia was a hopeless romantic.

"Sorry about my aunt," Kathryn said once she and Stan were alone in the kitchen. "She's not exactly the most subtle person in the world."

"Subtlety is overrated," he replied. "I've got some good news."

"Good news?" she said, spinning around to face him. "What?"

"I've been offered a permanent position at the prison."

"Oh, Stan, that's wonderful." He seemed surprised by her enthusiastic response.

"There's only one problem, though."

"What's that?"

"You won't be here."

Kathryn felt her chest constrict and a lump form in her throat. "You never know what the Lord will do next." She'd tell him her news later.

"What can I do to help?" he asked.

"Help?"

"Yes. Help with dinner."

"Oh. Uh, no, that's okay. I have everything under control."

"Then I'll go hang out with your aunt until you call for us."

Every few minutes, Kathryn glanced outside to observe the heavy snowfall. The entire backyard was buried under a thick quilt of snow. No one with an ounce of good sense would be out there in this mess. She was glad she'd ordered extra food that had been delivered when the roads were still passable.

Just as she put the finishing touches on the lamb, the

kitchen door swung open. She half expected it to be Stan, but it wasn't. It was Aunt Celia, taking tentative steps, using her walker. Kathryn quickly dropped what she was doing and rushed to her aunt's side.

"Why don't you wait a few more days before attempting this?" she asked.

"I don't believe in waiting for anything," Aunt Celia replied. She dropped into the nearest chair and exclaimed, "Whew! Who knew walking a few steps could be so exhausting?"

Kathryn wished her aunt would be more careful, since not even an ambulance would be able to navigate the streets of New York during such a heavy snowstorm. "Stay right there. I'll get Stan and see if he wants to have dinner in here."

"That would be cozy," Aunt Celia agreed. "There's no point in hauling all the food to the dining room for just the three of us. There are some things I need to discuss with you and Stan, anyway. I hope you don't mind."

Chapter 12

S tan had just finished saying the blessing when Aunt Celia piped up. "I've had a very generous offer on this place."

Kathryn froze, her fork suspended by the tips of her fingers in midair. "Offer? What kind of offer?"

"With the price of property skyrocketing in Soho, this place is worth a fortune. Plus, I'm afraid this boardinghouse is the last of a dying industry."

Stan frowned. "But where will you go?"

She flashed a smile toward Stan, then reached out and placed her hand on Kathryn's arm. "As I'm sure you're aware, I'm not getting any younger. My accident opened my eyes to the fact that it's time for me to look into other. . .living arrangements."

"Like what?" Kathryn said.

"My church sponsors a retirement center. The place stays pretty full, but there's an opening coming up. I'd like to move there, and the executive director said she'd hold it for me."

"I'm familiar with the place," Stan said. "It's nice."

"But you can't move to a retirement home, Aunt Celia. What about all your boarders?"

Aunt Celia shrugged. "I've stayed open for them as long as I can. I'm sure they'll find someplace just as nice."

"But what about all these great meals? There's nothing else like the food here—at least not in the city."

Kathryn caught what appeared to be a warning glance from Stan, but Aunt Celia smiled, looking back and forth between them. "Maybe I can talk someone into opening a restaurant and using my recipes. Besides, things change all the time. I can only do so much."

"I'm sure you've prayed about this, Miss Celia," Stan said. "I'll support whatever you decide to do."

"Yes, I know you will," she replied. "I was hoping I'd get a blessing from both of you." She tilted her head forward as she looked at Kathryn.

"Yes, of course," Kathryn said quickly. "I just hope you don't regret it." Her appetite quickly vanished.

"I'm ready for your fabulous cheesecake," Stan said a little too cheerfully.

"Me, too," Aunt Celia said.

Kathryn stood quickly, nearly knocking over her chair. She couldn't help but notice the glance exchanged between Aunt Celia and Stan as she scurried toward the counter.

Both of them made all the right appreciative sounds as they ate dessert. Stan had seconds, and Aunt Celia said she wished she could, too, but that she wasn't getting enough exercise to work off the calories. Finally, she asked for help to her room so she could go to bed early.

"Why don't you two have a little Bible study?" Aunt Celia said. "Take advantage of the blessings of this weather and spend it in prayer?"

"Sounds like a wonderful idea," Stan said as he steadied her on her walker. "But first, I want to make sure you're safe and warm in your bed. I'll be right back to help with the dishes, Kathryn."

"You're such a lovely boy," Kathryn heard her aunt say as they left the kitchen. "Any girl would be blessed to have you."

Kathryn's shoulders sagged as she realized how right her aunt was. Stan was a real keeper. He'd been through the most trying of times—much worse than anything she'd had to face— yet he never lost his faith in God. The saddest part of her real- ization was that she'd blown any chance she had with him by being so stubborn in the beginning.

Kathryn slowly bowed her head and whispered a prayer for forgiveness. "Lord, I've been selfish. Please show me what You want for me and make me pay attention." As she said the short, simple prayer aloud, she heard a shuffling behind her.

"I think you know what He wants for you," Stan said softly. "Both of us have been fighting it, but we can't any longer."

Kathryn turned around and faced him, trying hard to will her cheeks not to turn pink. But she couldn't stop them. They heated up just like they always did when she was alone with Stan.

"I didn't want to fall in love with you, Kathryn. You have all these big plans to make your way in the culinary world."

"What about you?" she asked. "You've got mighty big plans of your own."

"Yes, but until now, I never thought my dreams would come true. I had to wait for the Lord's timing to get this great offer. The only thing that bothers me is that you'll be down in sunny Florida."

"I almost forgot to tell you."

"Tell me what?"

"I got a call from the chef at the Don Cesar in Florida. He wanted me to come down there immediately, but I told him I was no longer interested."

Stan took a step closer. He tentatively reached out and touched her cheek. "What does this mean?"

"It means I'd like to stick around New York for a while."

"There must be dozens of places in the city that would love to hire you," Stan said, his grin widening.

"That's not what I had in mind. In fact, I might even open my own restaurant. Aunt Celia was throwing enough hints."

"Excellent idea," he said.

She twisted her mouth as she thought some more. "Of course, I have to find a place to live, and I just gave up my apartment in Midtown."

"Maybe we can go apartment hunting together," he said.

Kathryn nodded. "Yeah, and bounce ideas off each other."

"We can visit each other and talk about our new jobs. Maybe you can cook for me, and I can help you do a few things around your place."

She swallowed and nodded. "Great idea."

He glanced down at his feet and then looked back at her. "Who am I trying to kid? I don't want to visit you."

"You don't?"

"No, I don't. What I really want is. . ."

Kathryn watched him expectantly as his expression changed. "What do you really want?"

"What I really want is. . .Kathryn, I love you. I want you to be my wife. . .then we can get an apartment together."

A bolt of joy flashed through her. As soon as she realized her chin had dropped, she clamped her mouth shut.

"Well?" he said. "I guess I did spring that on you without

warning. Will you marry me?"

Kathryn was overcome by a fit of nervous giggles. "Yes, Stan, I'll marry you."

He blew out a sigh of relief. "For a moment there, I was afraid you'd say no, that you didn't want to be tied down."

"For a man of faith, that doesn't sound right," she said.

"I'm only human." He pulled her into his arms and dropped a kiss onto her forehead. "Who would've thought that such a wonderful thing would come of being snowbound for Christmas?"

"It just goes to show how prayer works."

Epilogue

How's it going?" Stan asked as he entered the kitchen of the tiny restaurant and catering service Kathryn had opened three months after their wedding. Their first Christmas as a married couple was coming up fast, and Stan had hoped they'd have some quiet time together. . .but from the looks of things, that wouldn't happen for a while.

"I'm swimming in sugar," she replied.

Stan chuckled. "I always wondered what made you so sweet. Now I know."

She cast a coquettish glance at him and giggled. "You know what I mean. I have so many orders for cheesecakes, macaroons, and crème brulees, I'm not sure Bonnie and I can handle it."

"Sure you can, sweetheart," Stan said as he reached out and grabbed one of the macaroons she'd placed on a platter to cool. "I'm just glad you came to your senses and hired someone who could keep up with you in the kitchen."

"Have you told Aunt Celia the news?" Kathryn asked.

"No, I thought you might want to be with me when I do."

"She'll be happy for us."

"And she'll be even happier when she finds out that if this

baby is a girl, we're naming her Celia Rose, after her and your mother."

Stan came up behind her and and gently patted her slightly protruding abdomen, letting the warmth of their love and God's blessings envelop them.

Crust
　1 c. graham cracker crumbs
　¼ c. granulated sugar
　¼ c. melted butter
　¼ t. vanilla extract

Combine graham cracker crumbs, sugar, and vanilla. Mix well. Pat into the bottom of a 9-inch buttered springform pan. Trim. Bake at 400°F for five minutes to set. Cool.

Filling
　2 lbs. cream cheese
　1⅓ c. sugar
　4 eggs
　2 T. all-purpose flour
　2 t. grated lemon zest
　¼ c. heavy cream

In a mixer, combine cream cheese and sugar until blended. Add eggs and blend until smooth. Mix in flour, lemon zest, and cream. Pour into crust-lined pan. Bake in a preheated 400°F oven for ten minutes; reduce temperature to 300°F and continue baking 35 minutes longer. Let cool. Chill before serving. To serve, remove pan sides and cut into wedges. Garnish with fresh fruit.

DEBBY MAYNE

Debby has been a freelance writer for as long as she can remember, starting with short slice-of-life stories in small newspapers, then moving on to parenting articles for regional publications and fiction stories for women and girls. She has been involved in all aspects of publishing from the creative side, to editing a national health publication, to freelance proofreading for several book publishers. Her belief that all blessings come from the Lord has given her great comfort during trying times and gratitude for when she is rewarded for her efforts. She lives on the west coast of Florida with her husband and two daughters.

A Letter to Our Readers

Dear Readers:

In order that we might better contribute to your reading enjoyment, we would appreciate your taking a few minutes to respond to the following questions. When completed, please return to the following: Fiction Editor, Barbour Publishing, Inc., P.O. Box 719, Uhrichsville, OH 44683.

1. Did you enjoy reading *Holiday at the Inn*?
    ☐ Very much—I would like to see more books like this.
    ☐ Moderately—I would have enjoyed it more if _____

    _____

    _____

2. What influenced your decision to purchase this book?
    (Check those that apply.)
    ☐ Cover   ☐ Back cover copy   ☐ Title   ☐ Price
    ☐ Friends   ☐ Publicity   ☐ Other

3. Which story was your favorite?
    ☐ *Let It Snow*   ☐ *Mustangs and Mistletoe*
    ☐ *Orange Blossom Christmas*   ☐ *Christmas in the City*

4. Please check your age range:
    ☐ Under 18   ☐ 18–24   ☐ 25–34
    ☐ 35–45   ☐ 46–55   ☐ Over 55

5. How many hours per week do you read? _____

Name _____

Occupation _____

Address _____

City _____ State _____ Zip _____

E-mail _____